Silent Ears,
Silent Heart

Blair LaCrosse and
Michelle LaCrosse

Silent Ears, Silent Heart

A deaf man's journey through two worlds

Blair LaCrosse and
Michelle LaCrosse

Silent Ears, Silent Heart

A deaf man's journey through two worlds

Published by: Deaf Understanding
Roseville, Michigan

www.deafunderstanding.com

Cover Photograph by: Blair LaCrosse

International Standard Book Number: 0-9740111-0-X
Library of Congress Control Number: 2003093762

Acknowledgments

We would like to thank our family for their support and encouragement during the six years that we struggled to nurture an idea to the point of becoming a book that will touch the hearts and affect the lives of those who read its pages.

Thanks to Lynda Karr, our copy editor, who helped make *Silent Ears, Silent Heart* not just a "good read" but also a story that inspires its readers to empathize with the Deaf.

We would also like to thank Todd Mucurio of Graphical Media for his help in the digital preparation of the cover design and manuscript. For without him, *Silent Ears, Silent Heart* could not have gone to publication.

Special thanks goes to the members of the Deaf community who shared their stories, hoping to bring a measure of understanding between two worlds—the Deaf and the Hearing.

FOREWORD

Silent Ears, Silent Heart brings tears to my eyes and with them a great sense of relief. Upon reading it, I am overwhelmed with many fond memories—especially the ones that I never realized would have such a powerful impact on my life. There are many instances throughout the book that accurately typify the experiences of a successful deaf individual in a world of ignorance and marginalization.

Throughout the book, there is an undeniable correlation between the socio-psychological development of deaf children and the degree of parental support and involvement. The importance of collectiveness in decision-making, consistency in providing loving support, and compliance for the best of the deaf child is manifested, vividly demonstrated and observed in the relationship of the deaf son and his father.

A parent's lack of awareness of a profoundly deaf child's needs results in his or her life being not only more difficult than his or her hearing contemporaries, but simply more difficult than necessary and often accompanied by dejection.

The expectation of hearing parents for their deaf child to communicate as a "normal hearing" person is unrealistic. Interestingly, many forget or are unaware of the fact that the average person lip reads with only thirty-percent accuracy.

Imagine having to watch the television without volume all day and night. Imagine talking unintelligibly in front of your hearing peers because you are unable to discriminate speech sounds. Imagine being forced to wear something that you unequivocally know does not benefit you. Imagine being deaf.

An excellent allegory would be that of a blind child. Would forcing a blind child to wear glasses help him or her to see well? As with the deaf child, the blind child's eyesight is beyond repair, but that fact is neither realized nor recognized. A doctor or a parent believes that putting on corrective lenses will solve this problem. To make matters worse, the blind child is frequently apprised of the need to persevere with the lenses with the presumption that he or she will soon be able to use sight to function normally. The child can actually do many other things individually without the preposterous expectation that the lenses will correct his or her sight, but rather than be encouraged to do those things, he or she is forced to conform to the standards of those with sight. As unrealistic as this seems, this is comparable to how a deaf child is treated by the hearing world.

For the deaf, sign language communication comes to the rescue. As an extremely effective communication method, American Sign Language (ASL) maintains the same unique properties of language as any spoken language, including American English. It is a visual-gestural language that accurately exchanges abstract concepts and has been passed on from one contemporary to the next. ASL is able to convey "sounds," or phonemes, discretely in the form of handshape, movement, location, and orientation of the wrist, not to mention some non-manual facial expressions. In this book, ASL has helped the deaf son to lead a successful life in both the hearing and Deaf worlds.

I am extremely grateful for the love and understanding that my parents provide me and very fortunate to have such dedicated and compassionate people in my life. Also, many thanks go to some of my former teachers who tirelessly and patiently trained me to speak. In addition, I want to acknowledge that if it were not for my friends, especially my former roommate and trusted friend, I would not be able to communicate freely and effectively in a language with which I feel very comfortable. Because of these people, I have been able to function in two worlds—the hearing and the Deaf.

Blair and Michelle, it has been a privilege to read *Silent Ears, Silent Heart* and write this Foreword. Thank you.

Read and enjoy.

Michael A. Weingart

Michael Weingart became profoundly deaf from spinal meningitis just before age three. He is currently teaching American Sign Language at Monroe Community College in Rochester, New York.

Table of Contents

Preface

Imagine living in a world where everyone around you speaks a different language, and you can't master it. The culture of those around you is very different from your own, and you can't be a part of it. No matter how much you struggle to fit in, you never will. And what if this is your lot in life not by choice, but by chance? How would you feel?

This is the very same world that millions of deaf persons are born into, including Christopher Cline. Christopher's journey through life highlights the challenges that a deaf individual growing up in a hearing world faces on a daily basis, including the most difficult, yet most important, challenge of all—gaining the acceptance and approval of one's hearing parents.

Though a work of fiction, *Silent Ears, Silent Heart* gives the reader a glimpse into the language, culture, and life of a Deaf person, but it does more than that. The reader's heart becomes intertwined with Christopher's so that he or she is inspired to be empathetic toward the plight of Deaf individuals.

Blair LaCrosse is a deaf person born into a hearing family. He has experienced firsthand the challenges of trying to communicate, understand, and succeed in a hearing world. Michelle LaCrosse has been a sign language interpreter for more than twenty years and is aware of the hardships that the Deaf face in medical, legal, and financial settings. Through our personal experiences, as well as the experiences of the many deaf individuals who have touched our lives over the years, *Silent Ears, Silent Heart* was conceived, drew nourishment, and incubated, until it finally broke free, demanding to be presented.

It is our hope that this book will give the hearing world insight into the minds of the Deaf, at least some understanding of their culture, and empathy with their situation, in order that they may feel accepted.

Blair LaCrosse and Michelle LaCrosse

Chapter 1
<u>First Memory</u>

It was a bright spring day, but bittersweet for Jack. As he looked from the cold gray monument to the handsome young man at his side, he wondered for the millionth time why he couldn't have seen it before it was too late . . .

~ ~ ~ ~ ~ ~ ~ ~ ~ ~ ~ ~ ~ ~ ~ ~ ~ ~ ~

"Nineteen sixty eight is going to be a very good year." His wife, Margaret, was glowing as Jack spoke of the child she would bear. "Soon I will have a successor who will eventually run Crownline Glass."

Rod smiled graciously and then proceeded to discuss the company's rising sales. "Our net sales for last month . . ."

"Excuse me Rod," Margaret turned toward Jack. "I've finished planting the marigolds out front. Now I'm going to head home and work on our yard."

"All right dear; don't wear yourself out. I'll see you later."

As Margaret left the office, Jack and Rod resumed their discussion.

Margaret had been having contractions on and off for the past week. Twice she and Jack had gone to the hospital only to be told she was experiencing false labor. Now Margaret was again having contractions. She didn't mention anything to Jack, since it was probably another false alarm.

Margaret went home and began preparing the ground in her flowerbed. As she worked, she was startled by a sharp pain and tightening in her abdomen. When the pain continued to recur, she decided it was time to take a break.

Since her contractions seemed to be coming at regular intervals and were getting stronger, Margaret began to time them. An hour later, her contractions were five minutes apart.

When Jack arrived home, he and Margaret agreed that it was time to go to the hospital.

Margaret didn't know quite what to expect after she was admitted, since this was her first pregnancy. She had been in the labor room since she arrived at the hospital. The contractions, now coming every two-to-three minutes, were lasting from 60 to 90 seconds. The pain was almost unbearable.

In the waiting room, Jack was on his third cup of coffee and second magazine as he nervously awaited the birth of their child.

The day was May 6, 1968, seven months after Margaret's first visit with Doctor Gracie. He had seemed more sympathetic to Margaret's feelings than her previous doctor had been, so she had decided to have all her prenatal visits with him. Margaret had sensed genuineness in this doctor right at the outset, when he had taken the time to discuss with her the concerns that both she and Jack had regarding their baby. Now Doctor Gracie was about to deliver, literally hand to her, her child.

"Margaret, it's time . . ." Doctor Gracie, along with an orderly, moved Margaret into the delivery room.

After two hours of intense pushing, Margaret heard the most beautiful sound she had ever heard. It was the sound of her child.

"It's a boy!" exclaimed Doctor Gracie, as he proudly held up the baby for Margaret to see. He could see that this baby was strong and healthy.

Margaret was overcome with joy as she saw her beautiful son. She reached out to touch his hand. "Hello, my dear Christopher! Hello!"

Jack, who had been told that Margaret had been taken to the delivery room, was even more fidgety than before. He repeatedly inquired at the nurses' station as to Margaret's condition.

Finally, one of the nurses approached Jack, "Mr. Cline, congratulations! It's a boy. He's seven pounds five ounces."

"I have a son," Jack repeated as if to congratulate himself. "How's Margaret?"

"She is doing just fine. She and the baby have been moved to her room. Would you like me to take you there?"

"Yes, of course!" As they walked toward Margaret's room, Jack noticed a doctor who had just stepped up to the nurses' station. "Isn't that Doctor Gracie?"

Doctor Gracie turned when he heard his name being mentioned and stepped forward to meet Jack. "Congratulations, Mr. Cline. You have a beautiful baby boy."

"Thank you, Doctor, for taking care of my wife and son. How are they doing?"

"They both are doing just fine." Doctor Gracie continued, "Your son is perfectly healthy, and what a fine looking boy he is too!"

Doctor Gracie turned toward the nurse, "I'll take Mr. Cline to see his wife." He then turned to Jack, "Let me show you to your wife's room." Doctor Gracie guided Jack down the hall to Margaret's room.

There they were. Margaret looked tired, yet so content, holding Christopher in her arms. "Oh Jack! He's beautiful! Our Christopher is so beautiful!"

Jack stepped forward to admire his son. "He is beautiful," he thought, "And he has my eyes." Jack held his son ever so close, just staring at this little person, so much a part of himself. He then lifted his son so that Christopher's little head rested on his shoulder, and he whispered, "One day you will stand by my side as my business partner. You will be a successful business man, just like your daddy." Jack admired his son for a few more minutes and then gave him to Margaret. He sat down on the edge of Margaret's bed and put his arm around her. They both sat speechless, watching Christopher as he rested ever so peacefully, cradled in his mother's arms.

Chapter 2
<u>Resentment Starts</u>

Christopher sat on the kitchen floor, playing, while Margaret prepared dinner. He had stacked his blocks precariously, one on top of another, and now he planned to ram his stuffed doggy into the side of the structure. This was a game he enjoyed and would repeat time and again.

As Margaret worked in the kitchen, she usually would take some time to stop and play with Christopher. Today would be different.

Jack was having a prospective client over that evening to discuss a contract for building a science center in Dallas, Texas. This one account could establish him as the most reputable glass manufacturer in the Midwest.

Stan Pratt, sole architectural designer for the city of Dallas and designer for a handful of other Midwestern cities, was a man from the big land of Texas. Whenever cities needed advice on how to expend their funds on city enhancement . . . Stan was their man. Serving on a number of building committees, he was hired for his name alone. He merely had to offer a few minutes of counseling and recommend a few nationally known contractors, and the project would be underway. Stan was well established in the field and was as dependable as any building with which his name was associated.

Now Jack was becoming involved with Stan. Jack had been chosen for his zeal in pioneering more durable types of glass while preserving aesthetics.

By four o'clock, Margaret had dinner ready. She wanted to have everything done before Jack came home. She planned to transfer the food to serving dishes which she then covered with foil, place the dishes in the oven, and then turn the oven on warm to keep the food ready until time for the meal to be served. She would then dry the preparation dishes and set the table, and all would be ready when Jack got home.

She had washed the preparation dishes and stacked them in the dish drainer earlier. Now, after spooning the contents of each pan onto a serving plate, she had washed each empty pan and piled each on top of the rest of the dishes in the drainer. The resulting mountain of pots and pans had grown so high, in fact, that it almost touched the cabinets just above. As Margaret reached to get out the last serving dish, she opened one of the cabinets and brushed against the spire of stainless steel. It toppled over, crashing into the sink.

Margaret, startled by all the noise, ran over to Christopher, expecting him to have been frightened by all the clanging of pots and pans . . . but he was oblivious.

Puzzled, Margaret sat down at the table and watched Christopher as he played. "Was he so preoccupied with his blocks that he wasn't aware of all the noise?" she wondered. She called, "Christopher. Christopher, darling, look at Mommy."

There was no response.

Margaret became uneasy as she wondered what could be wrong with her Christopher. She called him again, louder this time, "Christopher!"

He continued playing.

Margaret walked quietly over to the sink, where the pots were still strewn about. She picked up her frying pan and a wooden spoon and casually walked to a position behind her son. Clutching the pan's handle firmly, she lowered it so that it was directly behind Christopher's head, just inches from his ears. She struck the pan, hoping that the sound would surprise Christopher, but it didn't. She struck the pan again and again.

Christopher continued playing, unaware of what was happening behind him.

For a moment, reality escaped Margaret. She sat back down on her chair and reflected on Christopher's progress in the past eighteen months since his birth. "Although he hasn't yet learned how to say 'Mama,' everything else he has accomplished—rolling over, sitting up, teething, walking—has been the same as other kids his age," she thought. "He always seems so engrossed with other things that he just doesn't listen when I speak to him . . . or maybe . . . he just isn't able to hear me."

That revelation hit Margaret like a runaway train. She fell down to her knees, wrapped her arms tightly around Christopher, and cried.

"Oh my baby, this can't be happening! Oh baby, don't worry." She looked at Christopher and whispered, "Mommy is here." They were words like those she often spoke to soothe Christopher, but she would soon come to realize that her words could only calm herself.

Christopher, startled by the tightness and quickness of his mother's grasp, jumped, and as his big blue eyes snapped toward her face, she could see his fear as he began to cry.

"I'm sorry Christopher. Mommy didn't mean to scare you."

Margaret carried Christopher into the living room, where they sat on the couch, holding one another. She rocked him and began to sing, "Hush little baby, don't say a word—" She stopped. Her son couldn't hear her singing . . . and . . . "what if he never does say a word?" Margaret thought. She couldn't sing any longer. They sat in silence . . . rocking . . . until Christopher fell asleep.

Half an hour had passed. Pots and pans were still scattered about in the sink, the table had not been set, and dinner had not received the benefit of a warm oven. The meeting with Stan Pratt had been forgotten. Margaret's only concern now was for her son.

Jack arrived home thirty minutes before Stan was scheduled to arrive. This meeting was the opportunity of a lifetime for Jack. The only thing running through his mind was how he would present his designs for the new science center. He had drawings, window specifications, and numerous other papers to support his presentation.

As Jack entered his home, he had no idea what was in store for him. "Margaret, I'm home!"

With that introduction, Margaret usually came running with Christopher in her arms to greet Jack, but today everything was quiet.

"Margaret?" Jack walked through the kitchen noticing the pots and pans in the sink, one on the stove, a frying pan on the kitchen table, and Christopher's blocks still in the middle of the kitchen floor.

"Jack! Jack! Come here!" Margaret's fearful call from the living room was alarming.

Jack ran to the living room. "What is it, honey? Where's dinner? What's going on?"

"Jack, something is wrong with Christopher. I was in the kitchen preparing dinner and . . ."

As Margaret was explaining what had happened just an hour earlier, Jack experienced the full spectrum of emotions from anger, to confusion, to shock, to guilt, and back to anger.

"I thought Doctor Gracie did a thorough examination of Christopher at birth! He's a doctor. He should have picked up on something like this! What is it with these incompetent doctors? Didn't you take Christopher to the pediatrician for his check-ups?" Jack demanded.

"Yes. Yes I did! I don't understand how this could happen. Maybe he has an ear infection. I don't know!"

"Are you sure he can't hear?"

"Jack! I told you. I did it inches from his ears, and he didn't flinch."

By now Margaret's demeanor was no longer that of a concerned mother. She was becoming more agitated and tense with each of Jack's accusations. Christopher, sensing his mother's emotional distress, was roused from sleep.

Now that Christopher was awake, Jack wanted to see for himself how loud noises would affect his son. Reaching out, he snatched Christopher from his mother's arms.

"Jack, what are you going to do?"

"Come on," Jack said, as he grabbed Margaret's hand and practically dragged her off the couch. "Show me what you were saying."

"Jack, please! Calm down. You're going to upset Christopher."

Jack hurried to the kitchen and set Christopher on the kitchen floor. He picked up the frying pan off of the table and began beating it with the wooden spoon.

Christopher, still drowsy and very flustered at his father's abrupt actions, couldn't understand why he had been snatched from his mother's warm embrace and plopped so unceremoniously onto the cold kitchen floor. He began to scream.

"Jack! Jack! Please stop! You're scaring him! Stop! Please!"

Jack stepped back and watched his son, who was sitting in the middle of the floor, screaming, with arms and legs flailing. He ran his hand through his hair, took a deep breath, and looked Margaret straight in the eye. "Margaret, I'm not going to have a retard for a son!"

Scooping Christopher up in her arms to console him, Margaret hushed, "Jack! How could you say such a thing? We don't even know what's wrong with him!"

Feeling frustrated, Jack announced, "I don't want to continue this discussion. Stan is going to be here any minute, and I don't want to lose this deal!"

"Is that all you care about . . . 'your deal'? Christopher is your SON!"

At that moment, the doorbell rang. It was Stan.

"Jack, tell him this isn't a good time."

"Cancel my meeting with Stan Pratt? Margaret, I can't do that. This is important!"

"And your son is not important?"

"Margaret, don't do this to me!"

"Don't do this to you? Jack, something is wrong with our Christopher!"

The doorbell rang again.

Jack walked toward the front door. As he opened the door, he looked back at Margaret and then turned to Stan, standing expectantly outside. "Hi Stan. I'm real sorry, but I'm going to have to reschedule our meeting. My son suddenly took ill."

"Oh . . . all right," said Stan, "Give my office a call, and we'll see what we can do."

Though he did call Stan's office, that was the last Jack heard from Stan. The following week Stan signed a contract with Ellis Windows, a company operating out of Nebraska.

From that day forward, Jack's resentment would never again allow him to view his son in the same way.

Chapter 3
<u>Rumors Spread</u>

The very next day Jack and Margaret, deeply concerned, took Christopher to his pediatrician, Doctor Sherwood, to have his ears checked. "It isn't a cold or ear infection. It isn't a temporary hearing loss. It is a neurosensory loss in the inner ear . . . intrauterine exposure to the German measles . . . born profoundly deaf . . . unable to be remedied by any kind of surgery . . . no treatment . . . irreversible." These are the words that rang through Jack and Margaret's ears.

Christopher was deaf. There was nothing that either Jack or Margaret could do to change his condition. Jack was so angered, embittered, and frustrated that he was unable to focus on what Christopher really needed—acceptance. Jack blamed Doctor Gracie and the hospital for not doing something at birth. He thought the non-detection of the impairment by Doctor Sherwood had resulted in this now irreversible condition. He threatened legal action, only to have his attorney advise him that charges could not be brought because there was no malpractice or negligence involved.

Much happened to Jack after that ill-fated day when he

and Margaret had realized their Christopher would never be able to hear. The word about his child's deafness and Jack's inability to accept it made its way around the workplace. Except for a few instances, which were difficult for Jack to face, everyone usually chose to remain silent on the subject.

One of those instances happened during the annual open house of Crownline Glass. Building planners from several cities around the country had been invited to visit Crownline and to view various types of glass designed and manufactured by Jack and his team of designers and scientists. It was a day to "roll out the red carpet" to several prospective clients. The annual open house was so important to its future growth that the company had hired a team of full-time personnel to work throughout the year to prepare everything, from displays and lighting to factory tours and hors d'oeuvres.

Fifteen hundred visitors were expected, including not only potential clients but also architectural apprentices from universities nationwide, all of whom wanted the privilege of seeing the inner-workings of such a renowned manufacturing company. All Crownline Glass employees and their families had also been invited to "tour the facility and see what makes Crownline the success it is today".

Christopher was now two years old and very active, like any other child his age. He stared up at the high ceilings, looked down at the marble floors, and then examined all the people in between. It was all so exciting to Christopher, who looked up at Margaret with inquisitive eyes. The puzzled expression on his face was the same as that of any other two-year-old, which usually is accompanied with the question "Why?" Christopher, though, was unable to even shape his thoughts in words, let alone express them verbally or ask for reasons.

At this crucial time when his young mind was absorbing everything his senses detected and language should have been developing, Christopher was falling behind. The only way he could express himself was through grunts and high-pitched squeals. Not knowing what he was trying to convey, Margaret often found herself discouraged.

As Margaret and Christopher strolled down the corridors through the various departments, Margaret searched for Jack. Unable to find him, she approached some of the employees. She identified herself as Margaret Cline and asked where she might find her husband. No one seemed to have any knowledge of Jack's whereabouts.

Each time Margaret asked one of the employees for assistance, she noticed fleeting glances down toward Christopher in his stroller. They were strange glances, sort of furtive, as if to hide the fact that they had even looked down at him. Their unusual behavior made Margaret feel uncomfortable.

Moving through one of the rooms, she finally noticed someone she thought could help. The East-Coast sales manager, Alan Underwood, was speaking with a prospective client, a building designer from Boston, Massachusetts. Randy Rhodes was his name. He had been hired by his city to design an aquarium for exotic marine life.

Alan had met Margaret a few weeks earlier at a company-sponsored dinner and was happy to see her again today. He introduced Margaret to Randy.

"It's a pleasure to make your acquaintance, Mr. Rhodes."

"No, Mrs. Cline; the pleasure is all mine."

Randy then bent down to shake Christopher's hand. "It's a pleasure to meet you too." Christopher's eyes lit up, and he began laughing.

"You have an adorable little boy, Mrs. Cline. I have two children myself."

Appreciating Randy's obvious warmth and his fondness for children, Margaret saw this as a good time to excuse herself so that she could freshen up while Randy and Alan enjoyed the privilege of overseeing Christopher's entertainment.

Jack, meanwhile, had been making the most of what was always a big day for him. As he worked his way around the displays, he spoke to building designers from several cities that were interested in contracting Crownline Glass to manufacture the glass used in their structures. He was engaged in conversation with prospective customers at the display just behind Alan and

Randy when he overheard what he had suspected his employees had been feeling but would never express to him directly.

Randy looked down at Christopher and then back at Alan. "What a sweet kid . . . And to think this whole multimillion-dollar company will one day be his."

Bending down again to speak with Christopher, Randy added, "Yeah, little guy. One day you're going to be the big boss of your daddy's company."

"It's highly doubtful that Christopher will even be able to work in the warehouse, let alone own this company," retorted Alan.

Randy stood up with a look of surprise on his face. "What do you mean? He's their only child, and most likely, he will follow in his father's footsteps."

Alan proceeded to explain, "Christopher was born deaf and dumb. His disability retards his mental development and his ability to communicate. He will never be able to manage his own life, let alone this company."

"I can't imagine how hard that must be on the Clines, knowing that they will have to care for their son for the rest of their lives! I have two children, but I'm not planning on caring for them much past twenty" . . . Randy chuckled . . . "then they're on their own."

"It's rather sad when such things happen."

"Yes, that is sad. I never knew." Randy again looked at Christopher. "He looks fine to me. Isn't there something the doctors can do?"

Alan shook his head. "No. From what I've heard, there is no hope for him. Jack's child will always be handicapped and will never be able to handle responsibility."

Alan turned around just as Jack, having finally managed to extricate himself from the other clients while trying to keep them from also overhearing this discussion, walked up from behind the Thermopane glass display. "I'm sorry, sir. I had no idea you were . . ."

"We will take this up later, Mr. Underwood. Where is my wife?"

"Here she comes." Randy pointed toward Margaret as she approached.

"Jack darling, we have been looking all over for you! How has your day been?"

"It's been busy. If you'll excuse me, I have an appointment with my sales managers. Mr. Underwood, would you please come with me?"

The conference room where meetings were held was on the first floor, but Jack proceeded to the second floor. Alan knew he wasn't heading to a meeting with the other sales managers. None had been scheduled. He followed Jack into his office and closed the door behind him.

Jack walked behind his desk and then invited Alan to sit down in the chair directly across from him. Jack paused for a moment, which to Alan must have seemed like an eternity, and then in a calm but firm voice said, "Mr. Underwood, I will say this only once. My family life is of no concern to our present or prospective clients, to you, or to anybody else. You are to refrain from discussing my private affairs with anyone. As far as you are concerned, you know only me. I have no family, no wife, no son . . ."

Chapter 4
<u>Mocking Me</u>

The open house had been exhausting for Margaret and Christopher. Looking at the numerous displays and demonstrations had taken most of the afternoon.

Margaret knew from experience that Jack would be home late, probably 11 o'clock. The open house lasted until 8 o'clock in the evening, and then it would take time to close up the building and meet with the various department managers. She was sure that he too would be exhausted, since the day of Crownline's open house is the most stressful day of the year.

The sky had become dark and ominous. A storm was approaching, accompanied by thunder and lightning.

Margaret began to worry when, at almost midnight, Jack had not yet come home. She went to check on Christopher. Sound asleep; the distant rumbling of thunder would not awaken him.

"There are some benefits to having a hearing loss," Margaret thought. "Sleep tight, my dear Christopher."

It was one o'clock in the morning when Jack finally arrived home. Margaret noticed that Jack had been drinking and that he'd had more than one drink to help him relax. She attempted to come to his aid. "Darling, let's get you to bed." As she was helping Jack to the bedroom, Margaret said, "It looked like there was quite a crowd at the open house today. Christopher and I really enjoyed ourselves. How was your day?"

"My day? How was MY day?" With each word, Jack's voice tightened. "Everyone looks at me. Everywhere I go they look at me. I sense it."

"What do you mean? Who looks at you?"

"They do! Everyone at work! They talk about me . . . about us! And they laugh."

"Dear, why do you think that?"

"Alan and Randy . . . They know! Everyone knows my son is a retard! And they laugh. They say 'How can that retard take over Crownline Glass?'"

"Is that what's upsetting you? How other people view our child? Jack, they are only speaking out of ignorance. You would be able to see that, if you would stop thinking so much of yourself and how others view you."

"What can I do? I have a retarded son! He'll always be deaf and dumb. He'll never be able to manage anything or take care of himself!" Jack, becoming even more agitated, looked directly at Margaret. "You know the worst part of it? You just keep babying him. The world isn't going to treat him with compassion. He's going to be ridiculed and abused. That's reality. Your babying him will distort his view of the cold hard facts of the world he lives in!"

Margaret wondered how Jack could say such cruel things about his son, his only son. "Our son is not retarded! Don't ever call him that! He is as bright as any child of his age. Jack, don't ask me to downplay my love for Christopher. He is my child! I know the world will ridicule and abuse him, which is all the more reason we need to be there for him. You have never been there for him!"

"Don't say that! I love our son too. I work hard to take care of him. He isn't lacking anything he needs."

"Anything he needs? What do you mean? The most important thing he needs is YOU, Jack, but you haven't given yourself to Christopher. He needs your time, your attention, your support, and your acceptance. You give him none of what he really needs!"

Christopher woke up frightened, not by the sounds of his parents' heated argument in the hallway or the cracking of the lightning, but from the thunder's vibrations. Startled by the visual display of light flashing like a strobe into his room, he shrieked in terror as the dark gray shadows from the oak tree outside his window reached monstrous arms over his bed.

As his night-light went out, the ensuing darkness combined with Christopher's inability to hear caused his world to be profoundly silent . . . as silent as a stony heart.

Chapter 5
<u>State Recommendation</u>

It had been almost two years since Jack and Margaret had discovered that their son was deaf. Christopher seemed to be growing just like any other child . . . yet at the age of three, he was unable to speak. Margaret wondered if she would ever hear him say "Mama" or "Daddy."

At Christopher's next check-up, Margaret asked Doctor Sherwood about Christopher's inability to speak.

Doctor Sherwood explained, "The speech of hearing-impaired children varies depending upon the amount of their residual hearing. When a young child undergoes a hearing test, he is unable to give a clear indication of what he can actually hear, thus we cannot fully measure how much hearing he has left. The amount of residual hearing would determine how much speech he can replicate. It is very difficult, if not impossible, to reproduce sounds that have never been heard. So . . . only time will tell if Christopher will ever be able to speak and to what extent."

As Margaret thought of the possibility that Christopher may never be able to speak, she was saddened. Her son's grunts, groans, and squeals were becoming more troublesome as his mind was growing and desiring an outlet. He was unable to express himself in a way that she could understand, and Margaret was certain that her frustration would intensify as Christopher became older and was still unable to ask questions or communicate his thoughts and feelings.

The letter from Roosevelt school was a surprise to Margaret. Through bureaucratic procedure, the record of Christopher's deafness had been reported to audiologists, speech therapists, and numerous other specialists, who were recommending that Christopher be placed in the special education program at Roosevelt school. Margaret was sure a mistake had been made, considering Christopher's tender age. She called the school to inform them of their error.

Margaret first spoke to the school's guidance counselor, who told her that Christopher was eligible for the special education program because of his deafness. "A child who is deaf misses basic information that a hearing child gathers through auditory stimuli, but we can help him to catch up to the level of children his age."

Margaret then asked to speak with the principal, who informed her, "Deaf children lack the input that hearing children receive. Early schooling helps to counteract this, in order that the child may reach his or her full potential."

Margaret still wasn't satisfied with the answers she was receiving.

She then spoke with Mrs. Hood, the head coordinator of the Special Education Department. "Mrs. Cline, don't you want Christopher to learn how to speak so you can communicate with him?"

"But I do communicate with him . . . maybe not like other mothers communicate with their sons, but Christopher and I understand each other just fine."

"That is fine for now, but as he grows older, I believe you will no longer be satisfied with his grunts, squeals, and groans. You will want to be able to communicate your feelings, concerns, ideals, and beliefs."

Though Margaret recognized the truth behind Mrs. Hood's words, she could not imagine sending her baby to school. "Don't you think Christopher could wait and have a speech therapist aid him once he enters kindergarten? It just seems that leaving the security of his home and family so early in his life would be too traumatic for him."

Mrs. Hood spoke kindly, yet firmly, "Mrs. Cline, please remember that we are not asking you to send Christopher away to an institution. He would be attending Roosevelt school, which is a local school, where he would be educated and cared for a few hours each day, and then he would return home. Have you contemplated the outcome of waiting until Christopher is the age that other children would normally begin schooling before aiding him to speak? How will the other children view him? Children can be very cruel you know. You need to look at Christopher's situation objectively. What would be more traumatic for your son? Early schooling to prepare him so that he has a chance to fit in and function in a hearing world, or the ridicule of his peers?"

Margaret understood, but she wasn't ready to send her little Christopher to school. She cordially reminded Mrs. Hood that it was just a recommendation of the state, and not a law, that her child attend school at three years of age. Then she hung up the phone.

Margaret had not shown Jack the state's recommendation to send Christopher to Roosevelt school. In fact, she tried to dodge his involvement for as long as she could, knowing that he would agree with the state's recommendation. Unfortunately, though, a decision needed to be made, and the recommendation letter needed to be signed by both parents before being returned to the state. As the deadline approached for returning the letter, Margaret realized that the time had come to let Jack know what was happening so they could make a decision as to Christopher's education.

After having dinner and allowing them both some time to unwind, Margaret approached Jack with her concerns. "We received a letter from the state recently. It seems that Christopher is eligible to participate in the special education program at Roosevelt school."

Handing the letter to Jack, Margaret waited nervously for his response. "Isn't Christopher a little young to be attending school?"

Margaret, pleased with Jack's reply, added, "That's what I thought too."

"Did you contact the school to see why they feel Christopher should start school at such a young age?"

"Yes . . . I did."

"Well . . . what did they say?"

Margaret began stammering, "I called . . . and was transferred from one person to another. I spoke with the school's guidance counselor, the principal, and the head coordinator of the special education program. They seem to think that, because Christopher is deaf, he needs early schooling."

"After giving it much thought, I don't think that it's necessary. If he's put in school now, he'll just be grouped with other deaf kids. He won't receive individualized training . . . like I could give him at home."

"Margaret, Margaret . . . These people are experts. What do we know about the proper way to educate Christopher?"

"Jack, we're his parents!"

"Yes, and I think, as his parents, we need to make responsible decisions for our son so that he will get every advantage out of life. We obviously don't know how to teach Christopher to speak, since he still can't say 'Mama' or 'Dada.' Remember, Margaret, Christopher is our first real contact with deafness. The staff at Roosevelt school has years of experience . . . experience that we can benefit from."

"I know, but . . ." Margaret began crying, "I just can't let him go."

"Dear, I know that it's difficult watching him go to school when he is so little, but it really is the best thing for Christopher."

Margaret sat silently while Jack reread the state's recommendation and signed his name at the bottom of the form. He handed the letter back to her. Holding the letter tightly in her hands, as if afraid loosening her grip would be letting go of her dear Christopher, Margaret sat quietly until Jack went to bed, and then she tucked the letter away in her desk to consider at a later time.

Chapter 6
<u>Control Lost</u>

A few weeks had passed since Jack and Margaret had discussed the state's recommendation. They had been carrying out their daily routines, and everything was continuing as usual until one particular afternoon when Margaret took Christopher to Claire's home.

Claire and her husband, Eric, lived a few houses down the street from Jack and Margaret. Their son, Eric, was an energetic two-year-old. The couples had met at a block party the summer before and had become friends. Since Christopher and Eric always had such a good time playing, Margaret and Claire had made it a point to get together every week.

Margaret would put a few of Christopher's toys in his diaper bag so that when they went to Claire's, the boys would each have some of their own toys to play with. Today, Margaret quickly grabbed up a few toys and stuffed them into the diaper bag, without taking notice as to which toys she was bringing. When they arrived at Claire's, the two young mothers began discussing plans for a jewelry party that Claire was hosting the following week. Margaret was looking forward to getting to know better other mothers in the neighborhood with whom, until now, she had only spoken briefly in passing. Talking to Claire, Margaret absent-mindedly placed Christopher's toys on the floor for the two boys.

After a few minutes, tears began streaming down Christopher's cheeks. He soon began to scream uncontrollably, his arms and legs flailing as if to protect himself from something.

Margaret, startled by Christopher's sudden reaction, bent down and picked him up. His face was pale. She held him tightly, trying to console him, but it was to no avail. "Christopher, what's wrong? What are you afraid of?"

Christopher continued screaming.

Margaret didn't understand. Something was definitely upsetting Christopher, but she had no clue as to what had triggered such a reaction. Margaret checked Christopher's diaper pins to make sure one of them had not come undone and poked him. No, the pins were closed. She thought that maybe he was hungry, so she pulled out the animal crackers and tried to give one to Christopher. He pushed the cracker away and continued screaming. Margaret didn't know what to do. She tried to keep her composure as Claire reassured Eric that his little friend would be all right.

Margaret carried Christopher into the kitchen and sat down at the table. Settling him down on her lap, she held him tightly. She stroked his head in order to comfort him.

After a few moments, Christopher began to calm down. He looked up at Margaret with his big blue eyes. She wiped the tears off his face and asked, "What is it baby?"

Christopher just kept looking into his mother's reassuring eyes. Even if he had known what she was saying, he would, of course, be unable to answer.

Margaret, seeing that Christopher had calmed down, decided to take him back to play with Eric.

Christopher put his arms around Margaret's neck and hugged her tightly. As they entered the living room, he cautiously lifted his head off of his mother's shoulder and looked around. All of a sudden, he began screaming and trembling.

Margaret, perplexed by Christopher's reaction, took him back into the kitchen. "I'm sorry Christopher. I don't understand. Please help me understand. Tell Mama what's wrong."

Christopher continued crying. This time he would not let go of Margaret.

It was happening sooner than she had expected. There was something that Christopher needed to tell her but was unable to communicate. He had no way to convey his fears to his mother. Margaret, feeling helpless, could no longer control her emotions. She began to cry as well.

By that time, Claire had come into the kitchen. Standing behind her friend, she gently patted Margaret's shoulder. "It will be all right. Just give Christopher some time."

Margaret didn't want Claire's pity or her advice. She just wanted to be home.

"Claire, please get Christopher's diaper bag. We need to go home now."

Claire went into the living room and gathered up Christopher's toys and put them into the diaper bag. Within a few minutes, Margaret and Christopher were back in the safety of their home.

After putting Christopher down for his nap, Margaret sat down at the kitchen table with a cup of tea. The only thing out of place in her spotless kitchen was the diaper bag sitting on the chair next to her, so she decided to take Christopher's toys out and organize its contents.

There it was . . . that had to be the cause of Christopher's anguish. It was a small, colorful wooden train that she would have sworn she had thrown away after Jack had thrown it against the wall and broken it in a moment of rage a few weeks earlier. It was once Christopher's prize possession, his favorite toy. Evidently, Jack had found the train and mended it as best he could, hoping to redeem himself. The memories now connected with the wooden train affected Christopher so deeply that his once-prized toy now sparked fear in him.

Margaret sat in silence. The scenario of Christopher's reaction to the wooden train played over and over in her mind.

Her feeling of helplessness increased as she realized that the frustration of not being able to express himself or make himself understood had intensified Christopher's fear. Christopher needed to learn to communicate.

Margaret, feeling responsible for Christopher's ordeal, remembered the state's recommendation that Christopher attend Roosevelt school. She took the letter out of her desk, reread it, and then signed it. She called the school to set up a consultation with the head of the special education program, Mrs. Hood. A follow-up date was set when Christopher could go with his parents to see the school, and a tentative date was set for Christopher to begin his schooling.

That day came all too soon for Margaret.

Chapter 7
<u>Little Bus</u>

When the little yellow school bus pulled up in front of the Cline home, Christopher was excitedly waiting by the front door. He was wearing his new coat and shoes. Margaret had packed Christopher a lunch, which he was holding by his side.

Christopher thought he and his mother were going somewhere—to the grocery store, to the playground, or to Jack's office. Anywhere he went with his mother was enjoyable.

Margaret knew Christopher had no idea what was about to happen.

Bending down, Margaret caressed Christopher's cheek and kissed his forehead. She looked into his eyes, "Oh baby, you are going to school today. You will have a lot of fun and make new friends. It will be fine." There was no way Margaret could communicate these concepts to Christopher, but hearing herself say the words seemed to ease her conscience.

Margaret, taking Christopher by the hand, walked him to the school bus. Christopher had never seen such a big, brightly colored vehicle before. He gazed at the bus, looking at it from front to back and then back to front. A large door opened on the side of the bus. Unsure of what was about to occur, Christopher tightened his grip on his mother's hand.

A friendly looking woman stepped off the bus and approached Margaret and Christopher. "Hello. My name is Ruth. I'm going to be your son's bus driver."

"Oh, hi. I'm Margaret . . . Margaret Cline, and this is my son, Christopher."

Ruth held her hand out to Christopher. "Come on cutie." Christopher smiled shyly as he backed up and hid behind his mother, never letting go of her hand.

"I think . . . maybe I should walk him into the bus myself, and . . . he should be fine . . . This is all new to him."

"Oh, yes, of course."

Margaret looked at Christopher, then at the school bus, and back at Christopher. She tried to give him a reassuring look as she gently pulled him forward and led him to the bus.

Christopher looked up at the steps leading into the bus. They seemed insurmountable. As he was contemplating how he would overcome this obstacle, he felt himself being lifted up to the landing by his mother.

Christopher looked around for something or someone familiar, but found neither. The little bus was empty. It was all right, though, because his mother was by his side, leading him to the seat adjacent to the bus driver, sitting down with him. This would be fun.

Margaret put her arm around Christopher, leaned forward, and kissed his cheek. Standing up quickly, she walked out of the bus. The door closed behind her.

Christopher climbed up on the seat to look out the window. His mother was walking away. He was left behind. Feeling scared and alone, he leaned his head against the window and started crying.

As Margaret walked away from the bus, it took everything she had to control her emotions. Turning around, she waved at Christopher and blew him a kiss. Because everyone had said sending Christopher to school at such an early age was the right thing to do, she had put on a facade of bravery; however, inside she still questioned their judgment.

The bus pulled away and Margaret, no longer able to hold back the tears, ran into the house sobbing.

Chapter 8
Traumatic Day

Pulling away from the Cline home, Ruth glanced in her rearview mirror. She could see that Christopher was quite upset and confused. She tried consoling him. "It's okay, little guy . . . I'm your friend." She knew he couldn't hear her, but she had adjusted her mirror so that Christopher could see her smiling face and that she was waving at him. It was of no use. He was still looking out the window trying to find his mother.

Being only three years old, Christopher still needed Margaret. He was hardly prepared to deal with the wave of emotions that resulted from being separated from her.

After looking out the window and being unable to find his mother, Christopher decided to search the bus. He wiped the tears from his eyes, turned around in his seat, climbed up on his knees, and looked around. All he could see were a few rows of empty seats. Climbing down and walking toward the back of the bus, he looked in each of the rows. When he reached the last row of seats and realized his mother wasn't there, he laid his head down on the seat and began crying. "Maaa ma maaa ma ma aaa ma." All Christopher knew was that this warm and loving person who had been at his side all his life and taken care of him was gone . . . maybe forever.

Ruth, not knowing what to do, tried to imagine what it must be like for Christopher. Having no means of communication, he could not ask for explanations. His inability to hear barred him from fully knowing what was happening around him, and it prohibited him from receiving reassurance from the voice of a friend. Those thoughts were almost too much for Ruth to bear. The situation was obviously overwhelming for Christopher, whose cries now echoed throughout the bus.

Ruth pulled off the main highway onto a deserted side street that led to an abandoned warehouse, where she parked the bus. Glancing around, she hoped for the impossible: that Christopher's mother would miraculously appear.

Christopher was lying face down in the last row of seats, crying, when Ruth approached. The vinyl seat was covered with tears. Bending down, Ruth stroked his hair.

Christopher felt Ruth's hand comforting him much like his mother's had done numerous times before. He turned quickly, expecting to see his mother's loving face, only to find the woman who had taken him away from her. Quickly turning away from Ruth, Christopher tried to bury his head in the seat. He began crying even harder than before. The more Christopher cried, the more helpless Ruth felt.

"Hey sweetheart . . . it will be okay." Sitting down beside Christopher, Ruth gathered him into her arms, and tried to console him. In a soothing voice, she said, "You will be back with your mommy soon." Though she knew Christopher couldn't hear the tone of her voice, Ruth hoped that somehow he could sense her compassion.

He had, and he began to relax in the arms of this woman who acted as a temporary surrogate for his mother. Though no words had been exchanged, Christopher had correctly interpreted her smile and her touch.

Ruth was overwhelmed by the whole experience. Her eyes began welling up with tears. She feared that if she yielded to her emotions, she would be sacrificing the reassurance that

Christopher now needed. Still, choosing to share his suffering . . . she cried.

Ruth continued holding Christopher. As he was looking up at her, their eyes met. Christopher gazed for a long time directly into her eyes, to the point that she began to feel uneasy. He seemed to want to tell her something, but he was unable to utter the unknown words, " . . . aahmmma . . ."

Ruth knew what Christopher meant. The temporary time for a surrogate was completed, and he wanted to be back with his real mother. "You'll be with your mother . . . soon." Secure in Ruth's arms for several more minutes, Christopher fell asleep. Ruth then laid him back on the seat and continued driving to the school.

Roosevelt was much like the stereotype: bright red bricks, three stories high, a circular driveway for the buses to park, a tall flagpole in the middle of the schoolyard, and children running and playing.

Christopher was still sleeping in the back of the bus when Ruth approached him.

"How unfortunate that this little boy must face the world at such a young age," Ruth thought. Kneeling next to Christopher, she rubbed his back. She moved in closer and whispered, "Be brave, little Christopher."

He slowly opened his eyes.

"Hi sweetie. We're here at your new school." Ruth reached out her hand to Christopher. With nowhere else to turn, he took hold of her hand and followed.

After clumsily climbing down the school bus steps, Christopher was greeted with a mountain of cement steps rising ever upward. Perceiving that Christopher was overwhelmed as he surveyed the task set before him, Ruth picked him up and cradled him in her arms. He was still light enough that she could carry him up the steps. When they reached the pinnacle, she put Christopher down. But faced with two doors that towered over him, Christopher was still anxious.

As Ruth and Christopher stepped inside the school, a teacher walked to the door and began yelling something to the students outside. The children that had been playing in the schoolyard began lining up on the stairs.

Ruth took Christopher to the office, where Mr. Novak, the principal, then directed them to Room 16, "the classroom for handicapped and retarded children." Room 16 was located in the school's basement.

As Christopher walked through the halls, he became flustered; there was so much for him to see. There were colorful pictures lining the walls, children hurriedly drinking water from fountains while teachers were ushering them into their classrooms, and one man overseeing it all. Christopher, feeling intimidated by everything, held tightly to Ruth's hand. They walked down the stairs and through a long corridor to Room 16.

The teacher, a middle-aged woman with a friendly smile, approached Christopher. Bending down, she looked him in the eyes. She spoke directly to him, enunciating each word, so that he could understand what she was saying . . . if only he had known the words.

"Welcome to school! My name is Mrs. Turner." She smiled and repeated her name, "Mrs. Turner. That's me." She held out her hand to Christopher.

Unsure of what to do, Christopher looked at Ruth, who smiled, nodded in approval, and then nudged him toward the teacher. He reluctantly took Mrs. Turner's hand.

Mrs. Turner led Christopher into the classroom. There he saw many children sitting around tables and many brightly colored toys neatly lining the shelves.

Christopher turned around to see the friendly woman from the bus, but she was gone. He ran, screaming, to the door. Looking down the hallway, he was unable to find the one person who had brought him a measure of comfort since being separated from his mother. Now he felt extremely frightened and alone. Unable to communicate with anyone, he fell to the floor and began crying uncontrollably.

No matter what Mrs. Turner tried to do, it seemed that it only made the situation worse. She had no other choice than to remove Christopher from the classroom and take him to the nurse's office.

After consulting with the nurse, Mrs. Turner decided that it would be in Christopher's best interest to contact his mother. She called Margaret and explained the situation to her.

"I'll be there right away. Oh, my poor baby." Margaret wondered what kind of effect such a traumatic experience would have on Christopher's emotional development. Once again she questioned whether sending Christopher to school at this time was really the best thing for him.

In the time it took Margaret to reach the school, Christopher had exhausted himself from crying and was fast asleep in the infirmary.

Mrs. Turner took the time to introduce herself to Margaret and to discuss ways in which to help Christopher become acclimated to his new surroundings. She suggested that Margaret and Christopher go home, eat their lunch, and then come back to spend the remainder of the day looking around the school. Hesitantly, Margaret accepted Mrs. Turner's suggestion.

They did follow the plan laid out for them by Mrs. Turner, but after their little excursion through the school, Margaret and Christopher were glad to be back home.

Margaret, still searching for answers to Christopher's school dilemma, called Dr. Sherwood. She explained in detail how traumatic the day had been for Christopher . . . and for her. Dr. Sherwood recommended that Margaret accompany Christopher to school for a few days while he familiarized himself with his new environment.

Margaret decided to take Dr. Sherwood's advice a step farther. She not only took Christopher to school and sat in his class for a couple of days, she also volunteered to work in the principal's office for the entire school year.

Chapter 9
Four Wheels

Christopher was now four years old and had recently finished his first year of school. Since he had done so well, his father wanted to reward him.

After work, Jack went to the toy store and found a riding truck. It was a red fire engine with four yellow-and-red striped wheels. The large white steering wheel had a bright red horn in the middle. "Christopher will like this."

Patiently waiting for his father to come home from work, as usual Christopher was leaning over the back of the couch looking out the front window. He looked up the street and then down the street for Jack's big brown car. When he looked back up the street, he saw his father turn the corner onto their street and then turn again into their driveway. Christopher, excited to see Jack, began waving frantically to him.

Jack got out of the car and waved back. He shut the driver's door and looked back at the window. Christopher was gone. He no doubt had run to the side door, where he always greeted his father. Jack took the fire engine out of the trunk and walked toward the house. Placing the new toy just outside of the doorway, Jack opened the side door.

Christopher jumped up and gave him a big hug.

"I've got something for you," Jack said as he stepped back outside and brought the fire engine into the house.

Surprised by his father's actions, Christopher's eyes opened wide as he looked wonderingly from the new toy to his father.

Jack, putting his hand on Christopher's shoulder, looked him in the eyes and said, "It's for you."

Christopher read the invitation in his father's eyes. He was so excited that he immediately sat on the fire engine and began racing around the house. His little legs just kept going and going, pushing him into the living room, his bedroom, and back to the kitchen. He zoomed all around the house in his new little fire truck.

Thinking it might be nice for Christopher to burn up some of his energy outside, Margaret decided to take him and his truck for a walk around the block.

Jack, preferring to use the quiet time inside to relax, read his newspaper.

After Margaret and Christopher had taken their walk, Margaret sat outside on the front porch, watching Christopher drive his fire engine up and down the driveway.

The phone began to ring. Margaret expected Jack to answer it, but it continued ringing.

"Christopher is so busy racing up and down the driveway, he won't even notice I'm gone . . . and I'll be just a few seconds," Margaret thought. She ran inside.

Hurrying through the living room, Margaret saw Jack sleeping on the couch. She picked up the telephone. "Hello."

"Hi, Margaret. This is Julie." It was Margaret's Avon representative. "I wanted to let you know about a new line of cosmetics that are coming out next month."

After chatting for about two minutes, Margaret realized that Christopher was still outside by himself. "Julie, I hate to cut you short, but I left Christopher outside playing. Listen, I'll call you later. Okay?"

Margaret hung up the phone and went back outside.

Christopher wasn't in the driveway. Margaret looked up and down the street. He was nowhere to be seen. "Jack, Jack! Did Christopher come inside?"

"Wha . . . what?" Jack groggily tried to respond.

"Where's Christopher!" By now, Margaret was running through the house checking all the rooms. Her heart was racing as fear started to overtake her.

"I thought Christopher was outside with you."

"I came in to get the phone . . . now he's gone!"

Jumping off the couch, Jack ran outside in his stocking feet. He began scanning the neighborhood. "Margaret, check the backyard. Then you go down to the corner, and I'll check this way."

Jack and Margaret split up. Looking up and down the street, they asked the neighbors if they had seen Christopher. They called out to Christopher, which they knew was of no avail, but it helped to alert others in the neighborhood that he was missing.

Linda from across the street, as well as Claire and her husband from down the street, began searching for Christopher. Eric, who was checking the yards on the opposite side of the street, yelled to Jack, "Do you think the police should be notified that Christopher is missing?"

"Yeah; that's a good idea. Can you call them? I have to keep looking."

"Sure; I'll take care of it."

Within a matter of minutes, the police arrived at Jack and Margaret's house. The officers questioned them as to what Christopher looked like, what he was wearing, and when they had last seen him.

Giving the police officers Christopher's school picture, Margaret told them he was wearing a pair of blue overalls without a shirt underneath, white socks, and navy gym shoes.

Jack described the fire engine that Christopher had been

riding. He also told the officers that Christopher was deaf.

The officers' biggest concern, as well as Jack and Margaret's, was Huron Road, just three blocks west and one of the most heavily traveled roads in town. Radioing the dispatcher, the police officers had all the patrol cars put on alert that Christopher was missing.

When two hours had passed and Christopher had not yet been found, Jack and Margaret were terrified. They were preparing for the worst.

Finally, the dispatcher radioed to all the officers that a little boy fitting Christopher's description had been found seven blocks away on Huron Road just north of Mack Avenue.

Jack had been riding in a patrol car with one of the officers that received the call. The patrol car immediately headed back to the Cline home.

Nervously waiting at home, in case Christopher should make his way back, Margaret was unaware of what had been happening . . .

A police officer driving south on Huron Road noticed a young boy on the opposite side of the street. Riding a red fire engine, the child was not accompanied by an adult. "This may be the missing boy," he thought. The officer switched on his flashing lights, turned his car around, and pulled up next to the young boy. Getting out of his car, he slowly approached the child.

Christopher, noticing the flashing lights, stopped to see what was happening.

The officer smiled and waved at the boy.

Christopher waved back.

"Hi, little man. What is your name?"

Christopher smiled, impressed with the uniform and gear of the man approaching him.

Knowing the missing child was deaf, the officer waved at him again. He pointed at the red fire engine and made a thumbs-up sign. "That is a nice fire engine you have there."

Christopher kept watching the officer.

Pulling a lollipop out of his pocket, the officer removed the paper and showed the candy to the child.

Christopher, anticipating the familiar taste, smiled and reached out for the lollipop. He immediately started licking it.

Now, being on friendly terms with the young boy, the officer picked him up and put him in the front seat of the patrol car. He then put the toy fire engine in the back seat. The officer radioed the dispatcher to let the other officers know that the missing child had been found.

On the way to what turned out to be his home, Christopher was enthralled with the patrol car. The nice officer let him inspect the CB radio and turn the flashing lights on and off. Though he hadn't words for any of it, meeting the police officer and riding in the patrol car was a great adventure that Christopher would remember for a long time.

In the meantime, Margaret had been sitting on the couch crying. She wondered how she could be so careless as to lose her son. The emptiness she felt when she thought her son was gone forever was a feeling she hoped she would never experience again.

While agonizing over what had taken place, Margaret heard a familiar squeal of delight. She jumped up and raced to the front window. Seeing her giggling Christopher on the shoulders of a police officer, Margaret again began to cry. Her tears were no longer tears of grief, but tears of joy. Running outside, she grabbed Christopher and held him so tightly that he could barely move.

Another patrol car pulled up in front of the house, and Jack jumped out. He ran over to Margaret and Christopher. Relieved to see that Christopher was unharmed, Jack and Margaret held Christopher and each other.

The next morning, Jack went to the pet store. Christopher, of course, was unaware of his father's plans until later that afternoon, when his mom took him out to play. Discovering that he had to wear a dog's harness and that his play area was only as long as the leash attached to the door of the house, Christopher, for the first time, was disappointed with what his father had bought him.

Chapter 10
<u>Abusive Treatment</u>

Christopher's summer vacation was much like that of the other kids who were freed from the routine of going to school: excitement . . . amusement . . . refreshment . . . monotony. Nonetheless, the first morning that the school bus arrived to pick up Christopher for the next school term came much too soon.

Margaret had tried to explain to Christopher that he would be starting school again. She had drawn a picture of the yellow school bus with a woman stick figure in the front and a smaller stick figure in the middle of the bus. Pointing to the smaller stick figure and then to Christopher, Margaret said, "That's you."

She had two other papers laid out on the floor. One had a picture of a red brick building. "Your school." The other picture was a house. "Our house, here." Margaret said as she pointed toward the floor. Taking the yellow bus, she moved it from the house to the school. After a few seconds, the bus returned to the house. Margaret then drew a woman stick figure with a big smile on her face in front of the house. Christopher understood.

Still feeling anxious, Christopher, accompanied by his mother, walked to the bus when it arrived. He tried to be brave, but tears began to stream down his face. Climbing the steps into the bus, Christopher looked up and saw Ruth smiling at him. He remembered how friendly she had been to him and how much better she had made him feel on his first day of school last year.

Ruth held her hand out to Christopher. "Hi sweetie. Come with me."

Smiling through his tears, Christopher grabbed hold of Ruth's hand. She led him to his seat.

"Stay right there. I have a surprise for you." Ruth walked over to the driver's seat, grabbed something, and put it behind her back. Returning to Christopher, she pulled a stuffed toy from behind her and gave it to him. It was Snoopy.

Christopher's face lit up. Though he had no idea who Snoopy was, the little toy brought a broad smile to his face. He looked out the window to find his mother and showed her his new stuffed toy.

Margaret, waving to Christopher, said, "Oh yes, that is a very nice gift Ruth gave you."

Before the bus pulled away, Margaret wanted to tell Christopher how she felt about him. Putting her hands over her heart, she very slowly and distinctly said, "I . . . love . . . you."

Christopher put his head against the window and again began to cry. He did not know the words his mother's mouth motions meant, but he felt like putting his hands over his chest too, it hurt so. All he knew was his mother was his best friend. He missed her so much when he had to leave her for even one minute, and now he was going to be in school all day.

Watching as the bus drove away, Margaret waved to Christopher and blew him a kiss. It was the one thing she was sure he'd understand, because she had played with him since birth blowing him kisses and hugging him.

Linda, the woman who lived across the street from the Clines, saw Margaret outside. Wanting to make small talk, she walked over to Margaret, "Was that the school bus I just saw pull away from your home?"

"Yes. It was."

"Isn't your son too young to be going to school? Or is he

some kind of genius? My kids weren't ready to go to school until they were five years old."

Margaret, feeling disheartened because Christopher's deafness caused him to be treated differently than other children, managed to smile and respond to Linda. "Christopher is enrolled in a special program to prepare him for the future."

"What kind of program does the school provide for such young children?"

"We received a letter from the state indicating that because of Christopher's handicap, he qualifies to be a part of a special education program."

Talking for almost an hour, Margaret took the opportunity to explain to Linda how Christopher's deafness affected him and how Roosevelt school's program would teach him the skills he would need to communicate.

Impressed with Margaret's effort to help her son, Linda complimented her. "You're doing a fine job with your son, Margaret. Keep doing what you're doing. I'm sure Christopher will be all right."

Meanwhile, once Ruth had gotten the school bus well underway, she looked in her rearview mirror to check on Christopher. It appeared that he had stopped crying and was sitting quietly holding his Snoopy. She could see that he still had his head up against the window.

Staring out the window, Christopher watched the white lines on the street as they appeared to wriggle through the tears that were poised to spill from his eyelids. He felt safe holding his Snoopy; it gave him a measure of comfort and security as he was out in the world, away from his mother.

Mrs. Turner was Christopher's teacher again this year. There were ten students in her class, which was a relatively large number of students for a special education class. Three of the students were deaf, and seven students were hearing children with other handicaps. Last year had been an exercise in helping her students get along with each other and get used to the school routine. Because these students would be slow in learning for a few years, some forever, this would be a teaching year, even though most of her students would not normally have started kindergarten until next year. It was hoped that starting their learning skills earlier would keep them from falling too far behind the "normal" students. Helping the students to recognize words, Mrs. Turner had signs posted all around the classroom: DOOR, BLACKBOARD, CLOWN.

Mrs. Turner was a good teacher; she had worked many years in the special education department. Helping crippled children and slow learners seemed to be what she was meant to do. Unfortunately, not having had much exposure to the deaf community, when it came to the needs of her deaf students, she was not so adept. Speaking louder and enunciating her words while she taught, Mrs. Turner tried to help them progress. It seemed, though, that the deaf students' impairment was worse than that of the other students. The only time Christopher and the other deaf students could understand her was when she demonstrated exactly what she wanted them to do. Dividing her attention evenly between all of the students was almost impossible, since the deaf students required more of her time.

A few weeks into the school year, the frustration that Mrs. Turner was feeling due to the inability of the deaf students to understand her became apparent.

The morning started like any other day. The class attempted to say the pledge of allegiance and then all the students sat, coloring, at their desks.

Christopher was coloring a picture of his family standing outside their home. As he was coloring the blue sky, his teacher called for all the students to give her their undivided attention. Not hearing Mrs. Turner's directions for the students to put their crayons away, Christopher continued coloring.

Mrs. Turner pounded her fist on the desk. The deaf students sitting in the front row gave her their attention, but Christopher, who was sitting toward the middle of the classroom, was unable to feel any vibrations. Walking over to Christopher, Mrs. Turner grabbed the crayon out of his hand and confiscated the remaining crayons that were lying on his desk. She returned to the front of the classroom and began teaching the class how to write the letter "A."

Christopher, sitting quietly in his seat concentrating on coloring, had been startled by his teacher's actions. He looked around at the other students. Looking back at Mrs. Turner, he hadn't a clue why she had taken his crayons, what she was saying to the class, or what was required of him. He looked down at his seat and noticed his Snoopy sitting in the corner. Holding his toy close, he looked Snoopy in the eyes and smiled.

Mrs. Turner again came over to Christopher's desk. This time she grabbed Snoopy out of his hands.

At least he had seen her coming this time, and his chest wasn't pounding so hard. Christopher watched as she carried his toy off to her desk in the front of the classroom. He saw some of the distracted students laugh and rush up to Mrs. Turner's desk and begin touching Snoopy.

As he continued watching, Mrs. Turner, with a stern look on her face, said something to the students. Returning to their seats, they paid close attention to whatever she was saying.

Confused, hurt, and lonely, Christopher began to cry. His cries gradually became louder and louder as his need for support—some friendly face, some understanding of what he was supposed to do—skyrocketed.

Mrs. Turner, who was clearly frustrated with Christopher's emotional outburst, walked back to his desk. She looked him in the eyes, "Pay attention, Christopher."

Not understanding what Mrs. Turner was trying to tell him, Christopher sadly looked down at his desktop, wishing he could hide under it.

Suddenly he felt Mrs. Turner, thinking that her student was being obstinate, grab him by the chin and force his head up so that he was looking directly at her.

"You are in school now. It's time for you to stop playing and pay attention!"

Of course, the words meant nothing to him, and alarmed by his teacher's tight grip, Christopher closed his eyes and began sobbing.

Mrs. Turner began to shake Christopher. "Be a good boy and pay attention!" When he wouldn't stop crying, she yanked him out of his seat and made him stand next to his chair. "Stop crying!"

Feeling his teacher becoming even more angry, Christopher tried to quiet himself, but he couldn't stop whimpering and gasping.

Mrs. Turner was holding Christopher tightly by his shoulders. Unable to calm him, she again began shaking him and finally slapped him across the face. "The whole class is looking at you. Is that what you want?"

Christopher, thoroughly bewildered, was now really frightened and began to wail. He didn't know what she wanted, he didn't know how to tell her, he didn't know the words to express how he felt; in fact, he didn't even know there were words, for he'd never heard any. All he knew were gentle actions and violent actions, pretty sights and ugly sights, and how they made him feel. And right now he felt the need to scream and flee from the violence that threatened him.

Mrs. Turner again grabbed him by the chin. "Be quiet! Everyone can hear you!"

During Mrs. Turner's attempt to deal with Christopher, the other special education teacher from the next classroom, Miss Glenn, had heard all the crying and had come over to see if she could offer her assistance.

Looking through the classroom door, Miss Glenn could see all the children looking toward the center of the room. There was Mrs. Turner, holding a little boy by his shoulders. He was apparently crying uncontrollably. Shaking him, Mrs. Turner looked unsympathetic as she slapped him across the face.

Miss Glenn, unable to bear watching such harsh treatment of a young child, entered the classroom.

Hearing the door open, Mrs. Turner straightened up quickly and walked to her desk. Under her breath she had murmured, "What is it going to take to make him understand?" but looking at Miss Glenn, she asked, "How can I help you?"

Miss Glenn walked past Mrs. Turner to Christopher, who

was still sobbing. She could see he looked scared. As she moved closer, she also noticed he had a red handprint on his face, where he had been slapped. Wiping the tears off Christopher's face, Miss Glenn looked at Mrs. Turner. "What did he do that was so bad that you felt the need to treat him so harshly? You cannot expect him to learn anything under these circumstances."

"How dare you question my teaching methods!"

Miss Glenn held her hand out to Christopher, who, sensing her kindness in contrast to Mrs. Turner's violence, quickly grabbed hold. As she led him to the classroom door Miss Glenn said, "You won't need to worry about this young one any longer."

"Take good care of him. Oh, here; this is his," said Mrs. Turner as she handed Snoopy to Miss Glenn.

Miss Glenn had delivered her students to the gymnasium for their physical education class. Afterwards, their Gym Teacher would deliver them to the cafeteria for lunch. Taking Christopher into her temporarily empty classroom, she showed him her desk and the rest of the room. She noticed he had exhausted himself from crying, so she pointed to one of the floor mats and invited him to lie down on it to rest, demonstrating by lying on the mat next to it.

Once Christopher had fallen asleep, Miss Glenn returned to her desk and reflected on the treatment he had received at the hands of Mrs. Turner. She decided to report Mrs. Turner for her wrongful actions toward young Christopher. Afterwards she took her statement to Mr. Novak's office and made arrangements for Christopher to be transferred to her class.

Almost an hour had passed since Christopher had fallen asleep. He was beginning to stir by the time Miss Glenn returned from Mr. Novak's office. Opening his eyes, he examined his surroundings.

Miss Glenn approached Christopher and sat down on the floor mat next to him.

In order to teach retarded children who couldn't speak, Miss Glenn, in college, had learned sign language as a means of communication. Since Christopher was also unable to speak, she decided to try to communicate with him using sign language.

She put her hand up by her head like a salute, a sign that means "Hello."

Christopher, not understanding what Miss Glenn was doing, just stared.

Miss Glenn wanted to reach Christopher . . . somehow . . . and then she saw it. Christopher's little Snoopy was sitting on her desk. She retrieved the stuffed animal and brought it to him. Before handing it to him, she made a hand shape that looked like she was holding a ball in her fist. She put her closed fist over her nose. Moving her other cupped hand, she put it over Snoopy's big black nose. She again did the hand sign on her nose and this time pointed to Snoopy. "He's Snoopy . . . Snoopy."

Christopher smiled. In imitation of Miss Glenn, he pointed to Snoopy and then did the hand sign on his nose.

Miss Glenn was thrilled by Christopher's response. She patted Christopher on the back. "Very good!" She again pointed to Snoopy and did the hand sign on her nose. "He's Snoopy."

Miss Glenn next made the hand sign for teacher by forming the letter T with her left hand and with her right hand. Positioning her hands near her face at eye level, she moved them simultaneously forward and backward. She then said "teacher." Repeating the sign, but replacing the Ts for teacher with Gs for Glenn, she then pointed at herself. "My name is Miss Glenn," she said as she repeated her name sign.

Christopher smiled as he pointed to Miss Glenn and repeated her name sign.

Having never been exposed to sign language, Christopher did not have a name sign of his own, so Miss Glenn proceeded to make up a name sign for Christopher. Seizing on his smile, which lit up his whole face, she made a hand shape that looked like a "C," put it next to her mouth, and moved it along her smile line. Pointing to Christopher, she repeated the sign.

Christopher was delighted. He understood. That was his name. Excitedly, he pointed to himself and made a "C" with his little hand, put it next to his mouth, and moved it along his smile line. Christopher was so enthused by what he had just learned, he repeatedly pointed to Snoopy, Miss Glenn, and himself, showing Miss Glenn each one's name sign. He had no idea what words the signs were associated with, but he knew that those signs stood for the toy, his teacher, and himself.

Christopher's excitement was somewhat diminished when the rest of Miss Glenn's students returned to the classroom and he had to take a seat and share this new friend with the rest of the class. As he watched what transpired the rest of the day, he couldn't help wondering if everything he saw had a hand motion connected to it.

Miss Glenn felt truly satisfied with what she had been able to help Christopher accomplish that day. She was only in her second year of teaching, and this was her first year at Roosevelt school. What she lacked in experience, she certainly made up in her enthusiasm for teaching.

Learning that there were two other deaf children still in Mrs. Turner's class, Miss Glenn approached the school board to explain her qualifications in sign language and requested that she be permitted to teach all of the deaf children. The board unanimously approved Miss Glenn's request, and the deaf students were transferred to her class on the following Monday.

Jack and Margaret, appalled by Mrs. Turner's abusive treatment toward Christopher, refused to send him back to school until the school board took disciplinary action.

The following week Mrs. Turner was written up for harsh treatment toward her students and was suspended from teaching for a month.

Jack and Margaret were relieved that Christopher would no longer be in Mrs. Turner's class. They were thrilled to see Christopher's aversion to school change into an eagerness for learning.

Miss Glenn worked with Christopher and the other deaf students. She helped them to increase their sign language vocabulary. Walking around the classroom, she would point to objects—desk, paper, crayon—showing the students the sign for each object. She quickly realized that the deaf responded to learning sign language and that the visual aids impressed upon their minds the meaning of the signs.

Christopher and the other deaf students immediately began using the signs that Miss Glenn had taught them. Between signing and pantomime, the deaf students learned to communicate with Miss Glenn and each other.

Even the hearing students in the class were learning to sign. Of course, their advantage was that they could hear the words that each sign stood for, while the deaf students could not and therefore didn't even know what "words" were. The advantage for Miss Glenn was that she would be able to use both signing and speech so she could teach both groups of students at the same time.

Christopher was thrilled to have a means of communication. He had brought home a note from Miss Glenn, informing the parents that she was teaching her students sign language and encouraging especially the parents of her deaf students to learn it themselves. Every day Christopher would share what he had learned with his parents.

Margaret was delighted that she and Christopher now would be able to communicate. In addition to Miss Glenn's efforts to teach sign language to Christopher, Margaret had purchased a sign language book. Together, she and Christopher worked hard at learning sign language.

Jack was pleased that Christopher and Margaret could sign to each other . . . in the privacy of their own home. Considering deafness a defect and sign language as bringing attention to that defect, Jack didn't want Christopher using sign language outside of the home. He wanted his son to be able to speak. He wanted Christopher to be able to function and communicate in the world in which he lived—a hearing world. Thus Jack, along with the parents of the other deaf students, met with the school board to share their concerns.

After much deliberation, the board decided that, along with sign language, an oral program would be developed. All the deaf students would be required to meet with a tutor to learn how to vocalize sounds and eventually to learn how to speak.

After a month, the oral program was in place. Christopher worked with the tutor for an hour three times a week.

Starting with the letter A, the tutor tried to teach Christopher how to replicate the letter sounds. Using different techniques to teach different letter sounds, she and Christopher struggled through the alphabet. She would have Christopher feel the reverberation of her vocal chords and then his own as he tried to imitate sounds. For some letters such as the letter P, she would use a tissue, which she held in front of her mouth so that Christopher could see the airflow when the P sound was made. He then would attempt to imitate her.

Christopher found speech to be very difficult to replicate.

Struggling to teach Christopher the letter sounds, the tutor would practice one sound for a week or more before she would move on to the next letter. Oftentimes even after a week, Christopher was still unable to reproduce the letter sounds, but she would move on to the following letter anyway. In this way, Christopher would have the opportunity to master whichever letters he could, and those he could not master right now would have to be learned later.

By the end of the school year, Christopher had only learned to say about 25 percent of the alphabet. The remainder of the letters, he had been unable to master.

Though Margaret felt that sign language was more beneficial for Christopher at that time in his life, she had tried to compliment the tutor's work by practicing letter sounds with him at home. But she could see how difficult it was for him to discern the differences in some vowel sounds and letters like c, s, and z. And, of course, modulation of his voice was out of the question. Margaret's heart was overjoyed when Christopher spoke the words that she had been waiting to hear since his birth.

"Mama. Mama."

During the remainder of the school year, Christopher made great strides in his communication skills, and he had definitely found a friend in Miss Glenn. Christopher was a bit sad when the school year ended, but he was thrilled with the prospect of having Miss Glenn as his teacher the following year.

At the end of the school year, Miss Glenn applied to be transferred to Kennedy Elementary School.

Chapter 11
<u>Signing Banned</u>

During the summer months, Christopher and Margaret regularly visited the local park where he could run, jump, play, and keep active. He would also go play with his friend Eric, who lived a few houses down the street.

A few times, Jack took Christopher to work with him. Those times were always very special to Christopher. He felt important as he followed his father through the buildings with a hardhat on his head, a pencil in his front pocket, and a few papers under his arm, walking just like his father.

Summer went by much too quickly. The time had come for Christopher to begin kindergarten. He would no longer be attending Roosevelt School, but would be riding the bus about five miles farther south, to Kennedy Elementary School.

On the first day of school, the bus came to pick up Christopher. Feeling comfortable with Ruth, he was relieved to see that she was still his bus driver. Since he had begun school, two years earlier, there had been many changes in personnel, but the one individual who had consistently been there for him had been Ruth.

Ruth likewise felt close to Christopher, so much so, that she had wanted to learn how to communicate with him in his own language. She had purchased a sign language book and had attempted to learn a few signs. Now, on Christopher's first day back to school, Ruth awaited an opportunity to try out what she had learned.

As the bus approached Kennedy Elementary, Christopher could see it was quite different from Roosevelt. His new school was much bigger. There were many more children running around outside, and they all seemed to look older and bigger than Christopher.

Ruth dropped Christopher off in front of the school. As he stepped out of the bus, he apprehensively looked back at Ruth. Now was her chance to use her sign language. With a big smile on her face, she pointed at Christopher and then held up two tight fists in front of her. "You be brave."

Smiling, Christopher appreciated Ruth's efforts, though he thought she looked odd.

Christopher was walking toward the door when he noticed a teacher signing to a few students. He approached them.

Turning toward Christopher, the teacher signed, "Hello. What is your name?"

Christopher spelled his name and showed the teacher his name sign.

"Hello Christopher. Welcome. This is your new school. My name is Ms. Bennett."

It had taken Christopher most of last year to understand that the abstract concepts of "hello" and "welcome" were commonly used as greetings. Objects were easy to learn for they could be pointed to and then the sign made, but abstract concepts were much more difficult to comprehend since he had never heard people greet each other. Feeling a little uneasy, he stood quietly in line until the students were permitted to go into the school.

Christopher could see that Ms. Bennett was very different from Miss Glenn. Ms. Bennett was tall and thin, and she was much older looking than Miss Glenn. A pleasant-looking woman, except for the hairy mole on her chin, Ms. Bennett only vaguely reminded Christopher of the witch who lived in the gingerbread house in the picture book his mother had shown to him.

Although Christopher missed Miss Glenn, his new teacher seemed nice. He looked forward to the opportunity to learn from her.

As they were filing into the classroom, Ms. Bennett told her students to sit anywhere they would like. After the students were seated, she had all the students introduce themselves to the class.

Christopher knew a few of the students since they had attended Roosevelt together.

Ms. Bennett directed the students' attention to the blackboard, where she had written SIGN LANGUAGE ONLY IN THIS CLASS. Although the students had learned the letters of the alphabet, they had not yet learned to read, so they were unsure of what the words on the blackboard meant.

Attentively, Christopher watched Ms. Bennett as she used signed English to explain to the class, "There are rules we must follow in this class. The most important rule is that there will be no sign language used outside of this classroom. Do you understand what I am telling you? If I see anyone using sign language outside of this classroom, I will slap your hand with this ruler." She then picked up a wooden ruler and held it up so that everyone could see it.

Christopher looked at the students sitting around him. They looked as puzzled as he felt. The rules for their new school were quite different from those at Roosevelt. Christopher began to feel like he didn't belong in Ms. Bennett's class, and he wished he could be back with Miss Glenn.

Ms. Bennett began class by teaching the students a few English words and their corresponding signs.

Christopher sometimes had a difficult time understanding what Ms. Bennett was trying to explain—partly because he was not familiar with the signs she was using and partly because he only vaguely understood the concept of words (having never heard any) and therefore had not yet learned how to read lips. When people spoke, he could only think in terms of the alphabet letters he was trying so hard to learn to say. When the teacher showed him a picture of an object, he could learn the sign and even learn to spell the word, but he didn't understand why the letters were strung together as they were or how they related to the spoken word. When the teacher couldn't show him a picture of an object for a word she was trying to teach him, he was totally lost. Though his frustration was mounting, Christopher tried to remain composed as he practiced signing the words.

In the middle of writing the words on the blackboard, Ms. Bennett stopped suddenly and looked to the back of the classroom. The students followed her eyes to see a short, husky man standing just inside the classroom door. His facial expression was intimidating, like that of a pit bull dog. Ms. Bennett told the students to continue writing the words.

Ms. Bennett walked to the back of the classroom to talk with the man. After a moment of discussion, both walked to the front of the classroom.

The man began to speak to the class while Ms. Bennett translated his words to sign language. "I am Mr. Chuck. I am the principal here at Kennedy Elementary, and I want all of you to work hard and learn." Mr. Chuck then left as abruptly as he had come.

The students weren't sure what had just taken place, but Ms. Bennett clarified it in no uncertain terms. "This school has very strict rules that each of you must obey. If you don't obey the rules, you will go to Mr. Chuck's office to be punished."

Christopher came to realize that Kennedy Elementary School was, indeed, very different from Roosevelt school. Not only was the school itself different, but also the teachers' attitudes and styles of teaching. With so many rules to learn at this school, Christopher felt that he would go crazy before the day was done.

During lunch, Christopher and the other deaf students sat at a table in the far corner of the cafeteria. They could see the students from the other kindergarten classes talking and having a good time with their friends. Unsure if they were permitted to sign to each other, Christopher and his friends looked for   Ms. Bennett but were unable to find her. They wanted to ask her if they could sign to each other just as the hearing children were permitted to talk to each other during lunch. Deciding to sign to each other quietly, using very small signs and very little hand movements, they talked about their summer vacations and shared funny stories.

After about ten minutes of enjoyable conversation, one of the other kindergarten teachers approached the table of deaf students. Seeming quite perturbed, she waved her index finger and shook her head, "No, no, no."

Christopher and the other deaf students immediately understood that signing was not permitted. They sat quietly looking at each other for the remainder of the lunch period.

For the first time, Christopher experienced what he later would be able to identify as the injustice of double standards—one set of rules for the hearing students and another set of rules for the deaf. How he wished to be back at Roosevelt with Miss Glenn!

After lunch and some time in the school library, the kindergarten students were dismissed at one o'clock.

Christopher ambled over to the bus.

Ruth, greeting him with a big smile, tried her best to sign. "How was your day?"

Christopher looked at her and then looked down. He wasn't able to respond since he was carrying his jacket, lunch box, and two library books. Even if he could have responded, his mind was so preoccupied with the activities of the day that he didn't know what he would say to her. Sitting down in the back of the bus, he tried to relax.

Ruth realized Christopher must have had a difficult first day of school, but she was sure that he would quickly adjust.

The bus pulled up in front of the Cline home. As Christopher emerged, his mother came running out of the house to meet him. Giving him a big hug, she asked how his day at school was. "You like new school?" she signed.

Tears started streaming down Christopher's face.

Margaret hugged Christopher again. She knew immediately that the first day at his new school had been difficult for him; however, she didn't know that the school controlled when and where the deaf students could communicate. How deeply this affected him, Margaret couldn't have had a clue.

Two months after Christopher had begun attending Kennedy Elementary School, he still had a difficult time understanding why the deaf students were not permitted to use sign language outside of the classroom. Not being able to converse, he and the other deaf students were compelled to walk "silently" from class to class while the hearing students were seen talking to their friends on the way to their classes.

As Christopher and his friend Donny made their repressed walk through the hallway from their art class back to Ms. Bennett's classroom, they again noticed the hearing students talking. Christopher looked at Donny and then at the hearing students. He signed with one hand so that Donny could see him. "Boys and girls, they talk talk talk, but we can't." Christopher, feeling very upset by this difference, again looked at the hearing students and then shook his head.

Donny followed Christopher's eyes and then signed, "I agree."

Ms. Bennett suddenly appeared out of nowhere. She grabbed both boys by their arms and turned them toward her. Looking very upset as she spoke, she enunciated each of her words. "Both of you go back to the room." She pointed down the hall toward the classroom. "Put your head on your desk, and there is to be no talking!"

Christopher and Donny walked dejectedly back to the classroom and laid their heads on their desks until Ms. Bennett returned with the rest of the class. Ms. Bennett looked at Christopher and then signed to the class, "If I see any of you using sign language outside of this classroom, recess will be canceled. All of you will remain in the classroom with your heads on your desks. You understand?"

In a school where there is a program specifically established to assist deaf students in communication skills, Christopher was being choked by the inflexibility of its rules.

Chapter 12
<u>Clowning Around</u>

One day after lunch, all of the kindergarten students were taken to the gymnasium and told to sit in a semicircle in a particular area. After everyone was seated, a clown came in to entertain the children.

Christopher loved the clown because it made him smile, just as his toy Snoopy always brought a smile to his face.

The clown was acting crazy—jumping up and down, twisting, and spinning on one foot. The children were all laughing.

Christopher was enthralled with all the action and humored by the clown's merriment. Excitedly, he jumped up from his seat and ran toward the middle of the room, where the clown was performing. As he stood nearby watching the clown perform, it turned and looked at him. Walking right up to Christopher, the clown tickled his tummy, which made him laugh even more. Gently pushing him in the direction of his class, the clown went back to entertaining the other students.

Christopher wanted more interaction with the clown. He walked right up to the clown and pulled on its pant leg.

Turning, the clown looked down at Christopher.

Now that he had the clown's attention, Christopher wasn't sure what to do, but he mustered up courage to sign something. He made a hand shape that looked like a ball and put it over his nose. He then took his index finger, put it on his upper lip, and moved it down to his chin. "Nose red," he signed as he pointed at the clown's big red nose.

Having never seen sign language before, the clown watched Christopher with amazement. It then tried to copy Christopher's hand shapes and movements. The clown looked at the other children and signed, "nose red," as it pointed to all the students.

The deaf children squealed with delight.

All of a sudden, Ms. Bennett, who had been standing at the side trying to figure out how to gracefully get Christopher to sit back down, abandoned any appearance of poise or kindness and simply walked over and grabbed Christopher by the arm and told her students to go back to the classroom.

The clown didn't understand what was happening and tried to block the doorway. The hearing students still seated in the gymnasium were laughing at the clown's antics.

Ms. Bennett was not amused. Saying something to the clown, she moved it out of her way. She led Christopher back to the classroom at such a quick pace that he had to run beside her to keep from being dragged through the hallway. The other students followed, more slowly, behind them.

Christopher wasn't sure what he had done, but he knew he would soon find out.

When the students were back in the classroom, Ms. Bennett told them to sit down and pay attention.

Christopher was quietly sitting at his desk.

Ms. Bennett walked over to Christopher, grabbed his arm, and pulled him over to her desk. She opened her drawer and pulled out a wooden ruler. Holding Christopher's hand down, she hit it with the ruler.

Christopher winced from the pain, but she wouldn't let go.

Ms. Bennett proceeded to strike Christopher two more times, until he started to cry. She was clearly unhappy with him.

Christopher didn't understand why he was being punished, since he had been enjoying the clown just like everyone else.

Ms. Bennett then signed, "Sign language outside of this classroom is prohibited."

Even after all these months at Kennedy Elementary, Christopher still didn't understand the reason for this rule. Looking at Ms. Bennett, he signed, "We can't signing, why?"

Ms. Bennett scowled at Christopher and then turned toward the blackboard where she wrote "No Recess for Christopher on Tuesday", words that by now Christopher had learned to read well. She looked back at Christopher and told him to be quiet and sit down.

Demoralized by Ms. Bennett's treatment, Christopher sat quietly on the floor, waiting for the end of the school day, which couldn't come soon enough.

Ms. Bennett looked toward the classroom door. Someone was standing just outside. Everyone's eyes followed Ms. Bennett as she walked toward the door. When she opened the door, they could see the principal accompanied by the clown from the gymnasium. The three of them exchanged words, and then Ms. Bennett stepped aside to let the clown enter the classroom.

The clown walked over to Christopher, sat on the floor next to him, and picked up his hand.

Christopher was worried about the attention the clown was paying to him. Fearing he might be punished again, Christopher pulled his hand away.

Taking Christopher's little pink hand again, the clown gently rubbed it to relieve some of the pain. The clown looked Christopher directly in his eyes and smiled. It moved its hands up and down, then shook its head and frowned.

Christopher understood. The clown was trying to tell him that sign language was not permitted.

The clown then stood up and left the classroom with the principal following closely behind.

On arriving home from school, Christopher appeared sad. Margaret recalled how Christopher would often come home happy when he attended Roosevelt school. These days, though, he seemed so discontented.

Margaret discussed her concerns with Jack. He just reiterated his opinion that Christopher's life in a hearing world would not be easy and that he must learn to conform to the rules of the world in which he lives.

Chapter 13
<u>Close Call</u>

Snow fell early in 1974. By mid November, there were at least four inches of snow on the ground. Hunting season for deer was open, and Jack was raring to go. He and his childhood buddy Bill went together every year.

This time Jack had decided to take his family for a long weekend to visit Bill, Catherine, and their two daughters, who lived in a mobile home about four hours to the north. Jack and Margaret got up early, packed up the car, and then headed north.

The drive seemed to Christopher to take forever, but at long last, they arrived. He was happy to get out of the car and play in the snow. He wondered that the snow was even deeper here than at home. Plowing through banks that were higher than his knees he didn't even notice how cold it was.

After an early lunch, Margaret and Catherine washed dishes while Jack and Bill discussed their plans for the weekend.

Since Bill and Catherine's daughters were older than Christopher, and he had no interest in girls anyway, Christopher sat with the men. He knew that they were making arrangements to go out because his dad had put his special greenish brown pants on and his matching coat was lying on the floor next to him; he only wore that outfit when he went outside with Bill. Christopher, wanting to know where they were going, watched them as they spoke, but he couldn't understand what they were saying. The combination of the difficulty of learning and "seeing" sounds and the limited number of words Christopher had learned in school made lipreading impossible.

After a few minutes, Bill got up and went to the door. When he opened it, there were some other men wearing the same special coats and pants as Christopher's dad.

Christopher was thrilled to be with all these men. They obviously had something exciting planned, and he wanted to be a part of it.

Jack went over to the door, shook hands with each of the men, and then put on his boots.

Christopher tried to ask his dad if he could go outside, but Jack was too busy conversing with the other men to notice him. Deciding to put on his boots and coat anyway, he pulled them on and waited patiently by the door, while his dad put on the coat that had come to represent adventure in Christopher's mind.

Jack said something to Margaret. She smiled and waved.

As Jack headed out the door, he noticed Christopher standing there. "You stay home with mother. Father go out, but I'll be back."

Though Christopher didn't understand his father's words, he understood his expressions and gestures. He wanted so much to go with his dad, and not being permitted saddened him. He couldn't stop the tears that welled up in his eyes and spilled onto his cheeks.

Jack wanted to explain to Christopher that he was too young to go hunting, but he figured it would be a waste of time, since Christopher most likely would not understand. "You have to stay home with your mother. Okay?" Jack patted Christopher on the back and walked out the door.

Determined to be with his dad no matter what, Christopher finished buttoning his coat and followed Jack outside.

Jack, Bill, and their friends stood outside in a huddle. Christopher stood next to his dad while the men had a quite animated conversation. After a few minutes, Jack and Bill put some supplies in the back of Bill's truck.

Turning back toward Christopher, Jack reiterated, "I'll be back. You stay home." He got in the truck with Bill.

Christopher walked around to the front of Bill's truck. He could see his dad through the windshield.

Jack looked at Christopher and waved, mouthing that he would be back.

Feeling left out, Christopher just stood there watching his dad.

Margaret and Catherine, who were sitting inside at the dining room table, could see everything that was going on outside. As Bill and Jack backed out of the driveway, the women could see Jack wave to Christopher. Slowly Christopher raised his hand and waved back to his dad.

Bill and Jack drove off down the road.

"Jack, I was just wondering why Christopher couldn't come hunting with us. Legally, he's old enough to accompany us."

Jack smiled, "Someday it might be nice for Christopher to join us. The problem is that he can't hear the rifle shots. But what worries me more is that he could get lost in the woods. He wouldn't be able to hear me calling him. Then what would I do? Even if I put him on a leash at my side, either we would get tangled up in the bushes or he'd get so tired trying to keep up that I'd end up having to strap him to my back."

Bill grinned.

"Honestly," Jack continued, "I have a real hard time conversing with Christopher. He always misunderstands what I'm trying to tell him. It is actually better that he stays home so I can enjoy a little peace and quiet."

Bill agreed, "Yeah, it's probably better he stayed home. He would get bored with all us tranquil guys."

Both men started laughing.

The women continued to observe Christopher, standing

in the driveway looking gloomy. Margaret, watching for understanding and hopefully agreement in Catherine's expression, explained, "Christopher couldn't go with Jack because they have trouble communicating. I know Jack would like to take Christopher, but he worries about the dangers of not being able to hear rifle shots. Besides, Christopher is such a sensitive boy, I personally don't think he needs to see a deer being bled and butchered."

Glancing back out the window to check on Christopher, Margaret could see he was still standing in the same place, looking forlornly down the driveway. Bill and Jack's friends had loaded their gear into their truck and were slowly backing out of the driveway. Margaret thought that they would stop, but they kept backing up. They were headed right for Christopher. Margaret screamed, "Christopher!"

Bill's friend was driving a truck with four-wheel drive. Because the truck rode higher than a normal truck, and since Christopher was short for his age, the driver couldn't see him.

Margaret ran outside screaming for the truck to stop, but it was too late. The truck hit Christopher from behind, and he fell face-first onto the ground.

Christopher was shocked. Everything happened so fast. He turned his head and saw the rear wheels of the truck pass by him. Seeing the whole underside of the truck out of the corner of his eye terrified him. He started screaming.

Margaret was running toward the truck yelling for the driver to stop. When the driver saw Margaret approaching the truck with no coat or shoes on and saw the look on her face, he slammed on the brakes.

Falling to the ground, beside the truck, Margaret grabbed Christopher's coat and tried to pull him out. The driver, who had put the truck in park and had jumped out, now helped Margaret pull Christopher from underneath the truck. Margaret stood Christopher up and hugged him. She signed, "You all right?"

Shaken and crying, Christopher could only nod in the affirmative."

All of a sudden, the seriousness of the situation hit Margaret. She loved Christopher so much that the thought of losing her only son, her Christopher, was too much to bear. Hugging him even tighter, she began sobbing.

After a few minutes, Margaret began to feel chilled. Realizing she had put on neither coat nor shoes, she decided they better go back inside the house to warm up.

The friend of Bill's who had been driving the truck stood outside still in shock. He had never even seen Christopher. Terror washed through him as he thought about what could have happened. He was relieved to know that Christopher was all right, yet the image of Margaret running out of the house screaming and his horror as they pulled her son from beneath his truck were things he could not put out of his mind. With his brain so distracted, he decided hunting was out of the question. His buddies, similarly disturbed by the incident, agreed. Unpacking and repacking their gear and getting into their respective vehicles, they headed home.

Meanwhile, Margaret had taken Christopher inside and helped him remove his boots. When she took off his coat, Margaret could see that he was still shaking. She gave him a hot bath to help him relax, a cup of hot cocoa to cheer him, and her undivided attention to soothe him. In the bedroom, she held Christopher in her arms and gently rocked him until he fell asleep.

Later in the afternoon, Jack and Bill came home, wondering what had happened to Bill's buddies. Catherine started telling them what had happened. Concerned about Christopher, Jack rushed to the bedroom even before Catherine had finished speaking.

Margaret was still holding a sleeping Christopher in her arms. It was obvious that she had been crying for most of the afternoon. As soon as she saw Jack, her eyes welled up again. She wanted to tell him how much she loved Christopher and how fortunate they were to have him, but when she opened her mouth to speak, all she could say was, "Christopher was terrified. I was so scared. Please hold me . . ." Tears started streaming down her cheeks.

After Margaret composed herself, she told Jack in detail what had happened. As she related how she had felt while pulling Christopher out from underneath the truck, she began to cry again. "Christopher is so short . . . they couldn't see . . . he couldn't hear the truck."

Jack felt bad that he hadn't been there to protect and comfort his family. He put his arms around Margaret and Christopher and held them. The three of them stayed in the bedroom together until early evening.

Later when Christopher woke up, the room was dark. He could see a glow from the dining room light shining into the hallway. Getting out of bed, he followed the trail of light. The sudden change of light bothered his eyes, which he was rubbing when he saw Bill, Catherine, and his parents sitting around the dining room table playing cards.

Jack immediately stood up, walked over to Christopher, gave him a big hug, and scooped him up into his arms. He then took Christopher into the living room and showed him a big box. "Christopher, it's for you."

Having seen those words many times before, Christopher let out a squeal of delight and ran over to open the box. It was a remote-controlled police car. Remembering his earlier adventure in a police car, Christopher immediately began inspecting it.

Jack showed his son how to use the car, hoping that Christopher's new toy would engage his mind so that he would not remember the accident and he would be able to sleep peacefully that night.

Chapter 14
Bad Boys

Over the next three years, Christopher continued to meet with the speech therapist he had been assigned before kindergarten, three times a week. He struggled to learn the sounds of letters and then struggled to put the sounds together in order to vocalize words. Reading lips was even more of an effort for Christopher since so many letter sounds and words look alike. His signing skills, however, improved greatly. Along with the signs Ms. Bennett had taught in class, Christopher had intently watched the older deaf children signing to each other and had conversed with them on the bus ride to and from school. In this way, he was able to greatly expand his sign language vocabulary. Even though he didn't know the English words many of the signs represented, he certainly knew the feelings they expressed. The older students not only pointed out actions of other students and signed them, they pantomimed different feelings and then signed them for Christopher, something his staid and respectable teacher would never have thought to do.

Ms. Bennett continued to be Christopher's teacher. Throughout that time, Christopher had been caught numerous times signing outside of the classroom, and a pattern had developed: Ms. Bennett would take Christopher to the principal, who would ask him, "Why don't you follow the rules?" Not knowing how a response would affect the situation, Christopher would remain silent. Taking Christopher back to the classroom, Ms. Bennett would write on the blackboard "NO RECESS FOR CHRISTOPHER," and then she would continue teaching the class.

Miss Modak, the teacher who had dressed up as a clown when Christopher was in kindergarten, was a fourth grade teacher. She taught hearing students but had a fascination with sign language. When her students were at lunch or at the gym, she would often peek into Ms. Bennett's classroom to see what the deaf students were doing. Miss Modak had been entertaining thoughts of becoming a teacher for the deaf.

One day, Christopher and his good friend, Donny, went to use the restroom before their afternoon classes began. While in the restroom, they started a conversation about the food fight during lunch, involving a number of fifth-graders. Having forgotten where they were in relationship to the rule of no signing outside the classroom, they continued their conversation as they walked back to class.

Ms. Bennett, who had seen them signing, was obviously upset. She told them both to go to Principal Chuck's office to be punished.

Donny, who was afraid and didn't know what to do, just sat down on the floor. Ms. Bennett demanded that Donny stand up and go to the principal's office to receive his punishment, but he continued to refuse. He had become so frustrated by the "no signing" rule that he didn't want to listen to Ms. Bennett any longer. He closed his eyes and remained in his place.

Christopher was confused by the whole situation. He didn't want to get into further trouble, yet he didn't want to desert his friend.

Ms. Bennett tried to lift Donny up to his feet, but it was to no avail. He was like dead weight.

Now she was furious, and it could be seen on her face

when she said, "You are bad boys! You don't obey the rules. I am going to call Principal Chuck to come get both of you. You both are very bad boys!"

Christopher and Donny, comprehending little of what she had said, remained silent. Submitting to Ms. Bennett's unfair rules was something the boys felt they could no longer do.

Ms. Bennett turned around in a huff and walked into the classroom.

After a short time, Principal Chuck and Miss Modak came walking down the hallway toward Christopher and Donny.

The kindly face and demeanor of Miss Modak reminded Christopher of the clown that had entertained the students in the gymnasium when he was in kindergarten. He felt sure that Miss Modak and the clown were one and the same person.

Christopher stood off to the side while Ms. Bennett, Principal Chuck, and Miss Modak tried to get Donny to stand up and walk down the hallway. Donny would not cooperate with them and continued to throw himself on the floor after they literally picked him up. Miss Modak walked down the hall to the teachers' lounge, from which she returned with a wooden paddle.

It was usually the job of Miss Modak, who was an assistant principal, to train and, if necessary, spank disobedient children. She proceeded to do her job and, while Principal Chuck held him, paddled Donny three times for his misbehavior. Yet inside, Miss Modak felt the punishment was discriminatory, since it seemed to her the rules against using sign language outside the classroom had been devised solely by Ms. Bennett.

Ms. Bennett ordered Christopher to return to the classroom. Before doing so, Christopher turned to see Donny. Miss Modak, younger and stronger than Ms. Bennett, had picked up Donny and was carrying him back to Principal Chuck's office.

Suddenly Christopher felt a hand on the back of his neck.

Ms. Bennett grabbed him by the scruff of the neck and directed him back to the classroom. There she told him to return to his seat.

Frustrated, Christopher could no longer contain himself.

Looking Ms. Bennett right in the eyes, he signed to her, "You bad teacher!"

Ms. Bennett was furious that Christopher would have the gall to insult her in front of the entire class, but what she resented even more was that he did not appreciate her efforts to help him fit into the hearing world. He would have to be taught a lesson. She opened her desk drawer and pulled out her wooden ruler. Approaching Christopher, she grabbed his right hand and held it down on the desk. With this new sign of rebellion, Ms. Bennett was truly at the end of her rope and decided the relatively mild slaps she administered as the usual no-signing punishment simply would not suffice in this situation. This time, she lifted the ruler over her head, and brought it down with a whack.

The pain from Christopher's hand extended throughout his entire being.

Ms. Bennett then told Christopher to go put his head down on his desk.

Complying, Christopher put his head down on his desk, where he cried silently, unwilling to give Ms. Bennett the satisfaction of knowing how badly she had hurt him. His hand hurt so badly, in fact, that he wasn't able to move his fingers. Although, after she walked over to him and told him to sit up and pay attention, he kept his eyes focused on Ms. Bennett for the remainder of the class, he couldn't stop thinking about how much he wanted to be home in his mother's arms.

After school, Christopher looked for Donny. When he couldn't find him, he decided to board the bus and wait.

As Christopher climbed the stairs onto the bus, he noticed that there was a different woman driving the bus. Ruth was not there. Christopher later found out that Ruth had been fired because, although she loved the children, she was not a safe driver. The next thing he noticed was that Donny was not yet on the bus. Christopher began to feel nervous.

A few minutes later, Christopher saw Ms. Modak walking Donny to the bus. The new bus driver watched closely as Donny climbed into the bus and sat down next to Christopher. She then stepped out of the bus and approached Ms. Modak. After talking for a few minutes, the driver returned to the bus. Scowling at Donny, she prepared to drive away.

Christopher tried to ask Donny what was wrong, but the bruise on the back of his hand made movement very painful. Christopher used his left hand and clumsily signed, "Wrong what?"

Donny glanced up at the new bus driver and signed, "She my mother."

Both boys sat very still as the bus pulled away from the school. Christopher was thankful to leave the school behind him.

After driving for only a few minutes, the bus driver parked the bus on the shoulder of the road. She stood up and walked over to where Donny and Christopher were sitting.

Christopher was troubled by the driver's unexpected behavior.

The driver grabbed Donny by the arm, yanked him out of his seat, marched him to the front of the bus, and began signing very emphatically, "You bad boy! You not obey rules! You very bad boy!" Proceeding to turn Donny over her knee, she spanked him.

Christopher sat immobile for fear he too would be spanked.

When the driver was finished spanking Donny, she made him sit in a seat near her, returned to her seat, and continued on her route.

Christopher sat motionless as the bus dropped off student after student. When the bus finally pulled up to Christopher's home, he cautiously walked toward the front. Walking past Donny, Christopher wanted to say goodbye, but Donny sat with his head down. He wouldn't even glance up at Christopher.

Christopher stepped off the bus. As the bus pulled away, he looked at his house and saw his mother walking quickly toward him.

Margaret, having already been contacted by Ms. Bennett regarding Christopher's "inappropriate behavior," could see that the events of the day had proven to be very disturbing to him.

Christopher was relieved to see his mother, since he knew that, even if she was unhappy with him, she would provide the comfort he needed.

Margaret walked over to where Christopher was still standing, bent down, and hugged him. She held him so tightly, he knew he was safe at last.

Margaret signed to Christopher, "What happen? What wrong?"

His mother's gentle manner and kindly expression touched Christopher's heart. He buried his head in her shirt and wept. The day's events rushed through his mind like a whirlwind. There was so much that he wanted to tell his mother, but he didn't know where to begin.

Margaret lovingly looked Christopher in the eyes and took his hands in hers, but as she did, Christopher pulled his right hand back. She could see a bruise across the back of his hand. Taking Christopher's hand again, she ever so gently caressed it. "What happen? Someone hit you?"

Christopher nodded his head.

Margaret took him in the house, where Christopher told her everything that had happened that day at school. She was appalled that something like this could occur. School is supposed to be a place where children can receive an education in a safe environment, out of harm's way. Angered by Ms. Bennett's cruel punishment of Christopher—wounding the means he uses to communicate with her—Margaret shared her feelings with Jack. They decided to pay a visit to Kennedy's principal, Mr. Chuck.

The next day, Jack and Margaret met with Principal Chuck to discuss the incidents of the previous day. As they were talking, Ms. Bennett entered the principal's office and took a seat.

Margaret questioned them as to whose idea it was to punish deaf children by smacking their hands with a ruler.

Ms. Bennett stated that signing was not permitted outside of her classroom and children who do not follow the rules must be reminded of that and pain would remind them.

Margaret was furious with Ms. Bennett's demeanor. She told her in no uncertain terms that she was never to lay a hand on

Christopher again or it would be brought before the school board and reported to any other agency that deals with child abuse.

Ms. Bennett reminded Jack and Margaret that she was trying to teach Christopher and the other deaf students the English language so that they would be able to succeed.

Jack agreed that Christopher needed to learn English, but the whole point of this meeting was to make clear that no one had been given permission to administer corporal punishment to his son.

Later that evening, Jack sat down with Christopher. He tried to explain to Christopher that he needed to learn English like everyone else. Encouraging his son to improve his lipreading skills, Jack said, "One day you will grow up and become a man, and then you will take over father's business. You will preserve the name and reputation of Crownline Glass."

Christopher, not understanding what Jack had said, just smiled and nodded his head.

Chapter 15
<u>Lesson Learned</u>

Fourth grade was a more difficult year for Christopher.

Kennedy Elementary School was trying a new method of teaching deaf students by mainstreaming them into hearing classes. Ms. Bennett, who was an advocate for the program, readily arranged for Christopher and Donny to attend an English class taught by one of the fourth grade teachers. Provisions were made so that Donny and Christopher would sit in the front of the classroom. The English teacher would speak into a microphone that was directly connected to the amplifier box on hearing aids that had been provided to each deaf student. In this way, the teachers thought, the students could hear what was being taught. In reality, neither boy could hear any words, since they were both profoundly deaf. They could only feel the vibration of the teacher's amplified voice.

Christopher and Donny began attending the fourth grade English class with 15 hearing students. The English teacher would speak into her microphone as she taught the class. Both boys struggled to understand what she was saying. There was no sign language being used, and neither Christopher nor Donny was proficient in lipreading. Aside from their frustration with the inherent difficulties in learning lipreading, the boys had become so preoccupied with the unfair rules about signing that their rebellion had spread unconsciously into areas of learning that they associated with the injustice they felt. Lipreading was what their elders were trying to substitute for the signing they were being denied. It was only natural that their resentment would interfere with their ability to learn.

After a few frustrating days, they began occupying their minds with other things. They would lower their hands under their desks and sign to each other. They discussed what they would do after school and on the upcoming weekend.

The English teacher noticed that the two boys kept looking at each other rather than paying attention to the grammar lesson she was trying to teach. She began yelling into her microphone.

Christopher and Donny suddenly became aware of many vibrations from their hearing aids. They felt a number of strong vibrations that would subside briefly and then would repeat. Christopher looked at Donny, and then both looked up wide-eyed at the English teacher. Angered, she pulled the microphone from around her neck and began hitting it against the desk. Five times she banged the microphone on her desk, until it broke. Then she threw it away and stalked out of the classroom.

The English teacher returned a few minutes later with Ms. Bennett.

Christopher and Donny were escorted back to their classroom to receive discipline. Ms. Bennett pulled out her wooden ruler. Grabbing Donny's hand, she held it down on her desk and rapped him soundly. Donny returned to his desk crying.

Ms. Bennett then grabbed Christopher. Knowing that she was not permitted to administer any type of corporal punishment to him, she just stood holding his arm tightly. Then it came to her. She walked Christopher over to the coat closet, put him in it, and shut the door.

With the door closed, it was very dark inside the closet. At first, Christopher was scared, but after a few moments he started to think about everything he'd seen in the closet when he hung up his coat. He got used to the dark and, knowing there was nothing to fear, relaxed—so much so that he fell asleep.

The next day after school, when Christopher's bus arrived home, Margaret was waiting outside in order to talk to Donny's mother, Joyce, who was driving the bus again this school year.

"Joyce, could we talk for a moment?"

"Sure. What's on your mind?"

Margaret related the events of the previous day and asked Joyce how she felt about Ms. Bennett hitting her son's hand with a ruler as a course of discipline.

"Well . . . he learned his lesson."

Jack and Margaret had long been disturbed with Ms. Bennett's way of handling the deaf students, especially after they learned that she had been putting Christopher into a closet as punishment for signing. Two months into the school year, they took their concerns to the school board. The board decided that Ms. Bennett would continue to teach the deaf children who were oral and could read lips, but they would hire a new teacher, Miss Miller, who would be permitted to use sign language to assist those children who were behind in oral skills.

Miss Miller allowed the students to call her by her first name, Sally. In Deaf culture, referring to another person by his or her first name, regardless of age, is socially acceptable; however, Ms. Bennett was not comfortable with this lack of formality—just one of the differences between them. Miss Miller's familiarity with the culture of the Deaf and her love of interacting with her own young nieces and nephews enabled her to effectively communicate with her students and to compassionately care for them.

On the following Monday, Christopher and Donny were transferred into Miss Miller's class. Immediately Sally became Christopher's favorite teacher. He felt very comfortable with her.

After a morning of animated discussion about why the main character in the story acted the way he did, Sally guided the students outside for recess. As they walked through the hallway,

Christopher saw Ms. Bennett standing outside her classroom. She was watching Christopher and the other students as they were conversing among themselves. He kept looking at her as he chatted with Donny. When he got to the door to go outside, he smiled and tauntingly waved "bye-bye" to Ms. Bennett. Christopher knew he shouldn't have done that, but he couldn't help himself. In his mind, over the years she had come to represent, rather than vaguely resemble, the evil witches in fairy tales. He was very happy that Ms. Bennett was no longer his teacher.

Jack and Margaret had often wondered what had happened to Christopher's old teacher, Miss Glenn. They knew she had applied to be transferred to Kennedy Elementary and that the school had wanted to hire her to teach their special education classes, especially those with deaf students. Christopher and his parents, however, were deeply saddened when they found out that Miss Glenn was no longer teaching. At the time she had applied for transfer to Kennedy, she had been offered a promotion to assistant principal at one of the larger elementary schools. After some consideration, she had decided she could help more students as an assistant principal and so had accepted the promotion rather than transferring to Kennedy.

A few months later, Christopher noticed a substitute teacher caring for Ms. Bennett's class. He asked Sally where Ms. Bennett was and found out that she had fallen on the ice and had broken her left leg. She was out of school through the end of the year, after which she retired from teaching. One year later, Ms. Bennett died of a heart attack. Christopher couldn't help thinking that, because of the way she had treated him all those years, she deserved to be put in a dark closet—her casket would do.

Chapter 16
<u>Temporary Separation</u>

Joyce was Christopher's bus driver through all of fourth grade. Every day she would pick up the students, and every day Christopher and Donny would sit together. They would have lively discussions that usually ended up in laughter.

One day, glancing at the boys through the rearview mirror, Joyce tried to pick up bits and pieces of their conversation, but she couldn't keep up with their signing. She felt uncomfortable not knowing what the boys were talking about.

Years earlier when Donny had started school, Ms. Bennett had explained to Joyce that using American Sign Language, the language of the Deaf, would hinder Donny's progress in understanding and speaking English and it would prevent him from reading lips. Ms. Bennett had encouraged her to use Signed English, a word-for-word transliteration, in order for Donny to better fit into the hearing world. Joyce, thinking Ms. Bennett to be an authority on the subject, had accepted her assessment.

Wanting to help both Donny and Christopher to improve in their English, Joyce concluded it would be best to limit their time together. She decided to seat them separately on the bus to prevent them from conversing in American Sign Language.

That day after school, when Donny and Christopher got on the bus, Joyce told Donny, "From now on, I want you to sit in the seat behind me so we can be close." She then told Christopher to go sit in the back of the bus.

Christopher had noticed the way Joyce had looked at him when he would sit next to Donny, but he was still surprised that she would send him to sit in the back of the bus. "Me sit far, why?"

Joyce smiled and replied, "Because I said so, and I'm not changing my mind. Now go sit down."

Wondering what had prompted such an extreme measure, Christopher complied and sat down in the back of the bus. He looked for Donny, but was unable to see him since he was still too short to see over the high school-bus seatbacks, let alone the heads of the other students.

Joyce was relieved that the boys were now separated and hoped that this would encourage them to focus on speaking English and lipreading.

For the remainder of the week, Christopher sat in the back of the bus while Donny sat up front near his mother. During that time, the boys tried to find a way to see each other. Christopher sat on the left side of the bus near the window, so Donny did likewise. Christopher found that by standing up and leaning toward the window, he could see all the way up to the front of the bus where Donny was sitting. Being in view of each other, the boys could now chat.

The following Monday, after sitting in silence for the first half hour of the bus ride home, the boys leaned toward the window and started conversing. Christopher told Donny a joke he had seen earlier in the day, which Donny thought was funny; he began laughing.

Joyce heard him and, noticing what was going on, told Donny to turn around and face forward.

Now the hour riding in the bus to school and the hour back home seemed to get longer and longer. Christopher felt so lonely sitting silently in the back of the bus. He really wanted to converse with his buddy, but he didn't dare for fear of how Donny's mother would react.

Leaning toward the window, Donny looked back at Christopher, who was resting his head up against the window. Donny started waving to get Christopher's attention, which wasn't too hard, since most of the students had been dropped off already.

Christopher looked up at Joyce and then back at Donny. He stood up and signed, "Maybe your mom very mad."

Joyce glanced back in her rearview mirror and caught Christopher signing something about mom mad. She was furious that the boys were not only signing to each other, but also talking about her, maybe saying bad things. Deciding to teach Christopher a lesson, she slammed on the brakes so that the bus came to a screeching halt.

When the bus stopped, Christopher was propelled forward. He hit the metal bar on the back of the seat in front of him, lost his footing, fell to the floor, and slid under the seats.

Joyce put the bus in park and walked to the back. Christopher wasn't there. Joyce turned around and looked toward the front of the bus. Thinking that Christopher was fooling around and trying to sneak under the seats angered her. Joyce stood there waiting for him to come out.

Christopher found himself under the seats about four rows from the back of the bus. He was frightened and ashamed. Slowly pulling himself up, he sat down in the seat.

Joyce came up next to Christopher yelling, "Christopher, I want you to stop fool—" As she looked at Christopher, her expression immediately changed.

Christopher, who was bleeding from his nose and mouth, tried to wipe the blood off his face. Feeling bad for not following the rules, in pain from his injuries, and afraid he was in big trouble for signing to Donny, he started crying. He said "Sororrry, sororrry, sororrry." As he said the words, he also signed "sorry" by putting his bloody fist over his heart and moving it in a circular motion, which left a ring-shaped stain on the front of his shirt.

Joyce felt horrible.

Arriving at Christopher's house, Joyce explained to Margaret what had happened and repeatedly apologized. She said she had never meant to hurt Christopher. She just wanted him to sit quietly and not distract Donny. After apologizing again, she left.

Margaret took Christopher inside, cleaned him up, and cared for his wounds.

When Jack got home, he was upset at what had taken place; however, understanding Joyce's reasoning, he accepted her apology.

The next morning when the bus arrived to pick him up, Christopher was somewhat apprehensive.

Joyce was standing outside the bus waiting for Christopher. She seemed friendlier than usual. Smiling at Christopher, she signed, "Good morning. Bus has new rule. You and Donny can sit together from now on."

Christopher, smiling, climbed the stairs, and ran over and to sit next to his buddy.

Donny waved at Christopher to get his attention and then pointed toward the front of the bus as he mouthed, "Look, look, look."

Christopher saw a sign, posted on the front window above the stairs, which read: "No voice . . . Sign Language ONLY!"

Christopher and Donny looked at Joyce and then at each other. They were thrilled! Having a lot of catching up to do, they started signing and signing and signing . . .

Chapter 17
<u>Closed Caption</u>

Summer was always a fun time for Christopher. He would often play with Eric (the boy down the street), or he would spend the day with Donny. His favorite thing to do, however, was follow his dad around. Christopher would follow his dad to the office, the grocery store, the hardware store, the basement, the attic, or the garage. Anywhere that Jack would go, Christopher would follow; anything that Jack wanted to do, Christopher would try to do. He wanted so much to learn from his dad, but it was difficult without any real communication.

One evening, Jack was sitting in the living room watching television. Wanting, as usual, to be with his dad, Christopher sat down on the couch next to him. Jack would watch the television and then would start to laugh. He would watch some more and laugh again.

Christopher watched the same program, but he didn't understand what was so funny.

Jack continued laughing.

Christopher tapped his dad on the arm and tried to vocalize as he signed, "Daddy, you laugh why?"

Jack continued laughing, even harder now.

Christopher tapped his dad on the arm again. Determined to share in laughter with his dad, he started laughing too. Not understanding the basis for such laughter was frustrating to Christopher, but he watched the television, looked to see his dad's reaction, and then imitated it, hoping it would somehow make him feel closer to his dad.

Jack watched for a short while and then began laughing harder than before.

Christopher wanted to know what was happening. He grabbed his dad's arm and began shaking it.

Jack turned to look at Christopher, but he couldn't stop laughing. Glancing back at the television, he began laughing even harder, to the point that he could hardly catch his breath.

Christopher, continuing to copy his dad, began laughing hysterically—without knowing the reason why.

Margaret had heard Jack in the living room laughing. Assuming Christopher was probably with his dad, she had stepped to the door to see how they were doing. She saw Jack laughing and Christopher shaking his dad's arm to get his attention. Her heart broke when she saw Christopher start laughing just so he could be like his dad. How she wished Jack would learn sign language so that he could communicate with Christopher!

Margaret went into the living room, after watching long enough to give Jack a chance to respond to his son, and walked up behind Christopher.

When Christopher felt her hand on his back, he stopped laughing and looked up at his mom and signed, "Dad laugh, why?"

Margaret was disappointed with Jack's behavior, but now was not an appropriate time to discuss it. Now was the time to give her love and attention to her son. "You want with Mommy make cookies?"

Christopher was very agreeable. They walked into the kitchen together.

Margaret looked back at Jack. He had stopped laughing when he saw Christopher get off the couch and walk away.

Feeling bad for hurting his son's feelings, Jack put his head down, but his remorse was short-lived. The comedian on television said something that caught his attention, and he began laughing again.

A couple of hours later it was Christopher's bedtime, and after taking his bath and hugging and kissing his parents, he went to bed.

As Margaret was cleaning up the kitchen, Jack came in and started snacking on the cookies that his wife and son had made. Margaret, feeling she could no longer control her emotions, shouted at Jack, "Have you ever loved your son?"

Jack smirked. Knowing why she was upset, he very calmly replied, "I'm sorry dear. Christopher is deaf. I can't change that. Until he learns to concentrate on his English, our communication will never improve."

"Oh yeah! Put all the responsibility on Christopher—a child! Why don't you try learning some sign language?" With that she stormed out of the kitchen.

Jack did love Christopher. He wanted, more than anyone did, to be able to communicate with his son. He still held out the hope that Christopher would one day be his business partner, a father-son team, controlling Crownline Glass. But it was that very, worldly vision that made Jack determined to force, if he had to, Christopher to learn "normal" communications.

A month before Christopher would begin his summer vacation, Jack was talking with his friend Tony, who worked in broadcasting. Tony had asked Jack if Christopher enjoyed watching television. Jack explained that Christopher didn't watch television often because he didn't understand what was being said.

Tony had heard that there was a new device that had just gone on the market that put words on the bottom of the television screen. He didn't know what the device was called, but he was sure it would be helpful to Christopher.

Jack immediately began searching to find out what this new device was and where he could purchase one. After three weeks of phone calls and letters, he finally got the information he needed. Finding a closed caption decoder, he purchased it and brought it home for Christopher.

As Jack pulled his car into the driveway, he honked the horn to let Margaret know he was home.

Checking her watch, she was surprised that Jack was home so early—even before Christopher got out of school.

Jack was eager to show Margaret the surprise he had gotten for Christopher. He ran into the house, "Margaret, honey. Margaret, honey are you home?"

"Yes, I'm in the kitchen. What's wrong?"

Margaret had been sitting at the table where she had been looking through her new home and garden magazine. Running to the door to see what was wrong, she ran smack into Jack at the kitchen door. He laughed as he showed her the box containing the closed caption decoder.

Margaret could see how enthusiastic Jack was about this special surprise that could enable Christopher to better understand what's on television. In her heart, though, she wished that Jack would learn sign language in order for Christopher to better understand him.

Jack wanted to have the closed caption decoder connected to the television before Christopher got home from school. He excitedly anticipated Christopher's reaction.

After everything was connected, Jack turned on the decoder and the television. Checking the different channels, he finally found one with captions. He was so excited to see the words going across the bottom of the screen that he shouted for Margaret.

Seeing the captioning, she became as excited as Jack. Searching through all the channels, they wrote down the ones with captioning. They were a little disappointed to find only two channels that provided some captioned programs, but they figured that two was better than none. At least now there were some shows that Christopher would have a chance of understanding.

Jack and Margaret anxiously waited for their son to get home from school. When they heard the bus drop Christopher off, Jack ran to the front door and began waving his arms to get his son's attention.

Christopher was surprised to see his dad home from work so early and wondered what was happening. Going into the house, he put his lunch box on the kitchen table.

Jack ran into the kitchen to meet Christopher, "Surprise! Surprise!"

Christopher's eyes opened wide. He began looking around the room questioningly.

Jack waved to Christopher to come into the living room to see the television.

Christopher obliged Jack, but it looked like the same old television to him.

Jack turned it on and showed Christopher the words on the bottom of the screen.

Christopher wasn't sure what it all meant. He had never seen words on the television before. Sitting in Jack's chair, he watched the captioning.

Jack sat down next to Margaret on the couch. They watched and waited for Christopher's reaction. Jack expected Christopher to laugh or show some excitement at being able to understand the television program.

Instead, Christopher sat motionless watching the words go by.

Jack was disappointed. He thought, in time, Christopher would appreciate the value of this decoder in expanding his knowledge of the hearing world. He waited a little longer for a response. When there was none, Jack, a little hurt though he wouldn't have admitted it, lay down and took a nap.

Later in the evening, when it came time for Christopher to go to bed, Margaret approached him and put her arm around him. She signed, "You understand closed captioning?"

Christopher, looking at his mom, asked, "Words, what for?"

Margaret was surprised that Christopher didn't realize the purpose of the captioning. She explained "Words for you. Help you understand what we hear television say."

Christopher slowly nodded his head.

Margaret was confused by his lack of enthusiasm. She asked, "You understand words?"

Christopher shook his head, "Understand few."

Margaret couldn't believe that Christopher could not understand the words on the television.

The following day, Margaret made an appointment to meet with Christopher's teacher. Miss Miller explained that Christopher had a problem with reading comprehension since English was not his primary language. This news was discouraging to Margaret and devastating to Jack.

Chapter 18
<u>Severed Ties</u>

Fifth and sixth grade were Christopher's best years at school. Miss Miller made the information come alive for him and the other deaf students. He made great strides in his knowledge of American history and math, yet he still lagged behind his hearing peers in understanding the English language.

One morning in March, the bus came to pick Christopher up for school. When he got on the bus, there was a different woman driving. Seeming friendly, she reminded Christopher of his grandma.

Christopher assumed that Joyce was sick and that was the reason there was another bus driver. Looking around to see where Donny was sitting, Christopher realized that his buddy wasn't there either. He hoped they would both be back soon.

They weren't.

Donny had not been in school all week, and by Friday, Christopher was worried about his friend. He wondered what had happened to him.

After Miss Miller took attendance, the students divided into groups to work on their math problems. Christopher approached her and asked, "Why Donny not come school? He gone?"

Miss Miller knew how close Donny and Christopher were and she understood his anxiety. Trying to calm him, she explained, "Donny will fine. He back school next week. Now he lives with mother. She moved far from school. His parents split."

Shocked by the news, Christopher stood there for a few minutes. He remembered how depressed Donny would get because his parents argued and because he wasn't able to communicate with his father and could only communicate a little with his mother. Christopher felt bad.

The following Monday when Christopher arrived at school, he went into the coatroom. As he was hanging up his jacket, he felt someone hit him on the back. He wondered who it might be. His first thought was that his dad was there, because sometimes his dad would smack him on the back to get his attention. Turning around, he saw his buddy Donny. They were both very happy to see each other again.

Christopher, still worrying about Donny and his family situation, asked, "Sally told me your parents split; what happen?"

"My parents will divorce. My fault."

Christopher was confused. "Your parents divorce your fault, why?"

Donny seemed a little embarrassed when he responded, "Because my sign language."

"Divorce because sign language?"

Donny nodded his head.

Christopher was a little shaken by Donny's response.

The classroom lights began flashing off and on, meaning it was time for the students to sit down at their desks.

Donny looked down, as if he felt ashamed for what he had done. Shuffling to his desk with his shoulders drooping, he sat down.

Christopher wanted to cheer his buddy, but he didn't know what he could say to make him feel better about his parents. Sitting down at his desk, he waved to Donny to get his attention.

"Me sorry your parents divorce. Hey! You know our friendship never divorce!"

Donny started laughing. He was happy to have such a supportive friend.

After school, Donny and Christopher walked outside to where the buses were parked. Donny, explaining to Christopher that he and his mother had moved, got on a different bus. Both boys were saddened that they would no longer be able to share together the ride to and from school. Christopher's school-bus rides seemed much longer without Donny.

As the bus dropped off student after student, Christopher began thinking about how Donny's parents were getting divorced because of sign language. It seemed unfair to blame Donny when there was nothing he could do to stop being deaf. He began wondering what was going to happen to his parents, since it looked to Christopher as though they argued quite often about Christopher's use of sign language. Letting his mind wander, he began thinking about what would happen to him if his parents got a divorce. What an awful feeling that produced! How he hoped his parents would stay together!

When Christopher got home from school, he ran inside the house. "Mother! Mother!"

Margaret, as always, was glad to have Christopher home from school. She had baked chocolate chip cookies as a special treat for him. As he came into the kitchen, Margaret approached him with a plate of cookies. "Hi sweetie. You want cookies?"

Christopher grabbed up a handful of cookies, sat at the kitchen table and said in his usual rather loud voice, "Thank you."

Pouring a glass of milk for Christopher, Margaret asked, "How school today?"

Christopher shrugged his shoulders. Not wanting to relinquish his cookies, he all but shouted, "You know Donny's parents divorce?"

"Yes, Joyce called me today. I feel sorry for them," his mother signed in return, knowing this would be a fairly heavy conversation and he wouldn't understand her lips as well.

"Donny told me they divorce because sign language."

Margaret sat silently for a moment trying to decide how to respond to Christopher. Finally she signed, "I know. That not good idea. Divorce not Donny's fault—parent's fault they not work out. Maybe Donny need us help him. We need patient, see what happen Donny. I think Donny will all right."

As Christopher slowly ate his cookies, he stared at his glass of milk. He was trying to decide how to bring up what was bothering him. After a few minutes, he asked, "Will you, Dad divorce because me deaf or my sign language?"

Shaking her head, Margaret answered, "Dad and I love you very much. Now your father working hard. He no time learn sign language, but future maybe he learn. We not want divorce. If Dad and I argue, because our own problem, not because you. You understand?"

Christopher smiled, grabbed another handful of cookies, and walked off to his bedroom.

Later, when Margaret and Jack were lying in bed, Margaret began talking about Donny's parents. "You remember Christopher's friend from school, Donny?"

"Yeah, he seems like a nice kid."

"His mother called me today. She and her husband are getting divorced. Christopher says Donny's parents have made him feel that he is to blame for their divorce because of his use of sign language."

Jack shook his head. "It's too bad that they've made him feel responsible for their inability to solve their own problems. Donny is always welcome in our home. He can sign as much as he wants here."

Margaret continued, "Since Christopher found out about Donny's parents, he is worried about us. Being aware of our differing opinions on sign language, he is concerned about our future."

"Sign language is permitted in our home. You and Christopher can use sign language as often as you like. Myself, I would prefer Christopher learn to read lips. That way, when he becomes my business partner, he will be able to communicate with employees and clients alike. Don't worry Margaret. Christopher will be fine. Good night dear." With that, Jack rolled over and went to sleep.

Margaret was upset by Jack's lackadaisical attitude about Christopher's emotional stability and how it was tied to signing as a communications tool. Though he hadn't indicated he would, she thought that if he ever tried to eliminate sign language from their house, she would eliminate him.

Chapter 19
<u>Unconditional Love</u>

On Saturday, Margaret wanted to go window-shopping. Deciding to spend the day at the mall, she and Christopher browsed the little shops and larger department stores until early afternoon. Since they had not eaten lunch and were now beginning to feel the twinges of hunger pain, they made their way to the East corridor of the mall, where the restaurants were located. There was a quaint little restaurant that they liked. The food there was delicious and the atmosphere relaxing.

After they finished eating, Margaret thought this would be a good time to have a heart-to-heart talk with Christopher. She asked him how he felt about starting Junior High School in the fall.

Christopher was nervous, not knowing whether he would fit in with the other students at his new school. Out of the blue, he then asked the question that Margaret knew she would someday have to answer, "Why me deaf?"

Margaret had played out this conversation in her mind numerous times since she had found out Christopher was deaf, yet she still couldn't provide him with a simple answer. "Well, not your fault."

"How me born deaf?"

"Long time ago I pregnant. I excited. I already knew I cherish my baby. I love you much . . . I never want lose you." As she responded to Christopher's question, tears began running down Margaret's face.

"You crying, why?"

"Some people suggested I give you up. I loved you much. I refused."

"What you mean?"

"I pregnant, you inside me, happen I visited my friend. Her daughter inside sick but look fine. I stayed; we chatted. Her daughter I hugged. Later one week, her daughter got sick. She fever, body hurt. We thought she flu. Next day, she red spots on face, body. She went doctor. He examined her, found she sick rubella."

"R-U-B- . . . that what?"

"Other name German measles. Anyway, my friend called warn me. She encouraged me go doctor. I big worry my baby. I called your dad. He left work, with me went doctor. Doctor gave me scare. He said if I not vaccine, you will born retarded, heart problems, or other problems serious. I not know if should vaccine or not. Doctor recommended I give up my baby, let other people adopt you. I told doctor problems not matter; I want my baby. I felt doctor tried predict what happen your life, but he no proof. Again I go that doctor never. Many people offered opinions. I not care their ideas. I decided keep my baby."

Reflecting on what his mother had told him about people offering their own opinions as to what she should do, Christopher asked, "I wonder . . . my dad, how he feel?"

"Well . . . He concerned . . . He not yet know you . . . Now your dad loves you a lot."

Christopher sat quietly, meditating on what he had just learned. He began to appreciate his life even more, realizing that he might have never been where he was were it not for the love of his mother. Moved by his mother's unconditional love, he wanted her to know how much he appreciated her. "I know my world silent always. I deaf always, but I happy I alive. I love you."

Ordering their favorite dessert with two spoons, Margaret and Christopher continued to enjoy their time together.

Looking at Christopher, Margaret said, "You know that our family, you only one deaf not?"

"What? Really?"

"My grandparents, they deaf. I not remember them. I small, they died. They one son deaf. He my Uncle Tom. I remember, one time I met him. Later he moved east. I never saw again."

"That I didn't know."

After talking for a while longer, Margaret said, "We here chatting, always enjoy. We many memories, emotions share. Come on; we go shopping."

Chapter 20
<u>New Neighbor</u>

Spring was in the air. The weather was warming, and the lilacs were in full bloom. Christopher only had a few weeks of school remaining, and Margaret was feeling cheery. Deciding to surprise her men, she made one of their favorite desserts—blueberry pie. As she was preparing the crust, she happened to notice a moving truck unloading furniture next door. The 'For Sale' sign had been removed, indicating that the house had been sold, but for the past few weeks, it had been left empty. Today the new neighbors were moving in. Margaret, having enough blueberries to make a second pie, wanted to welcome them to the neighborhood.

After the pies cooled, Margaret got one ready to take next door. Approaching her new neighbor's house, she began to feel a little nervous. She knew they were probably busy unpacking, and she hoped that this wouldn't be an inconvenient time for introductions.

As she walked across the porch to the front door, Margaret saw two of the movers. "Excuse me, is the man or lady of the house here?"

"In the kitchen."

Margaret cautiously went in the front door. "Hello." She walked down the hallway toward the kitchen, where she saw a woman talking on the phone. Since the woman was facing the other way, she didn't see Margaret, so, not wanting to startle her new neighbor or disturb her phone call, Margaret silently stood in the hallway.

A young girl walked down the hallway toward Margaret. She looked to be about the same age as Christopher. She looked at Margaret briefly and then looked away.

Margaret said, "Hi. I'm Mrs. Cline, your neighbor. What's your name?"

Walking past Margaret, the young girl said something so softly that Margaret couldn't hear her. She went into the kitchen and tapped her mother on the back.

Turning around, the woman noticed Margaret standing just outside of the kitchen, in the hallway. "May I help you?"

"Hi. I'm Margaret Cline. I'm your neighbor. I just wanted to stop over and introduce myself. I also brought you a pie."

"Oh, could you wait just a minute while I finish this call?"

Margaret nodded her head.

The woman smiled, set up an appointment with the person on the phone, and then hung up. "Thank you for waiting. I'm sorry the house is such a mess. My name is Susan, and this is my daughter, Nicole. I'm sorry. What did you say your name was?"

"Margaret. Margaret Cline."

"Hello Margaret. It's so nice to meet you."

"I brought this for you. I hope you like blueberry pie." Margaret handed the warm pie to Susan.

"Wow! Thank you so much. We love blueberry pie. How thoughtful! You know, we could use a break right now. Would you like to come in and . . ." Susan looked around her house and noticed the couch and chairs had not yet been brought in, "Oh . . . I don't have anywhere for us to sit."

"That's okay. Why don't you come on over to my home. We can sit on the front porch and get acquainted."

"That sounds wonderful! This has been such a busy day." Susan looked at Nicole, who was nodding her head in agreement.

Margaret, Susan, and Nicole walked over to the Cline's home and sat down on the front porch.

"Would you like something to drink? I have iced tea." Looking at Nicole, Margaret continued, "and I have cherry Kool-Aid."

"Iced tea and Kool-Aid would be refreshing. Thank you."

Margaret returned with drinks and cookies.

Nicole smiled when she saw the cookies and immediately reached for one.

"Margaret, thank you again for inviting us over. This is a much-needed break. Today has been so busy . . . actually this whole move has kept us quite busy."

"Are you from this area?"

"No. We have lived down south for the past eight years. My husband works for the Food and Drug Administration, and he recently received a promotion. He was transferred here to manage the Great Lakes Region."

As the women were talking, Margaret could hear the school bus approaching their intersection.

"I hear the bus coming. My son, Christopher, will be happy to meet you."

"How old is your son?"

"Christopher just turned twelve."

Looking at Nicole, Susan said, "He's the same age as you."

Nicole, feeling self-conscious due to her mother's comment, wanted to change the subject. She asked if all the kids here had to ride the bus to school.

Margaret explained that Christopher was deaf and had to go to a school across town that had teachers who could use sign language.

"Really? Nicole's grandparents are deaf."

"Your parents?"

"No, my husband's parents."

"Do you know sign language?"

"No. Unfortunately I haven't seen my in-laws in almost ten years; they live on the West Coast. I never really had an opportunity to learn sign language, but I would like to meet your son."

"Well, here's your chance," said Margaret as the bus pulled up in front of the house.

When Christopher got off the bus, Susan commented on what a nice looking young man he was. Again embarrassed by her mother's comment, Nicole looked away.

Margaret stood up and waved to Christopher. When he came up on the porch, she gave him a hug. "School, what's up?"

Christopher looked at his mom and then looked at the woman and girl sitting on the porch. "School fine. Who they?"

"They new neighbor. Mother name Susan. Daughter name Nicole. You hello."

Christopher reservedly waved to them and then sat down next to his mother.

Nicole looked at him and smiled sheepishly.

Susan enjoyed watching Margaret and Christopher sign, though she didn't understand anything that was being said. "At Nicole's old school, they were teaching the students sign language." Turning to Nicole, Susan asked, "Honey, do you remember any sign language? Can you sign something to Christopher?"

Nicole shook her head. She actually did remember a few signs, but she was too embarrassed to try signing them.

"Oh, well, maybe Christopher can teach you some sign language."

Margaret, who had been interpreting for Christopher responded, "Yes, of course he will."

Nicole blushed.

As Margaret and Susan continued their conversation, Christopher and Nicole would stealthily glance at each other. When their eyes did meet, Christopher felt like his heart skipped a beat. Though he'd never experienced that before, he somehow knew it meant that he and Nicole would become the closest of friends.

Chapter 21
Formal Introductions

Over the next few weeks, Christopher would see his new neighbor, Nicole, in the yard playing, at the playground swinging, or standing near her mother while their parents conversed. He would smile and wave at her. Waving back, she seemed so shy. Christopher wanted to talk with her, but he couldn't get up the nerve.

Soon there were only three more days of school remaining. Christopher couldn't wait for summer vacation to start.

By the time the bus had dropped Christopher off, Jack had been home for a while. Lighting the barbecue grill, he saw Christopher walking up the driveway. "How was school today?"

Christopher answered with a resounding "Fine!"

Looking around to see if the neighbors had heard Christopher, Jack said, "You don't need to yell. Just talk normally."

Again in a rather loud voice, Christopher said "Sorry." Going inside, he gave his mom a hug. "Hi mom."

Jack, who had followed Christopher into the house,

reminded him, "We are in the house. You don't need to talk so loud."

"Jack, you need to be patient with Christopher."

Margaret's comment set Jack off. "Patient! I've been listening to his yelling for twelve years! How much more patient can I be?"

Jack and Margaret began to argue.

Confused, Christopher went into the dining room, sat down, crossed his arms on the table, and put his head down. He didn't know what he had said or done to cause his parents to get so upset, but he knew it was his fault.

Margaret tried to explain to Jack that since Christopher couldn't hear, and had never heard, he couldn't realize how loud he was speaking.

Jack understood the point Margaret was trying to make, but he wanted her to understand how he felt. Looking her straight in the eye, he asked, "How do you feel when people call Christopher deaf and dumb? I don't like hearing people speak that way about our son." Jack kept getting angrier. "I don't like people calling Christopher deaf and dumb! Do you know what dumb means? It means he can't talk! I want to be able to tell them my son CAN talk! I can't do that until he CAN talk—NORMALLY!"

Margaret didn't know what to say. She thought Jack should be more concerned with how Christopher felt rather than worry about what other people thought of him. Wanting Jack to calm down, she replied, "You have a point."

In the meantime, Christopher had gone into the living room to watch television. He had been catching on to closed captioning, but if he wanted to see the action, he couldn't spend much time trying to read. It was actually quite tiresome trying to see what others could hear. Cartoons were easier because the words were minimal. As he was watching cartoons, he felt funny, as if he were being watched. Looking toward the kitchen, he could see that his parents were still arguing. He looked around the living room. Thinking he saw some movement by the front window, he looked outside. No one was there. It was probably just the wind blowing the branches of the tree out front. He went back to watching cartoons on television.

Out of the corner of his eye, he again noticed movement by the front window. This time he walked over to the window, and he saw someone standing outside waving at him. It was Nicole. He went outside to see what she wanted.

Before Christopher could even say hello, Nicole grabbed his hand and began running toward her backyard. She led him to a tree house that her father had just finished building. She was so excited about it, she just had to share it with someone. Nicole climbed up the ladder and went inside. Christopher followed.

Inside the tree house, Christopher looked around and saw that it was full of girls' toys. There was a shelf with a teapot and teacups. Along one wall were dolls neatly arranged, and in the middle of the floor there was a pink blanket.

Nicole, sitting on the blanket, pointed to Christopher and then pointed to a spot on the blanket.

He sat down.

Getting her teapot, she poured some "tea" into the cups. She then handed a cup to Christopher, who played along with her and pretended to drink tea.

Christopher couldn't believe he was sitting in a tree house playing with a girl. He wasn't sure what to expect, but it was better than sitting at home trying to watch television . . . alone.

Nicole stood up, walked over to the shelf, and grabbed a little bag. Opening it, she pulled out some candy. She handed a piece to Christopher.

Slowly opening the wrapper, he put the candy in his mouth. Then he sat quietly looking around the tree house. Occasionally, he would glance at Nicole, but, as usual, they rarely made eye contact.

After a few minutes, Nicole looked determinedly at Christopher. She pointed to herself and then very slowly finger-spelled, "N-I-C-O-L-E." She kept watching him to see if he understood her.

Christopher's eyes opened wide. He couldn't believe she knew how to sign the alphabet. Dumbfounded, he just kept staring at Nicole, amazed that she was trying to communicate with him.

Nicole became embarrassed and looked away. When she looked back at Christopher, he was still gawking at her. Pointing to him, she spelled, "N-A-M-E W-H-A-T?"

Christopher, continuing to look at Nicole with the same blank stare, raised his right hand and slowly spelled, "C-H-R-I-S-T-O-P-H-E-R."

Excited that Christopher understood her, Nicole smiled and spelled, "N-I-C-E T-O M-E-E-T Y-O-U."

Christopher, beginning to come to his senses, showed Nicole how to sign "nice meet you."

Nicole pointed to Christopher indicating "You" and then she spelled, "L-I-K-E T-R-E-E H-O-U-S-E?" She waited for Christopher to answer.

Again Christopher sat with the same dumb, wide-eyed look on his face.

Nicole asked him again. "You L-I-K-E T-R-E-E H-O-U-S-E?"

Still there was no response.

Nicole thought Christopher might be crazy, since he was behaving so strangely. Since Christopher wasn't responding to anything she spelled, Nicole didn't know what else to say to him. Looking around the tree house and then back at her neighbor, she watched him for a few minutes wondering why he wasn't "talking" to her.

Soon she heard her mother calling her to come in for dinner. Relieved to have an excuse to leave, she finger-spelled, "Me G-O E-A-T," hoping Christopher would understand. Her mother had taught her not to be rude, even to those she didn't understand, so she waved to Christopher, climbed down the ladder, and ran to her house.

Christopher sat motionless for another five minutes. He still couldn't believe that Nicole had tried to converse with him using sign language.

The next day when the school bus dropped Christopher off at home, he saw Nicole going toward the tree house. Smiling, he waved at her.

Nicole, not knowing what to think of the strange boy next door who just sat staring while she tried to communicate with him, pretended she didn't see him. She climbed up the ladder and into the tree house. Stealthily peeking out the doorway, she saw Christopher walk up his driveway and into his house. Relieved, she decided to draw.

Opening a box where she kept some drawing paper and crayons, she began to draw a picture of a black horse running in a field. As she was coloring the background of her picture, she heard a noise down below, so she looked outside. Christopher was climbing up the ladder.

Christopher had felt bad about not talking to Nicole the day before. Seeing her trying to sign to him had taken him completely off guard. There were very few hearing people who had taken enough interest in him to try to sign. Wanting to show his appreciation, he thought he'd bring a bag of cookies to share with her.

Nicole sat back down and pretended she was busy drawing when Christopher came into the tree house. Casually glancing up at him, she smiled politely.

Christopher again smiled and waved at Nicole. Sitting on the floor across from her, he pointed to the paper bag he was carrying. He made a sign with one hand that looked like a "C" and placed it on the palm of the other hand.

Nicole looked at Christopher with a puzzled expression on her face.

Christopher repeated the sign and then opened up the bag so Nicole could see what was inside.

"Cookies! Oh, I understand. This is the sign for cookies." She imitated the sign that Christopher had just showed her and then picked up one of the cookies and began eating it.

Christopher smiled and nodded his head as he also ate a cookie. Afterwards, he began pointing to different objects in the tree house and showing Nicole the signs for each.

Nicole, thrilled to learn the signs for objects rather than just finger-spelling everything, began pointing to objects inside and outside of the tree house. As she did, Christopher would show her the signs. They continued like that until it began to get dark outside.

Christopher, pointing to his wrist and then his house signed, "Time, me home. Tomorrow, I see you."

Nicole didn't understand what word each sign represented, but she understood that Christopher had to go home and that he would see her again.

Climbing down the ladder, Christopher and Nicole walked to their respective homes. Before going inside, they looked at each other and waved.

During the days and weeks that followed, Christopher and Nicole got together often. When she would spell things to him, he would show her the signs for the thoughts she was so laboriously expressing. Christopher was thrilled to have a friend so close-by with whom he could communicate. By summer's end, Nicole had become quite proficient in sign language and the two of them had become best friends.

Chapter 22
<u>Junior High</u>

September came all too quickly. Christopher would be starting seventh grade, which meant he would be attending a new school this year.

Three days before school was to begin, Eastern Junior High held an orientation for the new students and their parents. They could come look at the school and meet the staff.

Christopher was a little nervous, but also very excited to be moving up to the Junior High School. Having heard that his teacher had previously worked at an elementary school teaching hearing students but was now learning sign language in order to teach deaf students, he looked forward to meeting her.

Jack, Margaret, and Christopher arrived early for the orientation. The principal directed them into the gymnasium, where chairs had been set up in front of the stage. In order for Margaret to interpret for Christopher without disturbing others in attendance, they sat toward the back.

When the program began, Margaret noticed there was a woman sitting off to the side signing for the deaf students. She encouraged Christopher to go over and join them.

Feeling a little uneasy about leaving his parents, Christopher walked over to where the deaf were sitting. As he looked for a seat, he noticed that all of the students looked just as anxious as he felt. Though Ms. Bennett had only taught at Kennedy, the other schools with special education classes had set up similar rules about not signing outside of the classroom; therefore, having all of the deaf sit together while the program was being interpreted was a new experience for most of them. Finding an empty seat right next to a student he knew from Kennedy Elementary, Christopher sat down.

The principal spoke first to the students, and then he directed some comments to the parents. Afterwards, he told all in attendance to feel free to walk around the school and become more familiar with their surroundings. At eight o'clock, all of the students and their parents were to go to their assigned classrooms to meet their homeroom teachers.

Jack, Margaret, and Christopher walked around. They found where the cafeteria, the principal's office, the library, and the art room were located. Shortly thereafter, the bell rang, which indicated it was time to go to their homeroom. Christopher had been assigned room 106, which was located directly across from the principal's office.

As each family entered the classroom, the teacher greeted them and introduced herself as Miss Modak. She invited them to look around while they waited for the other parents and students. When everyone was there, the teacher again introduced herself. Verbally and in sign language, she briefly explained the objectives set forth for the deaf students during the upcoming school year. After answering a few questions, Miss Modak invited everyone to the cafeteria for some light refreshments.

As everyone filed out of the classroom, Jack wanted to know how Miss Modak intended to help Christopher personally. "Ma'am, do you have any experience working with deaf students?"

Miss Modak smiled. She could see that Jack was concerned with getting the best education for his son. "When I taught at Kennedy Elementary, I had a few deaf students in my class. They needed a little extra help so I tutored them through the school year and also taught some of them during summer school. I believe the time I spent tutoring my deaf students, as well as taking classes in sign language and being trained to help students with special needs, more than qualifies me for being a teacher of the deaf."

Jack seemed pleased with Miss Modak's response, but he still had worries regarding Christopher. "You know, I want the best for my son. I think Christopher is a very smart young man and that he could learn anything if he puts his mind to it. I'm a businessman. I own a large manufacturing company, and I've always said that Christopher and I are going to run the business together. After I retire, he would take over operations for me. As it stands now, Christopher can hardly communicate with me, his father. I am having serious doubts as to whether he would be able to work in any type of managerial position. I really want Christopher to be successful. Do you think it's possible?"

"I remember Christopher from Kennedy. He stood out in my mind because he always strived to excel. Though he had some problem areas, he worked a lot harder than most of the hearing students his age. Christopher still has much to learn, but I think he is young enough that, if he puts forth the effort, he can be whatever he wants to be. Right now, the important thing is for you and Christopher to be able to have good communication."

Jack's main concern now came to the fore. "Can Christopher learn to read lips and speak clearly so that he can be successful in communicating with the hearing world?"

"Well, that would be up to Christopher. Here at Eastern Junior High we teach a program of Total Communication. He will learn to lipread and to speak, as well as learn more signs; that way he will be prepared to communicate with whomever he chooses, hearing or deaf."

Jack nodded his head and then thanked Miss Modak for taking the time to speak with him.

"I'm looking forward to having Christopher in my class this school year. If you have any further questions or concerns, please feel free to contact me. Meanwhile, your family and the other parents and students are in the cafeteria having refreshments, just down the hall, there. Why don't you join them?"

As Jack walked down the hall, he contemplated Christopher's future. He couldn't help but feel disappointed, since he wanted so much for Christopher to conform to the hearing world.

Chapter 23
Empathetic Friend

Eastern Junior High School's orientation had been on Friday evening, and Monday was the first day of school. When Monday dawned, Christopher was apprehensive. He was starting a new school where he would no longer be one of the older kids. At this school, the kids appeared much older and bigger than he was, and in actuality, they were. He was grateful that he had met Miss Modak briefly at the orientation and was comforted to know that she really was a nice person.

The junior high school's bus arrived almost an hour earlier than the elementary school's bus. Homeroom at Eastern began at 8:30 rather than 9:00, and the bus driver liked to get the students to school at least 15 minutes before homeroom was to begin.

When Christopher arrived, he had not yet received his locker assignment. Rather than hanging out in the halls with the other students, he went directly to his homeroom.

Miss Modak seemed eager to get to know Christopher. "Hello. My name Janice Modak." Showing her name sign, she continued, "You remember me taught Kennedy Elementary?"

Christopher looked at her face and thought for a few minutes, but he wasn't sure if he had seen her before. "I not remember. You taught class what?"

Miss Modak said, "I helped teach some deaf. You not my classes, but I remember teachers discussed you. I'm happy you join my class will two years."

The school bell rang. Miss Modak turned the lights off and on to let the students know it was time for class to begin.

Christopher sat down at one of the desks in the front of the class. He watched as the other students took their seats. The class was relatively small, consisting of just twelve students. He knew about half of the students in his class, since they had attended Kennedy Elementary together. The other students were brought in from a neighboring school district. Waiting for Miss Modak to give out locker assignments and textbooks, Christopher wondered why she had taken such an interest in him.

During the first semester, Miss Modak and Christopher became good friends. As she helped him to improve his English grammar, he helped her to improve her signing skills.

Miss Modak was constantly encouraging Christopher to strive to be the best he could be and to take advantage of any opportunities that opened up for him. One of those opportunities was the football team.

Christopher tried out for the team. Since he could outrun all of the other players, he was made one of the team's receivers. Being on the football team was a lot of hard work. Practicing every day after school, Christopher found himself training with weights, running, and learning to carry out different plays.

The other football players were constantly poking fun at Christopher. If he missed the catch they would say, "It's because he's the deaf and dumb player." In the locker room, his teammates would ridicule him. Slapping him on the back, they would get right in his face, rubbing their hands together and waving them in the air while saying, "Blah, blah, blah . . . Blah, blah." Then they would walk away laughing.

Christopher wished so much that he could hear like everyone else, but he couldn't, and he knew he never would.

After a while, he began to feel that the treatment he received was somehow deserved.

During football practice, Christopher had a difficult time understanding the quarterback's directions, especially since the quarterback didn't make any effort to look at Christopher when he was talking. Sometimes Christopher would pretend to understand what the quarterback was saying. Most of the time, however, in order to compensate for the lack of direction, he just trained harder, ran faster, and would do whatever he could to prove himself as good a football player as the hearing boys.

The quarterback knew Christopher was the fastest receiver on the team, yet he rarely used him. Halfway through the season, however, during the team's most important game against Redford Junior High—the number one team in the league—the quarterback asked him if he was ready to receive a long pass for a touchdown and the win. The score was Eastern 10, Redford 14, with 15 seconds left in the game.

Nervous, Christopher felt as if he had butterflies in his stomach. He had only played in two games this season, and this was the first time that he had been called on to receive a long pass.

The players stood on the line of scrimmage. It seemed so long before the ball was snapped, Christopher felt that time had stood still. Running as fast as he could, he made his way toward the end zone. The quarterback threw the ball hard and fast, over the players and directly to Christopher. As he turned to catch the ball, he felt it hit him square in the chest, but before he could get a good grip on it, the ball slipped out of his arms and hit the ground.

The game was over. Redford had won. The quarterback was furious. In the locker room, he walked over to Christopher and punched him in the eye. "Deaf stink!"

Christopher's eye quickly bruised, yet the bruise on his eye was not nearly as serious as the bruise to his self-confidence.

After showering and getting dressed, Christopher was ready to leave the school when the assistant coach pulled him aside. The coach didn't know sign language, but he tried to enunciate his words and use gestures so that Christopher could understand him. Pointing to Christopher's eye, he said, "I know what happened to your eye." He motioned, "Come with me." He got Christopher an ice pack to put on his eye and then led him into the coach's office, where the coach had been reprimanding the quarterback.

When Christopher and the assistant coach entered the office, the coach told the quarterback to put his hands on the desk and "take the stance." He then walked behind his desk and pulled a large wooden paddle out of his drawer.

The quarterback stood up nervously.

Handing Christopher the paddle, the coach again told the quarterback to bend over. He told Christopher to paddle the quarterback equal to his age—12 times.

Christopher held the paddle for a minute. He looked at the paddle and then at the quarterback and back at the paddle again. Deciding the problem was not with the quarterback, but with himself and his deafness, he dropped the paddle and walked away.

The quarterback stood up, thinking he was free to go, but the coach told him to bend over again. The coach proceeded to impress on the quarterback's memory a lesson he would never forget.

When Christopher arrived home, Margaret immediately noticed his eye. "What happened?"

Christopher signed, "My fault."

When Margaret told Jack what Christopher had said, Jack wondered why Christopher was at fault. "Was someone trying to teach you a lesson?"

Christopher, not understanding his father, looked at his mother. She signed, "Father want know someone try teach you lesson?"

"Yes, they teach me lesson." Christopher went into his bedroom.

Monday morning, Jack contacted the school to see what had happened. The coach explained that the quarterback had been frustrated because Christopher didn't understand him. He told Jack that the quarterback's feelings did not excuse his behavior, and he had been punished. Ending his phone conversation, Jack proceeded to explain to Margaret what had happened and then voiced his own opinion.

"I wish Christopher would use less sign language and work on his oral skills so that he can communicate better with hearing people."

Though she agreed that Christopher needed total communication skills, Margaret felt that his need to communicate with specific people was more important right now than the method he used to communicate. Oral skills wouldn't have helped Christopher catch the ball and the quarterback would still have been mad that he dropped it. The quarterback was just blaming his lack of self-control on Christopher being deaf. Their differences soon escalated into a full-scale argument. Jack packed a bag, told Margaret that he would be staying at the office for a while, and then stormed out of the house.

Seeing his parents' argument end with his dad packing a suitcase and leaving, Christopher asked his mom if his dad would be back. She told him his dad would be gone for a few days, but it was nothing that should worry him. Remembering how Donny's parents had divorced because of Donny's deafness and use of sign language, Christopher couldn't help but be concerned.

At school, Christopher didn't speak to anyone. Miss Modak pulled him aside, "Wow. Today you very quiet. You okay?"

Christopher's eyes filled with tears, "Dad left. Reason? I deaf. Parents big argue; he left." Christopher's tears finally overflowed.

Miss Modak gave Christopher a hug. She reminded him that he was not to blame for his parents' problems, and that no matter what happened, his parents still loved him very much. Miss Modak's continued encouragement helped him cope during the remainder of the week.

That Thursday the students at Eastern Junior High had only half a day of school. Taking a taxi, Margaret went to the school to pick up her son so they could spend the afternoon together on another of their adventures.

Christopher hadn't seen his dad much since the big argument between his parents, so he asked his mom if they could go visit his dad at the office.

Margaret was a little reluctant to go because she knew that Jack was always busy and that his hectic pace often affected his mood; however, understanding how much Christopher missed his dad, she agreed.

When he entered Crownline's lobby, Christopher ran past the receptionist, Becky, to his father's office. Opening the door, he began signing and saying, "Dad, Dad, my school half day. We go—"

Before Christopher could finish his sentence, Jack interrupted him. "Christopher, I'm having an important meeting here. Remember there is no sign language in my office. Keep your voice down." Pointing toward the door, he continued, "Go back to your mother, and I will be with you shortly, when my meeting is done."

Christopher was confused because it seemed that Jack wasn't happy to see him. Going back to the car where his mother was waiting, he explained what had happened and then asked, "Dad mad me why?"

Margaret was very upset. How could she explain to her son that his father really did care about him and wanted him to better himself, but that his father didn't understand the need for signing? Rather than answer his question, she tried to find a diversion to cheer him. Frustrated with the whole situation, she told him that they would go visit her mother and father for the weekend, since the last time they had seen her folks had been at the end of summer.

Christopher always enjoyed spending the weekend with his grandparents because they spoiled him with many gifts; yet his father's leaving still weighed heavily on his mind, even while he was there.

Monday morning during class, Miss Modak noticed that Christopher seemed troubled and unable to concentrate. His mind was obviously occupied with something other than schoolwork.

At lunch, Miss Modak went into the teachers' lunchroom to eat. The thermostat wasn't working properly, so the teachers had left the door open to allow more heat to come into the room. While chatting with another teacher, Miss Modak noticed Christopher as he walked by the door. He was walking very slowly, with his head down. Never having seen him look so dejected before, she excused herself and went to talk with him. She could see, as she approached him, that he was crying. "Wrong what?"

Christopher said, "Mom, Dad . . ." but then he got choked up and couldn't speak. He signed, "They separate." Looking down at the floor, he walked away.

Christopher, missing his dad a lot, was still feeling down the next day. At lunchtime, he sat at a table by himself. His lunch lay in front of him untouched.

Miss Modak, who was lunchroom overseer that day, watched Christopher for a while. Finally she approached him and asked him how he was feeling.

"My life lousy!"

"You know, other people problems hard, suffering same you. I notice other person feel lousy same you. Maybe he friend need."

"Who?" Miss Modak glanced at an overweight black boy sitting alone a few tables away. Christopher recognized him from the football team but didn't actually know him. He was one of the defensive linemen. "See boy wearing sweater red . . . he problem, sad. You go cheer him. Go on."

To make Miss Modak happy, and only to make Miss Modak happy, Christopher went over and sat down at the table across from the boy. Christopher noticed the boy had been crying. Trying to use his voice as he signed, Christopher introduced himself. "Hi. My name Christopher."

The boy, not understanding, looked at Christopher with a puzzled expression on his face.

Christopher wrote on his lunch bag "Christopher," and then he pointed at himself. He wrote "Your name?"

The boy wrote "Mike."

The boys began writing notes to each other. As they did, Christopher started to show Mike a few signs, which the other boy seemed to pick up rather quickly.

From the stage, Miss Modak watched the boys. She was pleased to see that they were able to help each other forget about their problems for the time being.

It was two and a half weeks before Jack and Margaret reconciled and Jack returned home. Though Jack's attitude toward sign language was unchanged, they realized their relationship with each other was more important than their differing opinions as to which language was to be used in or outside the home.

During Jack's absence, Christopher had begun to develop a new friendship with Mike. Every day the boys ate lunch together. Through their association, Mike had been able to learn and remember signs.

One day months later, as Christopher and Mike were on their way to the cafeteria, a couple of boys walked up to Mike, said something, and then walked away laughing. Mike's expression quickly changed.

Christopher asked Mike what the boys had said.

"They said I'm fat. They made fun me—said I don't eat too much healthy food. They always insult me."

Christopher smiled, "Their talk you accept, accept. You do nothing why? "

Mike replied that he was afraid; he didn't want to be making trouble.

Christopher said, "Watch me!" He approached the boys in the lunchroom as they were sitting at their table.

The boy that had insulted Mike looked at Christopher, "What do you want?"

Christopher stood motionless looking at their lunches spread over the table.

Another boy said, "He's one of those deaf dummies."

Christopher continued to stand next to the bully, smiling.

The bully was getting upset that Christopher was hovering over him. "Get lost!"

Christopher looked at him with a confused expression.

"Get out of here!" the bully snarled, giving Christopher a push.

Christopher fell to the ground. As he fell, he purposely knocked over an empty seat behind him, so as to make a loud noise that would get the lunchroom overseer's attention.

The lunchroom overseer for that day just happened to be Miss Modak. She saw Christopher lying on the floor and asked him what had happened.

Christopher explained he had just walked over to see what they were eating. The boys insulted him and then pushed him to the floor.

Miss Modak pulled the bully from his seat and took him up on the stage. She told the students that bullying other students is not tolerated in her lunchroom. She then asked the bully how old he was. He replied, "Thirteen." Walking over to a closet to the right of the stage, she pulled out a wooden paddle. She told the bully to bend down and hold his ankles. In front of all the students, she paddled him thirteen times.

Christopher had walked back to his table, grinning from ear to ear, and sat down next to Mike. "She my teacher. She cool—huh?"

Thursday was the day before the game against Harding Junior High. Miss Modak approached Christopher to talk to him about Mike. She wondered how their friendship was developing. Having heard from the football coach that Mike had decided to quit the team after the Harding game, she shared her concerns with Christopher.

Christopher was shocked and wondered why Mike would quit, since he was in the starting lineup of every game.

Miss Modak explained that Mike was tired of the name-calling and insults.

Christopher could relate to how Mike felt; yet he didn't want to see Mike give up a sport where he excelled.

In the locker room, while getting changed for football practice, Christopher saw Mike sitting quietly on a bench, tying his shoes. Walking over to Mike, he began signing, "I heard you quit team. You crazy! Look you! You quit why?"

Mike signed, "I play football, many tease me say, 'You fat.'"

"People insult me, call me deaf dummy. I ignore. You need same me." Christopher felt Mike was a great football player and could someday make it his career, but Mike needed to believe in himself and not give up because of other people's opinions of him. "Come on! Your body a lot meat, like ox. Whole school needs you support team! Come on, Ox. Show them what you do!"

Mike appreciated Christopher's encouragement and decided to tell the coach he would like to continue playing. The coach was thrilled to have his best defensive lineman back.

Years later, Mike played in the NFL as a defensive lineman. He had one of the best records for quarterback sacks. No longer considered fat, he was 300 pounds of pure muscle. The nickname that Christopher had given him in junior high school, the Ox, stuck with him throughout his NFL career.

On the day of the game against Harding Junior High School, Christopher was getting his books out of his locker when it suddenly slammed shut. The bully who had pushed Christopher in the cafeteria was now standing in front of him with two of his buddies. Christopher looked around. There were very few students in the hallway where his locker was located, and the ones that were there either didn't notice what was happening or didn't care to get involved.

Christopher was scared, but he tried to act brave. He took a step forward, looked the bully directly in the eyes, and said, "Excuse me." He tried to walk past the bully, but the bully grabbed him by the collar and pushed him up against the lockers.

"I'm going to knock you out if you ever make trouble for me again!"

At that moment Mike turned the corner and saw how the bully had Christopher pinned up against the lockers. Mike shouted to the bully and his buddies, "Hey! You got a problem?"

The bully turned his head to see who was speaking to him.

Following the Bully's eyes, Christopher also turned to see what he was looking at. It was Mike. Christopher had never been so happy to see Mike. He knew he'd be all right now.

The bully took a step away from Christopher, wiped off Christopher's shirt, and then said, "Hey man, there's no problem. We're cool."

Walking toward the bully, Mike mocked, "Cool, yeah, be cool man." Then he stood face-to-face with him and said, "Christopher is my brother. If you bother him, you'll deal with me. I'm not afraid of you anymore. Know why . . . huh? I'm 175 pounds, and you're what . . . uh, 95 pounds?" Mike punched the bully in the stomach so hard that the boy doubled over and fell to the floor.

Christopher was surprised at how brave Mike had become. Walking down the hall to class, they gave each other a high five and laughed at how they had beaten the bully.

Chapter 24
<u>Growing Brave</u>

The summer between seventh and eighth grades was rather uneventful. Christopher helped his mom around the house and watched a lot of television. Occasionally he visited his father's office. The remainder of his time, he spent with Nicole. They would sit in her tree house for hours at a time, talking, laughing, and playing games. She was becoming quite fluent in sign language, so he enjoyed being with her. Besides, she seemed to like the same things as he and was just fun to be around. They had quickly become best friends.

Miss Modak, being the only junior high teacher for deaf students, was again Christopher's teacher the following year. Although eighth grade proved to be a difficult year for him, it was one that empowered him.

After just a couple of weeks of school, Miss Modak approached Christopher at his desk. "I ask you," she signed, "Your mind always running fast how?"

Christopher thought that was a strange question. "You mean what?"

Miss Modak continued, "My class you pay attention. I

notice your mind always thinking. You talk positive, encourage many people. I wonder you want learn self more confident?

Christopher looked puzzled.

"Confidence help you go ahead do something."

Christopher still didn't understand, "Confidence what for?"

"You plenty time can learn 'what for'. Future you will more confident. Many goals will successful."

During the past few years, Miss Modak had become an assertive, confident individual. Standing before government officials and business leaders, in order to establish a total communication program for the deaf at Eastern Junior High School, she had gained experience in asserting herself. Wanting to put that experience to use, she was prepared to help Christopher learn how to control his thoughts, motives, and actions so that he could be successful, not only in facing the hearing world but also in dealing with his father.

A few weeks into the second semester, Christopher and the other deaf students were sitting at their desks waiting for class to begin. As she walked into the classroom, Miss Modak slammed the door. The sound of the door slamming resonated throughout the classroom.

Christopher, who had been organizing his papers in his folder, was startled. Thinking it was the boom of thunder that he felt, he looked toward the window, but the sun was shining brightly. He then looked toward the front of the classroom, where Miss Modak was standing. She looked very upset. Christopher realized the vibration must have been the classroom door. Sitting quietly, he waited to see what was going to happen next.

Miss Modak began signing very distinctly. "You all pay attention. My wallet put closet, it inside 35 dollars. Now money gone. I want—"

Suddenly Christopher stood up, walked to the classroom door, opened the door, and then slammed it shut. The classroom again reverberated. He pointed to the other eleven students. "If Miss Modak's 35 dollars you stole, give her, or I punch you."

Miss Modak knew Christopher was trying to help her find the culprit, but she wanted him to realize that aggressive behavior was not the answer. Getting Christopher's attention, she said, "Finish. You go sit. I teacher, you not. Go SIT."

Christopher's eyes opened wide. Surprised that Miss Modak would be upset with him when he was simply trying to help, he returned to his seat.

Miss Modak continued addressing the class, "Before lunch, my 35 dollars, I want put my desk. I don't care who stole money, but it must back my desk BEFORE lunch."

Christopher saw how Miss Modak asserted herself. She made her wishes known in a calm, yet firm manner. Before lunch, the money was returned.

The week before school was to let out for winter break, the students were in the cafeteria eating lunch. Fooling around, a few hearing boys started throwing little pieces of food at each other. One of them took his sandwich and threw it across the cafeteria to where the deaf students were sitting. The other boys followed suit. Laughing, the boys congratulated each other for the strength of their pitch.

Christopher had seen the students fooling around. Walking up on the stage, he stood looking at all the students in the cafeteria. The troublemakers, as well as some of the other students, began laughing at Christopher. Looking at the students, he stood undaunted.

Miss Modak, who happened again to be responsible for overseeing the lunchroom, approached the stage. "You stand stage why?"

Christopher smiled, "I see everything happening. Don't mind me assist you?"

"Why?"

"You want me learn self act confident, proper action. Right?"

"All right. Few minutes you can power assist me."

Christopher was excited to have this chance to prove himself. He wanted the students to look at him, so he started waving to get their attention. Once he had the attention of the troublemakers in particular, he tried to speak as he signed, "You throw sandwiches; you go pick up!"

The students all stopped when Christopher began talking, but his speech was difficult to comprehend. Many of the students began laughing, and some of the boys began mimicking his garbled speech.

Miss Modak walked up on stage next to Christopher. "I want the sandwiches picked up just as Christopher said. If the food that was thrown is not cleaned up, ALL of you will be given detention."

Many of the students were surprised by Miss Modak's firmness. Not wanting to be punished for the conduct of a few misbehaved students, they all started shouting at the troublemakers to clean up the mess. Finally, the mischievous boys walked across the cafeteria picking up the food they had thrown.

Miss Modak and Christopher watched from the stage. Turning to Christopher, she praised him, "You good progress."

Christopher felt proud that he was learning how to use power properly in order to be an assertive individual.

After enjoying a festive two-week break, the students returned to school only to find out that the teachers, who had been trying to negotiate a new contract through their union, were scheduled to go on strike Wednesday at midnight if their demands were not met.

Miss Modak hated to leave her precious students without proper education, but there were principles that needed to be upheld, and she hoped the time would be short. Informing them on Wednesday morning that negotiations were not going well, she told her class they would probably have a substitute teacher for a while. She encouraged the students to continue putting forth effort to learn all that they could while she was away.

Before school let out, Miss Modak pulled Christopher aside. "I miss you much will," she said. "I start teach until now, you best student. I see you focus education, thinking other students. I gone, my class same sheep; you watch, take care them."

Knowing he would miss Miss Modak, since they had become good friends during the past two years, Christopher replied, "I try my best."

Miss Modak gave Christopher a hug and then sent him outside to meet his bus.

Thursday morning, Christopher entered the classroom hoping that the School Board had conceded and Miss Modak would be sitting at her desk as usual, but there was another woman sitting in her seat. He introduced himself to the substitute teacher.

Many of the students were uncomfortable with the substitute teacher because she wasn't fluent in sign language and she didn't know how to relate to the deaf students. Having promised Miss Modak that he would take care of her "sheep," Christopher tried his best to help the substitute improve her signing skills. He also came to the aid of any students who didn't understand the teacher or the information being taught, once he figured it out himself.

Every day Christopher would come into the classroom hoping to see Miss Modak, and every day he would meet with disappointment and frustration. After about a month of waiting, he decided to go speak with the principal. Since the principal didn't know sign language and there were no interpreters available, he and the principal wrote notes back and forth to each other. Christopher wrote, "Teachers come back when?"

The principal tried to explain that it was not his decision. The teachers union had to reach an agreement with the School Board, and then the teachers would return to school.

Christopher was disappointed with the principal's vague answer; the principal seemed to feel just as disappointed.

Returning to the classroom, Christopher sat at his desk.

The substitute teacher approached him and asked if everything was okay.

Not wanting to rehash what he and the principal had discussed, he sat quietly thinking. All of a sudden, it hit him. He had an idea.

Approaching the teacher, he asked her if she would do him a favor.

Since he had assisted her so much during the past month, she didn't hesitate to offer her help.

During the remainder of the study period, he got some poster board and made two large signs.

When all of the students were assembled in the cafeteria for lunch, Christopher and his teacher stood on the stage. Getting the attention of the students, she told them that Christopher had something to show them. Looking at him, she said, "Go!"

Christopher held up a large sign that read, "End the Strike!"

Confused, the students looked around at each other. They couldn't imagine what they could possibly do to end the strike.

Christopher then held up another sign, "No School until Strike Ends!"

Some of the students stood up and began clapping in support of Christopher's idea.

Christopher began stomping his feet.

The students began pounding their fists on the table, stomping their feet, and chanting "No School until Strike Ends!"

As Christopher watched the students rally around him, he began to feel the power that Miss Modak had tried to teach him. Asserting himself for something he believed in, he was able to inspire the other students to take action. He then led the students out of the school.

News of the students' movement at Eastern Junior High School quickly spread throughout the school district. Soon all the students in the district took a stand in refusing to return to school until the teachers' strike ended.

Miss Modak received a phone call from the principal of Eastern. "Janice, did you hear how all the students in the school district refused to come to school until the teachers' strike ends? Imagine, they all refused to attend school until their teachers return!"

"Yes, I heard that on the radio. That's unbelievable! I heard it started at our school, is that true?"

"Yes it is, and you won't believe who lead the students in this strike . . ."

Miss Modak was very curious, "Who? Who was it?"

"It was Christopher Cline!"

Shocked, Miss Modak dropped the phone. "Oh my goodness!"

The principal went on to explain how Christopher had motivated the students to walk out halfway through the school day and not return until the strike is ended.

A week after the students had refused to attend school, the School Board acquiesced and met the teachers' demands. The teachers were then ordered to return to school first thing Monday morning.

Christopher's mother heard the news on the radio and immediately relayed it to him. He was thrilled to learn that the movement he had started had resulted in the teachers returning to work—which really benefited everyone.

Monday morning, as Christopher was walking down the hall to class, he could see Miss Modak standing outside the classroom. She smiled approvingly at him. He could read on her face that she was pleased that he had learned his lesson well.

The last few weeks of school seemed to be the longest, but Christopher had learned a lot this school year. Though his English was not as good as he would like it to be, he had improved academically. What was more important was what he had learned about himself. He had learned that he could accomplish almost anything he wanted.

Chapter 25
<u>Honor Awards</u>

The last week of school was exciting. Some of the students were stressed over finals, but most were looking forward to summer vacation and graduating from junior high school.

On the final day of school there would be an honors ceremony. Students who had excelled academically would be honored. In addition, one student would receive special recognition for the extraordinary effort he or she had put forth to become better educated despite adversity.

The students entered the gymnasium and took their seats. Finding seats on the far side of the gym near the interpreter, Christopher and Mike sat down. They were talking about what they planned to do on their first day of summer vacation, when Miss Modak motioned to Christopher to come with her. He followed her outside of the gymnasium.

Miss Modak told Christopher how privileged she felt to have been his teacher for the past two years and how proud she was of the progress he had made. "That reason all teachers choose top honor give you."

Christopher was stunned, "You serious?"

"Yes. Other student much effort, same you. Teachers must pick one. We pick you."

"Other student, who?"

"His name Tim LaBree. Last year his father died. He 13 years old. He work hard, help mother take care children, but he still finish homework. His report card always A's, B's same you. Right now his mother hospital, will surgery. He oldest child. He sisters two, brother one. Yesterday school finish, he take children visit mother. He go store buy food, get children, cook dinner, help kids ready bed. Every day neighbor check them okay, eat, go school, but he much work take care family."

Christopher was impressed. "Wow! He big effort!"

Miss Modak smiled. "We should go back gym. Program soon begin."

As Christopher walked back into the gymnasium, he noticed his parents sitting on the same side of the gym as he, but more toward the back. His mom waved at him. Smiling, Christopher sat back down next to Mike.

After the honor awards were given to those students who had achieved academically, the principal again spoke to the audience. "Every year the faculty chooses one student who has put forth an extraordinary effort to perform academically, as well as to assist others. You'll recall this school year how one of our deaf mute students was able to unite all the students in a protest that brought the teachers' strike to an end. He has also been on the honor roll for the past two years. The student chosen to receive this year's special award is Christopher Cline!" All the parents, teachers, and students began applauding.

As Christopher walked onto the stage, he felt good about all that he had accomplished this school year.

Shaking Christopher's hand, the principal gave him his award.

Christopher asked if he could say a few words to the students and the faculty.

The principal called Miss Modak to the stage to interpret for him.

"I want to tell my fellow classmates to enjoy your summer,

and I wish you all the best in the future. To the faculty, I want to say thank you very much for this special honor. I appreciate your recognition, but I feel there is another student who deserves it even more. His father passed away last year, and he has had to help his mother raise his three siblings. Right now his mother is in the hospital for surgery, and he is doing much of what she would do for them. During all of this, he has managed to stay on the honor roll. I would like to present my award to Tim LaBree."

Everyone began clapping as Tim came on stage. Shaking his hand, Christopher gave him the award, and then the audience gave them a standing ovation.

After the ceremony, the students were dismissed for summer vacation.

Standing in the hallway, Margaret waited for Christopher beside his locker. She gave him a big hug and told him, "I very proud you. I love you." They walked through the hallway and out the front door, where Jack was waiting for them.

Jack gave Christopher a hug and told him, "I watched you in the gym. You did a great job. I'm proud of you." The three of them walked away together.

Miss Modak watched the Clines walking to their car. She thought back to when Christopher had begun attending Eastern Junior High, two years before. Lacking confidence in his abilities, he had felt he was somehow a lesser human because of his deafness. Now he was a self-confident young man who was ready to take charge of his life and make it a success. Miss Modak knew she would never forget Christopher. As she watched the Clines drive away, she whispered, "Christopher, you deserve the best."

Chapter 26
<u>No Good-bye</u>

Over the past two years, Christopher and Nicole had become best friends. They spent all their free time in the tree house. Nicole had made it into a comfortable hide-away where they could get away from the world, and there they just enjoyed each other's company. Here is where he helped her learn sign language.

Christopher never wanted Nicole to feel pressured to learn how to sign. He was afraid of being too demanding when it came to sign language because he didn't want to lose such a good friend. He tried to make signing fun. They would take turns pointing to objects and signing what they were. Making up stories, they enjoyed trying to sign them to each other. Nicole had brought a radio up into the tree house when she first moved in. Now, instead of just listening to it, she would try to interpret for Christopher what was being said or sung. In fact, she liked to inform him of every sound that she heard: the birds, the cars driving past the house, or the crickets chirping. He was surprised by how noisy the world actually was.

Together, they would talk for hours at a time about school, family, their feelings, hopes, and dreams. Nothing could be better than spending the summer with your best friend.

During the third week of July, the Clines left to go camping in Canada with Bill, Catherine, their two daughters, and another family who had four children. Camping was always a great adventure, and everyone had a great time.

When Christopher arrived back home, he ran over to the tree house to see if Nicole was there. He wanted to surprise her and tell her all about his camping trip. He also had brought her some wildflowers from their campsite. Though Christopher waited until dark, Nicole never came out to the tree house. Christopher finally headed back home. He left the flowers in the tree house in case she came out the next morning before he got there.

During the next two days, Christopher visited the tree house at various times to see if he could catch Nicole, but she was never there and never came while he was there. The flowers he had left on the shelf were now wilted and the petals were beginning to fall to the floor. He was beginning to wonder what had happened to her. Maybe she was sick. He decided to go to her house and find out.

Christopher went to the front door of Nicole's house and knocked.

Nicole's mother, who always had a friendly demeanor, came to the door.

Christopher signed and tried to say, "Nicole, where?"

Nicole's mother smiled, "Nicole is away, but I will call your mother."

Christopher was confused by her answer. He wondered where Nicole was. Maybe she hadn't come to the tree house because she was upset with him. The only time she had missed going to the tree house before was when her family had gone to Florida over spring break.

Christopher went back home. His mom was in the kitchen, baking. "What happen Nicole? Her mother said she gone. Where she go?"

"I phone talked Nicole's mother. She told me Nicole with father. New house, they bought. This weekend they move will."

"Before move, Nicole back see me?"

"I don't know. Maybe she move finish."

Christopher was upset. He began shouting as he signed, "Nicole gone, why? She never tell me, why?"

Margaret could see how much Christopher was hurting. She knew she could say nothing to take away his pain. Trying to comfort him as best she could, she held him in her arms for a few minutes and then said, "Sorry Nicole gone."

Christopher was upset because Nicole hadn't even said good-bye. "She gone because I deaf."

Margaret wanted to remind Christopher that Nicole's moving was something beyond her control. Before she could say anything, however, he ran into his bedroom and slammed the door shut. Walking over to his bedroom, she could hear him throwing things around. She went into his room.

Christopher yelled, "Go away!" To emphasize the fact that he didn't want his mother there, he threw a book in her general direction. Margaret could see that losing his best friend was something that he was not prepared to bear. He continued to throw objects across the room.

Walking over to Christopher, Margaret put her arms around him and held him tightly. He struggled for a minute and then broke down crying. She continued to hold him until he calmed down. "You know that Nicole, she good friend. You deaf that reason she leave not. She with her family must. Her father's job transferred other state. That reason Nicole leave— not you fault. I feel you see Nicole again will."

Later that afternoon, Christopher and his parents sat down to dinner. There was almost no conversation as they ate.

Jack wondered why everyone was so quiet.

Margaret explained that Christopher was depressed because Nicole and her family were moving out of state, and he hadn't been given a chance to say good-bye.

Jack claimed to understand how Christopher felt. "You will be fine. I know Nicole has moved away, but I'm still here for you. We can be buddies. Don't feel bad. Everything will be okay."

Margaret interpreted what Jack was saying, but Christopher seemed even more upset by Jack's words. "My buddy knows sign language. You don't!"

Jack felt that Christopher was just being immature. "I want you to grow up. Nicole is not the only friend you have. Your mother knows sign language too. You will be fine."

Jack may as well have said "Blah blah, blah blah blah," because to Christopher, his words meant nothing. They only underscored his lack of understanding that, as far as Christopher was concerned, the people who really cared about him were the ones who would make the effort to learn to sign and at least try to make it easier for him to communicate with them.

The next day Christopher went up to the tree house. He felt as empty inside as the tree house now was. Apparently someone had come up and taken all of Nicole's things. As he looked around the tree house, his mind was flooded with memories of Nicole. He remembered all their fun times. Missing her so much, he felt like a puppy that had lost his way home. He lay on the floor, looking up at the ceiling. Soon he fell asleep.

When Christopher awoke, he noticed a white envelope lying on the floor to the right of the door. It had his name on the front. Recognizing Nicole's writing, he stood up and looked out the window and then out the door. Thinking that maybe she had come home, he climbed down from the tree house, ran to her house, and began knocking on the front door. No one answered. He walked across the porch to look in the front window. The furniture was gone, and the house was empty.

Christopher realized that Nicole was gone. He went back to the tree house. Picking up the envelope, he held it in his hands as he thought of his best friend. He opened it and read, "My friend Christopher, You helped me learn sign language—thank you. Now I must go with my family. I will big miss you. You, me will always best friends . . . Nicole."

Christopher felt as though an important part of his life had been ripped away from him. He knew Nicole was gone . . . forever.

Chapter 27
High School

The remainder of the summer was lonely without Nicole, but it didn't last long. Soon it was time to prepare for a new school experience.

Christopher would be starting high school this year. He would no longer have to take the bus to school. Since Madison High School was just a few blocks away from his home, he would now be able to walk.

Toward the end of summer, Christopher tried out for the football team. It was more difficult because there were students from the other two junior high schools vying for the same positions. When it came time to choose the running backs, the coach was more comfortable using hearing students, since he had no experience working with the deaf.

The coach's decision was okay with Christopher. Not having football practice every day after school, he would have more time to concentrate on his studies.

A week before school was to begin, Christopher and his parents were to meet with the guidance counselor for the deaf students to discuss his curriculum.

Entering the counselor's office, Jack and Margaret were greeted by a friendly looking woman who had been sitting at a round table in the middle of the room. She stood up, introduced herself, and shook their hands.

Looking at Christopher, the counselor then signed, "Hello, I Miss Tessler. My name," she showed him her name sign, which was the letter T placed on the back of her fist. "You Christopher, name sign what?"

Christopher showed Miss Tessler his name sign.

Miss Tessler voiced and signed, "It's good to meet you. Please sit down." She directed them to sit around the table. "I see from Eastern's records that you scored in the 92nd percentile overall on your most recent Equivalency Test and in the 99th percentile on your Math and Analytical Thinking portion of the test." She showed Christopher his test results. "I'm wondering . . . have you thought about your career goals?"

Jack took the paper with Christopher's test results and examined it.

"Yes. I want help deaf people life improve."

Miss Tessler asked, "You mean same social worker?"

"Well . . . I prefer lawyer or judge, set new laws support deaf."

Jack smiled, "Did you say you want to be a lawyer? Many young people think they can become lawyers, but I think you need to be realistic. Look at your English scores." Jack pointed on the paper to Christopher's English score and then he held his nose indicating his score stinks.

Miss Tessler explained, "Actually, Christopher's English scores and reading comprehension scores are average for a deaf person, but his scores in math and analytical thinking, as I said, are very high—"

Jack interrupted, "So you could get a job as a carpenter, a draftsman, a machinist, or warehouse manager. Then I could hire you to work at the factory."

Christopher rolled his eyes.

Miss Tessler looked at Jack, "That's true, but with some college training, he can improve his English, and I think he could be much more." She then looked at Christopher, "I recommend you goal career accounting, engineering, or social work. You want goal what? Understand, you not stuck that career. This help us pick courses lead your goal."

Christopher looked at his parents, then at Miss Tessler, and replied, "Really, I want goal lawyer or judge."

Jack laughed.

Margaret asked Miss Tessler, "Do you know of any deaf people who have become lawyers?"

"Well, I personally do not, but considering Christopher's test scores, I believe if he really studies hard and puts his mind to it, anything is possible."

Jack looked at Christopher, "If you want to become a lawyer, you are going to need to improve your English."

"I try best I can improve English, but that not my major."

Miss Tessler left the room so that Christopher and his parents could select his courses.

After much discussion, Jack and Christopher reached an agreement. Christopher signed up for English, Algebra I, U.S. History, Biology, Sociology, Physical Education, and Accounting. He would have a full schedule with his only free period being his lunch hour. He accepted the challenge in order to include the history and sociology courses that he wanted to take.

Miss Tessler came back into the room and sat down at the table. Christopher handed her his course selection form.

Carefully looking over Christopher's schedule, Miss Tessler signed to him, "Wow! This full schedule. You no free time for study means you probably will homework every night."

"Yes, I understand."

Miss Tessler suggested, "These courses you could divide over next five years."

"Five years? What you mean?"

"Most deaf students stay school five years earn credits need for graduate. Some students need more time."

Christopher shook his head. "I graduate four years WILL."

Miss Tessler smiled, "I hope you can."

Christopher looked her directly in the eyes and signed, "Four years, I graduate. Me honor student will. You watch me." Turning to his father, he voiced "Four years." He then looked at his mom and held up four fingers for emphasis.

Margaret smiled and signed, "I know you will."

A week later, Christopher's first day of high school was exciting, but it also made him nervous. The high school was much bigger than any of the other schools he had attended. The students also seemed bigger. At fourteen, he had not yet experienced his adolescent growth spurt, so he was still shorter than most of the boys and some of the girls at the high school.

Since Christopher's family had gone camping again the week before, he had missed the school's orientation program. Now he was supposed to go to his homeroom, but he had no clue where it was located. Stopping a couple of students who looked to be seniors, he showed them his schedule. He pointed to the room number of his homeroom and shrugged his shoulders.

One of the students pointed him down a long hallway. The other students with him began to laugh as Christopher walked away.

Following the boy's directions, Christopher ended up in the cafeteria. He asked another student for directions, but she was also a freshman and was just as lost as he was. Finally Christopher found a teacher, who gave him directions to the homeroom for the deaf students.

By the time Christopher arrived in homeroom, he was late, as was half of the class. They all had similar experiences getting to homeroom. He felt better knowing that he was not the only student to get lost that day.

The teacher introduced herself as Mrs. Sinclair. She was a tall woman in her mid 30's with a kind demeanor and a smile that was genuine. Wanting to befriend her class, she was extremely understanding toward the challenges her students had faced that morning; yet still commanding the respect that her position afforded her, she informed her students that after the first week of school, tardiness would no longer be excused.

Mrs. Sinclair used the homeroom period to hand out locker assignments as well as give her students directions to their classes. All of the deaf students were assigned to Mrs. Sinclair's English class and Mrs. Conklin's math or algebra classes since both teachers used sign language.

After approaching Mrs. Sinclair to get directions to his classes, Christopher sat back down at his desk. As he looked at his schedule, he became a little nervous. Not only was he going to be the only deaf student in his sociology and U.S. history classes, but also he would probably be the youngest student. Sophomores or juniors usually took these courses, but Christopher had chosen them in order to prepare for law school.

When the bell rang, a light began flashing in the classroom to let the students know that it was time to go to their first class.

The first few weeks of school were difficult. All of Christopher's classes, with the exception of math, English, and physical education, were interpreted.

Christopher had one interpreter in the morning, for his biology class, and another interpreter for his afternoon classes. Signing word for word what the teacher was saying, the morning interpreter used very little facial expression. The majority of the time, it was difficult to follow her. The only time she varied from her normal interpreting style was when the class was dissecting worms and frogs. She then became quite expressive. Although the monotony of her signing at times made Christopher's eyes very heavy, he fought the desire to take a nap.

Christopher's afternoon interpreter made an effort to use American Sign Language, which better conveys the concepts being taught. He appreciated his afternoon interpreter's efforts since his choice courses, U.S. History and Sociology, were taught in the afternoon.

By the time the first grading period had ended, Christopher had developed a study routine that had enabled him to get the most out of each of his courses. Excelling in math and history, he ended the first grading period with a 3.85 grade point average. Especially captivated by his U.S. history class, he looked forward to the next quarter when the class would learn about the establishment of the justice system.

Chapter 28
<u>Distanced Friend</u>

Halfway through the school year, a new student moved into the school district. She was sixteen years old and a sophomore. Because she was deaf, she was assigned to the same homeroom as Christopher.

When Christopher entered homeroom, he noticed a black girl, her mother, and Mrs. Sinclair sitting at a table. Glancing at this new student, he walked to his desk. He found himself curiously looking up to watch her response as her mother talked to Mrs. Sinclair.

Shortly thereafter the girl's mother shook hands with Mrs. Sinclair and then left.

After the tardy bell rang and the light in the classroom flashed, all of the students took their seats. Mrs. Sinclair introduced the new student to the class and encouraged them to make her feel welcome. She then directed her to take the seat next to Christopher.

As soon as homeroom was finished, Christopher turned toward the new girl to introduce himself and see if she needed any assistance getting to her classes. "Hello. I Christopher. Your name what?"

The girl looked at Christopher, but didn't respond.

Wondering what was wrong with her, he again signed, "I Christopher."

Looking at him, the girl said "So?" and walked away.

Bewildered by her callous response, Christopher walked to his locker wondering why she acted so tough.

The next day before homeroom, Christopher approached Mrs. Sinclair. "New girl, she act tough why?"

"Remember" she signed a letter D over her heart.

Christopher interrupted. He imitated the D over his heart. "That who?"

"New girl, her name Danielle. Name sign," she again signed a letter D over her heart. "Remember, before Danielle go other school. Recent she move, join us. Move new school, not easy for her."

Christopher, trying to understand how she must have been feeling, made it a point to be friendly to her, but it seemed to no avail.

Christopher and Danielle were in the same algebra class. Seeing that she was struggling with the math problems, he wanted to help her. It was difficult offering her assistance since she had set up an invisible barrier, and he had not yet figured out how to get past that in order to gain her trust.

One day Christopher was watching Danielle struggle with an algebra problem when she suddenly caught him staring. Glaring back at him, she asked, "You eye problems?" Embarrassed, he looked the other way.

Danielle found out from another girl that Christopher was the best math student in their class. His grades were higher than even the hearing students were. Though impressed, she was still unwilling to ask him for assistance.

One day Mrs. Conklin, the math teacher, was sitting with Danielle trying to help her work through one of the algebra problems. Christopher saw how hard she was struggling. Wanting to help her, he walked up to the blackboard behind Mrs. Conklin and began writing the calculations on the board.

Danielle saw him but continued to reject his help. Pointing at the blackboard, she told Mrs. Conklin, "Christopher cheating. He writing answers on the blackboard."

Mrs. Conklin turned around as Christopher wrote the answer at the end of his calculations. He didn't realize the teacher was watching him until he turned around to see if Danielle understood.

Mrs. Conklin asked, "Christopher, you writing answer on blackboard why? Danielle trying work hard, herself find answer. You cheating."

Christopher looked at Danielle, who was grinning from ear to ear because he had been caught. He was embarrassed and a little upset at her lack of appreciation for his help. Walking back to his desk, he sat down.

A few days later, Christopher noticed Danielle was again having trouble—this time with fractions. Wanting to help her, he first asked the teacher for permission.

Mrs. Conklin told him that he could help Danielle, but he was not to cheat and give her the answers. "She must learn. Herself problems solve."

Christopher was excited to help Danielle, even though she acted like she didn't want his help. He stood next to her while she endeavored to solve the first problem.

Danielle stopped writing, looked at Christopher, and for the first time signed to him rather than mouthing words to him. "Your problem what?"

Christopher was surprised to see Danielle sign. Her question gave him the perfect opportunity to get her back. "YOU!"

Danielle smiled because she realized that she had set herself up for that. "You try sit near me don't. You turn around, go away." She pushed Christopher back, but he wouldn't leave.

Christopher kept watching Danielle as she pretended to be working out her math problem.

Trying to get Mrs. Conklin's attention, Danielle began waving to her.

Christopher grinned and then grabbed Danielle's pencil out of her hand. Breaking it into four pieces, he put the pieces on her desk.

Danielle was upset that he had broken her pencil.

Christopher proceeded to take three of the pencil pieces and place them together on the left side of her desk. The other piece, he placed on the right side of the desk. He explained that there were three pieces of pencil out of a total of four pieces. "Fraction what?"

Danielle was beginning to understand how fractions work, but she didn't want Christopher to know that he really was helping her. She refused to respond.

Christopher didn't give up. He continued to explain to Danielle that there were a total of four pieces. The total would be the denominator—the bottom number of the fraction. The portion separated from the whole would be the numerator or top number of the fraction. The three pieces of pencil would represent ¾, and the other one piece would represent ¼. He then showed her how ¾ is larger than ¼. After demonstrating fractions, he smiled at her and then walked back to his desk.

Danielle liked what she had learned, though she wouldn't admit it to Christopher.

The next day, Christopher brought to school a pencil with a rainbow design on it and laid it on Danielle's desk with a note.

Danielle read the note. "Sorry broke your pencil. Won't happen again." She looked at Christopher and smiled.

After a few weeks of brief conversations, tutoring sessions, and joking around, it seemed Danielle was much more comfortable with Christopher. He had made another good friend.

One morning Christopher saw Danielle at her locker. Walking toward her, he could see something was wrong. She looked up at him, but she seemed distant. He smiled at her, but before he could say anything, she shut her locker and walked away.

Christopher wanted to cheer Danielle so he walked faster in order to catch up with her. He tapped her on the shoulder.

Danielle turned her head, looked at him, and without saying a word, turned back around and continued walking.

As Christopher again tried to catch up with Danielle, someone came up from behind him and grabbed his shoulder. Turning around to see who had grabbed him, he saw a tall black boy. He had never seen this boy before.

The boy looked Christopher in the eye and said slowly, "Knock it off! You stay away from Danielle!"

Christopher, not knowing what to think, just nodded his head.

The boy let go of Christopher and walked in the direction of Danielle.

Christopher didn't know why Danielle was avoiding him or who this boy was. Feeling confused, he walked back to his locker. He thought maybe he had said or had done something to insult Danielle or hurt her feelings.

All morning Christopher was troubled by the way Danielle had treated him. Wanting to see if she was in a better mood, he looked for her in the cafeteria during lunch hour. Finally, he found her in the food line with one of her girlfriends. He watched her as they walked over to a table and sat down. As he ate his lunch, he kept watching her.

Suddenly, the boy that had grabbed Christopher in the hallway that morning slammed his hand on the table. He spoke very slowly and distinctly, "That's my sister! You leave her alone!" Then he walked away.

Christopher sat minding his own business as he finished his lunch.

A few days later, Christopher approached Mrs. Sinclair and told her what had happened. Taking him to the office so that they could talk privately, she explained, "Danielle's father beat her awful. Happen she become deaf. Her old school no program help deaf, that reason come here school. Also her father sexually abused her. He now prison. Her experience terrible. Now on, she difficulty any relationships—especially friend males. Her brother vow no one advantage Danielle again. If she scared relationship too close, he protect her."

Christopher felt bad and wished he could do something to help Danielle forget her past and feel more secure, but he realized there was nothing he could do.

A few weeks before school let out for the summer, Danielle moved to the other side of the state, where no one knew what had taken place in her family. Christopher was disappointed that he had lost another good friend.

Chapter 29
<u>Deafness Accepted</u>

Tenth grade was much the same as ninth grade for Christopher.

Mrs. Sinclair and Miss Tessler reviewed Christopher's career goals. Still wanting to work in a legal or a judicial profession, he chose courses that would help him to attain his goal. Between the required courses and the courses that Christopher chose to take, he again had a full schedule.

Jack didn't think that Christopher could work in any type of legal profession because of his deafness, but he didn't discourage him. He felt the basic courses Christopher would be taking—English, history, business, and math—would benefit him when he took over Crownline Glass.

Mrs. Sinclair wasn't sure that Christopher's goals were attainable for a handicapped individual, but she encouraged him to make his dreams a reality.

In contrast to Mrs. Sinclair, many teachers, rather than encouraging their deaf students to exert themselves in their studies, disabled them mentally by giving them easy work and passing them onto the next level of study. For that reason, most of the deaf students failed their finals and had to stay in high school for at least five years. The School Board even had made provision for deaf students to continue their high school education until they were 21 years of age, if necessary.

Christopher didn't want to be like that. He worked hard so that he could graduate in four years, and he intended to do it with honors.

A few weeks before school was to let out for summer vacation, Margaret and Christopher spent a Saturday at the mall. They were shopping for summer attire for him.

After a full day of shopping, Margaret and Christopher went to the food court to get some refreshments before heading home. She noticed a group of people sitting at a long table. It seemed that they were all waving. They were very animated in their conversation.

Margaret, wondering if any of them were deaf, grabbed Christopher's arm, "Looks like those people signing!"

Christopher became excited, "Where? Where?"

Margaret pointed to the table.

Christopher saw them. He watched for a minute and understood everything that was being said. They were signing!

Margaret and Christopher walked over to the table. As they approached, the whole group stopped signing and looked at them.

Margaret, a little nervous about signing to other people, since up to this point she had only signed to Christopher, got up the nerve to sign, "Hello. This my son. He deaf."

Everyone began waving to them and signing. It was a little overwhelming for both Christopher and Margaret.

One deaf person waved to Christopher and then asked, "Your name what?"

"Me C-H-R-I-S-T-O-P-H-E-R." After spelling his name, he showed them his name sign. He also introduced his mother.

Everyone in the group was happy to meet them. Most of them were deaf; some of them were hearing, but all of them could sign.

A deaf man pulled up two chairs and invited Margaret and Christopher to join them. Others in the group began asking him all sorts of questions about his school, his teachers, his family, where he lived, and how he became deaf.

Christopher wasn't used to so much attention being paid him, but he thoroughly enjoyed himself.

The deaf in the group shared their experiences, such as how their parents wouldn't let them drive for fear their deafness would somehow cause an accident. Christopher was surprised at how similar their life experiences were to his.

One deaf man, Nick, wanted to tell Christopher a Deaf joke. He told a story about a deaf giant who was on an island where tiny people lived. Walking through the village, he mistakenly stepped on the occasional house or wagon. People were running for their lives. The giant then saw a small house and lifted off the roof. Inside was a tiny, yet beautiful, woman. Gently picking her up, he put her on his hand. Looking at her, he admired her beauty. As the giant held the girl in his hand, he signed "You, me married?" Since the sign for married is the palm of one hand facing up while the other hand comes down and clasps the upward-facing hand, when Nick signed this, Christopher and the others began laughing. Afterwards different ones joined in and began telling jokes.

Christopher was having a very good time. He was laughing and being understood. He seemed comfortable—like he finally fit in.

Margaret watched Christopher. He was so happy being able to communicate with others in his own language.

An interpreter approached Margaret and introduced herself. They talked for a while about Christopher and his situation. Explaining that there is a Deaf club that meets weekly on Saturdays in the multipurpose room at the mall, the interpreter invited them to visit.

After a very enjoyable afternoon, Christopher and Margaret headed home.

The following Saturday, Jack, Margaret, and Christopher headed over to the mall to visit the Deaf club.

Entering the conference room, Jack was surprised to see everyone signing. At first he felt somewhat uncomfortable, not knowing with whom he could speak. The longer they stayed, the more frustrated he became. People were approaching him, not speaking, but only using sign language.

Jack couldn't understand how they could live in a hearing world and not know how to speak English. He didn't understand that some of these people were considered very successful, and some of the deaf were able to speak and read lips fairly well; other individuals were interpreters or hearing children of deaf adults. It was the joy of being able to relax and just sign freely and understand everything that kept the Deaf club "silent".

Watching his son having a good time signing and laughing with everyone, Jack began to worry that Christopher would become like those handicapped people. He didn't want that for his son. He wanted Christopher to be successful in the hearing world and that meant being able to speak English so that he could communicate with hearing people.

Margaret walked around meeting different deaf individuals and interpreters. She again ran into Nick who she learned was the president of the Deaf club. Signing to Nick, she informed him, "Me, Christopher, we much enjoy come, associate Deaf club. I know Christopher happy socialize."

"Thank you. You, Christopher welcome always."

Margaret continued, "I ask you, Christopher's school require him hearing aids, but he not comfortable. I think hearing aids give him migraines. What I do?"

"Situation very difficult. Myself never want hearing aids because help me nothing. If person hard of hearing, hearing aid can help. If person born deaf, hearing aid help can't. Deaf kids stuck: must respect school rules. Parents must inform school kid's feelings."

She then asked Nick, "You think Christopher can match hearing world?"

"No. Think child nationality Chinese, but born Russia. He not fully belong Russia because holds Chinese culture. It same deaf person born hearing world. Christopher holds Deaf culture. He fully conform hearing world, never. I believe Christopher will comfortable match Deaf world. I hope my story not scare you." Nick swallowed hard.

"No, no. You not scare me." While it didn't scare Margaret, she knew that this kind of information would surely scare Jack.

After returning home, Jack walked into the kitchen where Margaret was preparing dinner. He seemed bothered by something.

"Margaret, I've been doing a lot of thinking. I know Christopher enjoyed associating with those people today at the club, but I think it would be in his best interest if he not get too involved with them."

Margaret, a little surprised that Jack was so bothered by Christopher's new friends, asked, "Excuse me. Are you saying that Christopher must stay away from other deaf people?"

"Well, I think it would be in his best interest."

Margaret was upset with Jack's unsympathetic attitude. "Don't you see how much Christopher enjoyed being with other deaf people? He had a wonderful time with them. Are you going to refuse Christopher happiness in his life? Or do you think "those people" will pull him away from our grasp?"

"I want Christopher to be happy, but not at the expense of his family or his being successful in life."

Wanting Jack to understand how hard it is for Christopher to try to fit into the hearing world, Margaret asked, "How did you feel when we went to the Deaf club today? There was no one speaking with his or her voice. Everyone was signing. How did you feel not being able to communicate or to understand? Weren't you feeling awkward, frustrated, and out of place? That's how Christopher feels every day of his life. He may never be able to compete in the hearing world. He may never be as successful as you would like him to be."

Jack felt that Christopher just needed to put forth more effort in learning English and improving his verbal communication skills, and then he would be able to accomplish anything. Feeling that Christopher's frequent association with deaf people would be self-defeating Jack expressed his decision. "Well, we're not going back to that Deaf club."

Margaret didn't want to argue with Jack, but she wanted him to understand that he could no longer control Christopher's life. "Christopher IS going back." Margaret then walked out of the kitchen.

Jack stood there and let out a deep sigh . . .

Chapter 30
<u>Challenging Father</u>

During the summer, Christopher visited the Deaf club every week. He enjoyed being with people who could relate to his experiences, feelings, and concerns.

Through the Deaf club, he met Sean, an 18-year-old deaf student who had just moved into the area and would be attending Madison High School. The two of them became good friends. Sean was the first male friend Christopher had made since Mike had begun attending the high school in a neighboring school district two years earlier. Sean and Christopher sometimes went swimming at the municipal pool. They would build model sports cars in Sean's basement or race their remote-controlled cars in the school's parking lot. They spent a lot of time together.

The summer of '84 was a carefree time, but it didn't last long. School was back in session by the 29th of August.

Christopher's schedule was full. He was working on getting another six credits this year. Supporting his goal of working in a legal or judicial profession, he chose Government and Politics, Civilizations and Cultures, Business Correspondence, and a psychology class, along with the mandatory English, math, and science classes. It was a struggle, but Christopher did well the first few weeks.

In mid-October, Margaret's father suffered a heart attack. While he was at home recuperating, Margaret went to stay with her parents for a week.

Jack and Christopher were on their own while Margaret was away. Jack took care of himself and felt Christopher was old enough to do the same. Every morning, they would go their separate ways until the evening, when they would both come home. Jack would read the newspaper and watch television while Christopher would do his homework, and then both would retire to their bedrooms until the next morning, when they would repeat the same routine. Hardly a word was spoken between the two of them.

One morning Christopher had overslept and was running late for school. Jack was already sitting in the kitchen reading his business news and finishing his morning coffee when Christopher came into the kitchen. He poured himself a glass of orange juice and then put two slices of bread in the toaster.

While Christopher was waiting for his toast, he felt a vibration on the floor. He turned in the direction of the vibration and saw Jack waving at him. His dad looked upset. He signed, "What's up?"

Jack trying to enunciate his words said, "I've been calling your name, trying to get your attention. Where are your hearing aids? You are supposed to wear them every day. What's the point of having hearing aids if you're not going to use them?"

"I not need. I told you, they not help."

Jack put his newspaper down on the table. He removed his glasses and looked at Christopher. "I want you to put your hearing aids on right now!"

Christopher couldn't understand his dad's insistence. His hearing aids didn't improve his hearing so he could see no purpose in using them. "I MUST wear hearing aids?"

"Those are the new house rules. Now put your hearing aids on!"

Christopher was aggravated. As he left the room, he let out a yell that sounded like a growl. When he returned to the kitchen, he had his hearing aids in his hand.

Jack was watching him to make sure that he put them on before he left for school.

Christopher walked over to the sink. Turning the garbage disposal on, he looked back at his dad.

Jack shook his head with a look on his face that said, "Don't do it."

Christopher looked Jack in the eye and said, "No hearing aids!"

Jack pointed at him. "No!"

Christopher, smiling, replied, "Yes," as he dropped the hearing aids down the garbage disposal.

Jack could hear the crunching of the hearing aids.

Christopher shut off the disposal, smiled at his dad, grabbed his lunch bag, and left for school.

Jack couldn't believe what Christopher had done. He sat motionless.

When Christopher got to school, he was in no mood to talk to anyone, not even to his best friend, Sean. Putting his coat and lunch in his locker, he grabbed his books and headed toward homeroom.

Sean ran up from behind him and purposely bumped into him. "What wrong? You grumpy why?"

"My father!" Christopher kept walking.

"What happen?"

Christopher didn't want to discuss his problems in the hallway where everyone could see. "Homeroom, I tell you." They walked down the hall to their homeroom. Sitting down, he explained his confrontation with his father. "Garbage disposal eat hearing aids. You never find again!"

Sean was shocked at Christopher's gumption. "You kidding me? Wow! I can't believe! That cool!" Sean started laughing.

Christopher began laughing too. "My dad not happy."

"Yeah, right." Sean said as he rolled his eyes.

After school, Christopher went into his bedroom to do his studies. When he opened his bedroom door, he saw his closed caption decoder on his bed. It was dented and the knobs were broken off. Next to the decoder box was a baseball bat. He knew his father was trying to get even with him for destroying his hearing aids. Christopher, even more upset than he had been before, picked up the baseball bat, got on his bicycle, and rode to Jack's office.

Walking into Jack's office, Christopher closed the door behind him. He was grasping the baseball bat tightly in his left hand.

Jack was sitting at his desk. When he saw Christopher, he took off his glasses, and rested his arms on the desk.

Christopher stepped up to Jack's desk and placed the baseball bat down on the desk in front of his father. Putting both hands on the desk, he leaned forward so that he was face-to-face with his father. Very slowly and distinctly, he said, "Thank you."

Furious, Jack slapped Christopher across the face.

Christopher glared at his father as he took a few steps backwards. Turning around, he opened the door, and stalked out of the office.

Jack took a deep breath, leaned back in his chair, and reflected on what had taken place. The fact that seemed to elude Jack was that Christopher had, up until today, tried very hard to please his father.

As Christopher rode home, he too reflected on what had happened and his relationship with his father. Knowing that his dad wanted him to be successful, he had endeavored to make wise choices in life; however, no young man wants his father to control him. He wanted his father to realize how hard he had tried to conform to the hearing world, but no matter how hard he tried, his deafness would always separate him.

The day after Christopher had destroyed his hearing aids, he was standing in the hallway at school talking with his deaf friends. Approaching him, the principal asked him to come to her office. He followed her to the office, the whole time wondering what she wanted to discuss.

When he entered the office, one of the school's interpreters was there. The principal walked over to her desk and sat down. She told Christopher to sit. The interpreter sat in a chair near him.

The principal began, "Your father called me today. He is very concerned with your education. He wants you to be able to manage in the hearing world. He worries that, if you associate solely with deaf people, you will lose, or at the very least, not continue developing your lipreading and oral skills."

Christopher was shocked that his father had tried to get the school involved with their personal dispute. He sat silently.

The principal continued, "We were discussing that it may be to your benefit for you to stay in school for an extra year. That way you could focus on your English language skills."

Christopher didn't appreciate the principal's interference in his personal life. "You know nothing my life. My life none of your business." With that Christopher walked out of the principal's office and left the school.

After sitting in the park for a while thinking, Christopher decided to go to his father's office to have a talk with him. Walking into the office, he sat in front of his dad's desk. Christopher signed and used his voice. "You worry me?"

Jack very calmly answered, "I do."

"I want you, me good communication, but . . ."

Jack interrupted, "Then put your hearing aids on. Wear them all the time so you can hear me."

"You not understand. I deaf. I hear can't. You give me hearing?"

Jack, sitting back in his chair, looked at Christopher, but didn't answer.

Christopher stood up, leaned forward on Jack's desk, and answered his own question. "No! Impossible!"

Jack still sat silently.

"I try best match Deaf world, match hearing world."

Jack began to get agitated. "How can you say that you are trying your best when you won't wear your hearing aids?

If you want to be stubborn and not work with me, that's your decision."

Christopher smirked, "I stubborn, not work with you? Crazy! I deaf! Hearing aids not work! Impossible me hear same you!" Turning around, he left his father's office.

Chapter 31
Baseball Championship

Senior year was exciting, yet challenging.

Since the curriculum had become more difficult, Christopher studied long hours after school. Once a week he had a student teacher tutor him in English. He worked hard, and it was paying off. He had been on the honor roll every semester for the past three years, and this year was no exception.

One Saturday in early March, while Christopher visited the Deaf club, he found out that the high school baseball league was forming a new team, the Wildcats, made up solely of deaf students.

The deaf students had made it known to the baseball league that they wanted their own team, but there were never enough students in any one school to fill the roster. At the insistence of the Deaf community, the league made an exception to form an inter-school team.

What an opportunity for Christopher to be involved in sports, but without the communication problems he had experienced in junior high football!

Christopher tried out for the baseball team. Baseball seemed to be the sport he was meant to play. He filled the team's shortstop position. Running with lightning speed, he tagged numerous runners out as they were making their way to third base. His keen concentration helped him catch almost every ball that came his way. That same focus helped him when he went up to bat. Becoming the team's leading hitter, he averaged one home run every game.

The Wildcats had an excellent first season. They had chalked up 27 wins and only 3 losses, which had won them the championship for their league. Now, having made it through the playoffs, the Wildcats were going to be playing the Lakeshore Lions for the State Championship.

The afternoon before the team was to leave for the championship game, Margaret came by the school to watch the Wildcats practice. Afterwards she asked Christopher if he wanted to grab a bite to eat.

As Christopher and his mom ate, he noticed that she seemed troubled by something. "You okay? What wrong?"

Margaret sat for a moment as if she were trying to decide whether she should broach the issue, and then she asked, "You try against hearing world?"

"You mean what?"

"You play against hearing world why? You hate them?"

Christopher was shocked. "I not hate hearing people! Wildcats play baseball challenge other teams—not challenge hearing. Other team black, white, hearing, or deaf, not matter; we play baseball. I prefer deaf team. If hearing team, one or two deaf, communication very hard. Why Dad think I hate hearing people?"

Margaret's eyes began to tear, "You never try work with father!"

"Not true. My whole life, I try work hard give Dad happy. You want me do what?"

Margaret stood up to leave. "Don't play state championship game."

Christopher sat at the table as his mother walked away. He gazed after her, shocked that his parents could think the baseball championship was somehow a contest between two worlds—the hearing and the Deaf. He couldn't leave the final game; he was only playing for the love of the sport! Leaving the restaurant, he went to the home of one of his teammates, Phil, where Christopher had planned on spending the night. In the morning Phil's dad would drop them off at the school where they were to meet the bus.

The championship game was going to be in Lansing, which was about a two-hour drive from Christopher's home. The bus, however, would arrive at the stadium early on the day before the game, allowing the team time to practice on the unfamiliar field. Everyone on the team was ready.

During the championship game, the Wildcats and the Lions both played well. Neither pitcher allowed more than three hits per inning. At the bottom of the ninth inning, the score was Lions 3 - Wildcats 2. There was one out and a man on second.

All of the fans in the Wildcats section of the stadium began cheering and waving their arms as Christopher walked up to the plate. For the first time, he felt nervous. The pitcher threw his first pitch . . . "STRIKE ONE!"

Christopher stepped away from the plate. He had always felt so confident of himself, but for some reason this time was different. He stepped back up to the plate. The pitcher threw a fastball, but it was out of the box . . . "BALL ONE!"

Christopher waited for the next pitch. Again, it was out of the box . . . "BALL TWO!"

The next pitch was a curve. Christopher swung at it . . . "STRIKE TWO!"

Stepping out of the batters' box, Christopher looked over toward first base. He felt as though someone were trying to get his attention. Looking at the fans seated near first base, he saw her, standing at the bottom of the bleachers—it was Nicole! He couldn't believe it, after all these years! Wiping his eyes, he looked again, but she was gone. Was it really Nicole or a figment of his imagination?

Christopher was standing there looking through the crowd, when someone grabbed his arm. It was the umpire. "You ready?"

Christopher wished Nicole were there to support him. After four years, he still missed her. Looking at the umpire, he nodded and then stepped up to the plate.

The pitcher was sure he could get Christopher out. He threw a curve ball.

Christopher focused on the ball. When the bat connected with the ball, he was sure it was a home run.

The ball was hit high. It looked as if it were going to go right over the center-field wall. The man on second ran to third and as he rounded third, the ball fell just short of the wall. Christopher stopped at second base and watched as his teammate safely slid home.

The score was now tied at 3 - 3. Everyone was excited. You could feel the fans' enthusiasm with every wave of their hands and stomp of their feet.

Phil was the next person up to bat. He hit the ball into right field. Before the outfielder could get it, the ball hit the ground and bounced twice. Christopher had begun running as soon as the ball was hit. At lightning speed, he rounded third base and headed home. As he neared home plate, he saw the catcher preparing to catch the ball. Just a few feet from home plate, he saw the catcher catch the ball. Sliding to the plate, he felt the catcher tag him.

Christopher lay on the ground. He was out, and the game would have to go into a tenth inning.

All of a sudden, Christopher felt himself being lifted off the ground. He looked around. His teammates were cheering, "We won!" He wondered how that could be possible.

Later one of his teammates told him that as the catcher made the tag, he dropped the ball. The Wildcats won 4 - 3, and Christopher was named "Most Valuable Player."

After the game, the word was passed that the Wildcats' players and coaches were going out to celebrate. Phil invited Christopher to hang out with him, but wanting to be alone,

Christopher decided to go back to the hotel. He couldn't stop thinking about Nicole and how much he missed her. He also wished his parents had been at the game to see how well he had played.

Christopher changed his clothes and headed to the hotel. As he walked across the baseball field, he saw his mother sitting in the first row of bleachers just behind third base. He walked over to her. "You here why?"

She smiled, "I thought about you, me conversation. I know championship game not Deaf against hearing. You love baseball. I not want miss your game." She looked so proud of him. "Congratulations!"

Christopher smiled and hugged his mom.

Chapter 32
<u>Failed Assistance</u>

Christopher graduated high school with honors. He graduated fourth in a class of 346 students, 338 of whom were hearing. He had taken his S.A.T. and scored very high. Sending applications to a few select colleges, including two colleges specifically for the deaf, he waited for their responses.

Margaret couldn't have been more pleased with Christopher's achievements.

Jack, on the other hand, couldn't just enjoy the moment. He was preoccupied with Christopher's college choice.

Christopher wanted to attend a university that was geared toward helping the deaf.

Jack felt that Christopher would do just as well at the community college. Though not expressing it, he thought that Christopher's choice of a legal or judicial career would be unobtainable for him. Feeling that Christopher's time would be better spent focusing on a more realistic profession, he had steadfastly agreed with the high school guidance counselor's suggestion that Christopher work toward becoming an accountant.

If Christopher could learn the accounting basics, he could be given an entry-level position in the company. In that way, he would be employed in the hearing world, which would give him confidence, yet he would still be under the watchful eye of his father—a situation Jack considered to be win-win.

Since his father was paying for his college tuition, Christopher knew his choices were very limited—either attend the community college or start working in one of Crownline's assembly lines. He chose the community college.

Christopher's schedule included English, government and politics, psychology, sociology, and his father's prerequisites of accounting and business management. An interpreter was provided for each of his classes, but oftentimes one or more of his regular interpreters would not be there, so another interpreter would substitute. The substitute interpreters were not always skilled in American Sign Language, which made it difficult for him to understand what was being taught. At other times when he got to class, there would be no interpreter at all. He would be forced to ask one of his fellow students to take notes for him.

English class was still difficult for Christopher, since American Sign Language was has primary language. There was an interpreter for the class, but the interpreter was only responsible to relay into sign language whatever was being spoken by the teachers or the students. She was unable to assist Christopher in any other way.

After struggling through the first semester and just barely receiving a passing grade, Christopher went to the college's Disabilities Office to see if assistance could be provided.

The Disabilities Office had been established to help students with disabilities attend and participate in their classes. This was the department that had provided Christopher with interpreters, but they weren't sure of what else they could do to assist him. They had a great deal of experience helping blind students and those who were crippled, but Christopher was the first deaf student to ask them for assistance.

Christopher, explaining that, because a deaf person is unable to hear how words are pronounced or used in sentences,

English is more difficult, suggested that the department provide him with an English tutor.

After much discussion with the head of the Disabilities Office, the head of the English Department, and the college dean, Christopher was finally able to get across the differences between American Sign Language and English, and how the two languages are different. In the end, approval was granted for Christopher to be provided an English tutor at the school's expense.

Two weeks into the second semester, the English professor asked Christopher and his interpreter to go with him to the Disabilities Office. There they met a man, Craig, who was to be Christopher's English tutor. Christopher was relieved and excited to receive the additional help that he so desperately needed.

The head of the Disabilities Office explained that Craig would be available to help him up to 25 hours per week, and if there were any problems, to feel free to contact the office for assistance.

For the next few days, Christopher met with Craig after his English class. Communication was very difficult since Craig knew no sign language. Rather than teach him the English language structure, Craig simply provided Christopher with the answers to his homework or wrote essays for him to copy. His homework grades were improving; however, he was still failing the tests since he really hadn't learned anything about the English language.

Christopher wanted to understand. He wanted Craig to use the dictionary, pictures, or historical writings—whatever it would take to help him better understand English as a language.

Craig felt that Christopher took up too much of his time, time that could be better spent tutoring students that were not "learning disabled," as he felt Christopher was.

It wasn't long before Craig began missing his tutoring sessions with Christopher. Sometimes he would put in an appearance and try to give Christopher a basic grammar lesson, but most of the time he would not even bother to show up.

Spending many hours every night in the college library, studying and trying to better understand the English language, Christopher managed to improve his grades a little. He went from a C average to a C+ in English.

Christopher's English professor, however, was not satisfied with the improvement. He felt that Christopher was capable of a lot more, and with all the assistance that had been provided him, he should have gotten higher grades in English.

At the end of third quarter, the professor met with the head of the Disabilities Office.

The next day, Christopher and his interpreter were directed to go to the Disabilities Office after English class. The college Dean was looking at Christopher's high school transcript and S.A.T. scores when they entered the office. "You know, when a student comes to college, we expect his grades to drop a little in the first quarter because the curriculum is designed to be more specific and intensive than in high school. Usually after the first quarter, students' grades return to their previous average. In all of your courses, your grades dropped drastically, and you've managed to bring them up to a B average except English. Why is that?"

Through the interpreter, Christopher explained, "I've been studying very hard, but the structure of the English language is very different from ASL. It's a real challenge for me."

"I guess we don't understand why you aren't taking advantage of the help the college has provided for you."

"You mean Craig?"

"Yes."

"I didn't want Craig giving me the answers or writing my essays for me. I told him that I wanted to learn to do my homework myself. I guess he misunderstood me."

"Why is that?"

"He stopped meeting me after English class."

"You mean he hasn't been tutoring you?"

"No . . . not for the past two and a half months."

The Dean looked at the head of the Disabilities Office. They then asked Christopher how long Craig had tutored him.

"The first week, we met three days. The next two weeks, we met twice a week. After that, he met with me maybe three more times."

"How long were your tutoring sessions?"

"Between one and two hours."

The head of the Disabilities Office began looking through his files. He pulled a manila folder out and looked at some paperwork that had been filed away. He then handed it to the Dean, who shook his head and then looked at Christopher. They both apologized to Christopher for the problems he had experienced, and they recommended that he take the English course again in the fall. At that time they would provide a different tutor and a sign-off sheet for each tutoring session.

A few days later, Christopher found out that Craig had billed the college and had been paid for tutoring him 25 hours per week for 15 weeks. He was shocked that someone would cheat the college, but even more than that, he was appalled that someone who was supposed to educate him instead had taken advantage of him. Thankfully, the administrators had believed him, and it was Craig whom they dismissed from school and not Christopher.

Chapter 33
<u>Lost Buddy</u>

After attending the community college for a year and having his grade point average fall below 3.0, Christopher felt it would be to his advantage to attend a university that taught the deaf in their own language. He sent his application to the two major universities for the deaf on the East Coast, and received a letter of acceptance from both. After considering his educational goals, he decided to attend the university located in the Washington, DC area.

Jack was certain that classes taught in sign language would be inferior to those at a "hearing" university. After numerous family discussions, a visit to the University, and several talks with the university's Dean and some of the professors, he reluctantly allowed Christopher to attend the university of his choice.

During Christopher's freshman, sophomore, and junior years, he lived in the college dorm. College was similar to high school, but more intense. The students studied harder and partied harder. He tried not to let himself get distracted by the wild life of the other students. Concentrating on his studies, he once again excelled.

During his senior year, Christopher got a part-time job working as an errand boy for a large DC law firm, Willard, Brendon, Miller, and Whitfield.

A few weeks after he was hired, Christopher had the opportunity to meet one of the company's senior partners, Mr. Robert Brendon. Though they only conversed for a few brief moments, he managed to convey to Mr. Brendon his desire to work in the legal profession. Mr. Brendon, impressed with Christopher's enthusiasm, encouraged him to use his free time doing research in their firm's library.

Using the money he earned from working at the law firm along with money his parents provided for him, Christopher was able to rent a small apartment near the university. It was a nice change for him, since he could now study with very little distraction. His classes, homework, job, and additional research in the law office's library allowed him little time for extracurricular activities.

One evening while Christopher was finishing up his studies, the light on his doorbell began flashing. Not expecting anyone, he was even more surprised when he opened the door to his elementary-school buddy, Donny. "Donny, that you?"

"Yep."

Christopher hugged Donny. "Good see you. I surprised you here. You find me how?"

"Your mom told me."

Christopher looked at Donny. He looked disheveled and sad. "What's up?"

"I want see you."

Inviting Donny into his home, Christopher asked, "You want eat, drink?"

"You any beer?"

"Yes." Christopher went into the kitchen. Coming back into the living room with a beer for each of them, he felt embarrassed at his clutter. "Sorry messy."

"Not bother me. I used messy."

Christopher organized his schoolwork and put it in his bedroom along with the clothes that he had left lying around. He got a garbage bag from the kitchen and picked up an empty pizza box, a few pop cans, and a newspaper that was spread over parts of the couch and coffee table. Afterwards, he sat down on the couch with Donny. "School since, what you do?"

Donny nonchalantly replied, "New nothing. My life same same."

Christopher began to worry about Donny; he seemed disconsolate and indifferent. He asked Donny where he was staying. When Donny said he would find someplace, Christopher invited him to stay at his apartment for as long as he needed.

Going to his bedroom, Christopher straightened up his desk and put his clothes in the laundry basket. He then brought out a sheet and blanket for Donny; however, when he returned to the living room, Donny was already asleep on the couch. Happy that Donny felt safe in his home, he covered his buddy with the blanket and went back to his bedroom to finish studying his English.

The next day Christopher left a note telling Donny to make himself at home and that he would be back at about five o'clock.

In the evening, Christopher picked up Chinese food and brought it home for the two of them. While they were eating, they reminisced about old times.

When Christopher wondered how Donny's family was doing, Donny started laughing. "You want know my family . . . they gone forever!" Suddenly his smile disappeared. He solemnly replied, "They don't want me!"

Christopher put his hand on Donny's shoulder in order to comfort him. "You, me best friends, no matter your family."

Donny didn't want to discuss his family any further, so he changed the subject. "You still want lawyer yourself?"

"Yes, but big struggle for me." Christopher could see how unhappy Donny was. Trying to be positive and kind, he reminded Donny that he was welcome to stay with him as long as he needed.

Donny did stay for a few weeks.

As Christopher watched Donny, he became more and more concerned. He would get up early, go to class, and then go to work. Every evening when he came home, Donny would be asleep on the couch. There would be empty beer cans on the coffee table.

Later Christopher noticed that a previously unopened bottle of vodka he had kept in the cupboard was almost empty. He was becoming more and more worried about Donny's drinking. When money began disappearing and more empty beer cans were being left around the apartment, Christopher decided something needed to be done. That Saturday he would make a nice dinner for Donny and himself, and when both were comfortable, he would bring up the subject of Donny's drinking.

Donny slept most of the day Saturday. When he woke up, Christopher encouraged him to go shower and shave so that he would feel refreshed. He reluctantly did as Christopher asked. When he was finished in the bathroom, he came into the living room to find that Christopher had cleaned up the room and had food waiting on the coffee table for both of them.

The men, focused on their food, ate their entire meal without a word. When they had finished, Christopher remarked, "I see you much drinking."

Donny smiled, "Drinking, you talk about what?"

Christopher very straightforwardly said, "You, me buddy long time. You need honest examine yourself. You addicted alcohol."

Donny didn't want to hear that—especially from his best friend. "You worry what? You worry me, huh? Remember I not little boy. Okay?"

Donny didn't want to continue this discussion, but Christopher didn't feel he could ignore what had been happening. He asked Donny, "If I addicted alcohol, you help me, right?"

Donny wished Christopher would back off. "Finish! I not want discuss!"

Christopher and Donny didn't talk much more after that. Donny watched television. Christopher cleaned up the kitchen and then sat down to watch television with Donny.

Before going to bed, Christopher told Donny, "Remember: you, me best friends many years. I care you. If you need talk . . . you can approach me anytime."

Donny didn't say anything.

Christopher wanted to remind Donny that they had spent many good times together and that Donny's life could be good again. Before going to sleep, he decided to look through his photo albums and find pictures of Donny and him when they were younger. After he gathered up the pictures, he went back into the living room. Donny had already fallen asleep. Looking through the pictures again, Christopher smiled and then left them on the coffee table for Donny to see when he awakened.

For the next week, Christopher and Donny didn't converse much.

Christopher's schedule kept him rather busy. His friend's arrival had prompted him to slack off on some of his extra research at the law firm. Now he was trying to get back into his regular routine of getting up early to study, going to class, going to work, and then staying after work an extra hour to study in the firm's library. He didn't know exactly what Donny did during the day, but he knew it included drinking and sleeping. Donny usually was asleep on the couch when Christopher arrived home in the evenings.

One night when Christopher returned home from the law firm, Donny wasn't there. He had hoped that Donny was doing something positive for himself; however, he was greatly disappointed when Donny stumbled into the apartment just after midnight.

"You drunk why?"

Donny smiled and sloppily signed, "Wrong what? You worry worry me?"

Christopher picked up his homework and took it to his bedroom. He wondered if there was any way to help Donny.

After about 15 minutes, Christopher felt a thump. Going into the living room, he found Donny passed out on the floor. He picked him up and dragged him into the bathroom. After lifting Donny into the tub, he turned the cold water on from the shower.

Donny barely woke up. He was moving very slowly, but he was trying to get out of the tub.

Christopher pushed Donny back under the cold water. He kept Donny there for about ten minutes until his friend started coming around.

"Okay! I freezing. Please me out!"

Christopher helped Donny out of the tub, dried him off, and then helped him back to the living room couch, where he immediately fell asleep.

The next morning when Christopher was getting ready to leave for class, he noticed the living room was cleaned up. Donny wasn't there. He found a note on top of the television, "Christopher, I sorry make problems. I know you not want me same my family! Donny." Disheartened, he wondered why his efforts hadn't been enough. He had wanted so much to help Donny to become more productive and satisfied with his life, but instead Donny had misunderstood his intentions.

Christopher never saw Donny again.

Two months later, Margaret called Christopher and told him that Donny had died. His car had run into the base of a freeway overpass. Witnesses said he was probably going 60 mph when he hit the wall.

After performing an autopsy and checking Donny's blood alcohol level, the coroner listed Donny's cause of death as a suicide. Though twice the legal limit, the blood alcohol level wasn't sufficient to cause Donny to pass out, yet there were no skid marks at the scene of the crash.

Donny was just 22 years old.

Christopher was overcome with grief.

The following week Christopher went back to Michigan to attend Donny's funeral. Thinking about Donny's life,

Christopher felt it must have been unbearable to have a family that didn't want him because of his deafness.

At the funeral, there was no interpreter for Donny's deaf classmates who attended. Margaret tried the best that she could to interpret for them.

Christopher watched Donny's father and mother for a long time. They were crying and acting like they missed Donny, though they hadn't had any contact with him since he had graduated high school. Anger welled within him at their hypocritical display of affection for their lost son.

After the funeral, Christopher stayed and talked with some of his old schoolmates, and then he went back to his parents' home.

Jack was sitting in the living room in his favorite chair when Christopher came in. He stood up and waved at Christopher as if he had something he wanted to say.

Christopher wasn't in the mood to talk, especially to his father, but he tried to be polite.

"I'm sorry about Donny."

"You happy I not Donny."

Jack didn't know what Christopher meant by that comment. "What do you mean? Can you please explain to me?"

Christopher sat down on the couch. "Donny, he gone forever. You understand?"

Jack understood Christopher's sorrow. "I thought he would do well in school and work hard just as you have done."

Christopher, feeling great anguish, wondered aloud, "Donny kill himself—WHY?" Then he passionately answered his own question, "His parents not want him because deaf. His parents don't care him. They not try communicate him. They learn sign language—never! His parents throw him away same garbage!" With that, he stood up and walked out of the living room. He went to his old bedroom to get some rest.

Jack watched Christopher walk dejectedly away. He looked at Margaret in the dining room and then he sat back down in his chair. Beginning to realize how sad Donny's life must have been, for a brief moment he was able to empathize with Christopher.

Chapter 34
<u>Legal Training</u>

After graduating from the university, Christopher continued working for Willard, Brendon, Miller, and Whitfield, Attorneys at Law. He was thrilled when they promoted him from errand boy to research assistant.

Christopher really enjoyed this job, not only because it paid more, but it also allowed him to learn about past cases. He could see which laws applied to certain cases and the line of reasoning used by the attorneys in defending these cases. Studying the newly enacted Americans with Disabilities Act in detail, he looked forward to becoming an attorney and using this law in defense of those who could not defend themselves.

Christopher researched numerous cases, but the ones that he was most eager to research were the cases involving deaf individuals.

One deaf couple had sued their landlord because he had not installed smoke detectors with lights in the apartment where they had lived. They had asked him numerous times to install the detectors, but he had just ignored their requests.

After the couple had lived in this building for about eight months, there was a fire during the middle of the night. The deaf couple was unaware that there was any danger until the firemen broke the door down to get into their apartment. The deaf couple was rescued, but by the time the firemen found their baby, she had died of smoke inhalation.

Because of the landlord's negligence in following the A.D.A. laws, the couple was awarded two million dollars.

In two separate cases, a deaf man and his employer sued an interpreting agency.

The deaf man had been working in a machine shop for four years. He was an exceptional employee, and his employer was pleased with his work. In order to be offered a promotion that he otherwise qualified for, he had to be trained on two other pieces of equipment.

The employer made arrangements for his deaf employee to go to a two-week training course. He also made arrangements with an interpreting agency to send out interpreters for the duration of the course.

The interpreting agency was informed a month in advance so they could have enough interpreters ready.

When it came time for the course, there were two days when the deaf man had no interpreter. Other days, the interpreters that came were not qualified to interpret such a technical course.

Because of the lack of quality interpreting, the deaf man did not fully understand everything that was involved in running the equipment he was supposed to use, though he thought he did. His first day back to work, he was assigned to use one of the new pieces of equipment. He programmed it incorrectly and caused $35,000 worth of damage to the machine.

The deaf man sued the interpreting agency for emotional distress due to this incident.

The employer sued for damages caused to the machinery, wages paid to this deaf man while attending class, all fees for class, and for losses due to the disruption of production.

Both the deaf man and his employer received undisclosed monetary awards.

Another deaf couple sued their landlord for molesting and raping their fourteen-year old hearing daughter.

The school counselor became suspicious of abuse when the normally studious, happy, outgoing teen became disinterested in her classes. She became introverted and began gaining a lot of weight within a short amount of time. The counselor called Social Services to look into the matter.

After a couple of visits to the home, Social Services wanted the young girl to see a child psychologist.

The psychologist quickly noticed the signs of sexual abuse. A number of sessions with the psychologist revealed that when this teen's parents were away or asleep, the landlord would let himself into the apartment using his master key. He started by fondling her breasts and eventually moved on to sexual intercourse. He told her that he would kill her parents in their sleep if she ever told anyone about his visits.

The landlord was found guilty of rape as well as the lesser charge of trespassing. He was sentenced to 35 years in prison, and the teen was given a large monetary award.

In another case, a deaf woman sued her employer for discrimination. She had worked for a corporation for twelve years. Her supervisor had always been pleased with her work. Her attendance record showed that she was never late to work and that she had rarely used her sick days.

This woman had been a productive employee, yet she had been given very minute raises compared to her hearing coworkers who did less work than she did. Her employer had told her that instead of receiving substantial pay raises, money was being put into a health insurance plan and pension plan for her.

After talking with a few coworkers, the deaf woman found that they all had the same benefits as she did plus a yearly pay raise of at least 75 cents per hour. She sued the corporation for discrimination.

The jury calculated how much of a raise the deaf woman should have received each year based on the raises of other employees who had a similar record of service, and she was awarded back pay for the past 12 years in the amount of $25,600.

Another case involved a 78-year old deaf man who had been misdiagnosed by his doctor.

According to the A.D.A. law, the doctor is responsible to pay for an interpreter to assist the doctor in communicating with his deaf patients. This particular doctor didn't see a need in having an interpreter present since he could write notes to his deaf patients.

The problem was that the deaf gentleman couldn't read or write English very well. He tried to tell the doctor that he had been vomiting since the evening before and was having abdominal cramps. He wrote, "Sick me blah long." The doctor told him that he had the stomach flu, and he should go home and drink plenty of liquid.

Two days later, the gentleman was rushed to the emergency room. His grandson had found him at home, so weak that he could hardly move and dehydrated as well.

The emergency room doctors had then run numerous tests on the gentlemen and found that he had a bowel obstruction. Emergency surgery had to be performed. He remained in the hospital for two weeks, recuperating. The doctors told him that if his grandson hadn't found him when he did, he probably would have died within 24 hours because of the toxins backing up into his system.

The deaf man sued his primary care physician for negligence because he didn't provide him with an interpreter. The court awarded him enough money to cover all of his medical bills and legal fees as well as enough money to care for himself for the remaining years of his life.

These cases, along with others that Christopher researched, helped him to better understand the principles behind the law. Thinking about the future, he knew he wanted to be an attorney whose focus was on civil suits involving those with disabilities.

The senior partners of Willard, Brendon, Miller, and Whitfield kept their eyes on Christopher; he was an asset to their law firm. In their opinion, he had the ambition and the drive to make himself into a prominent civil attorney.

Chapter 35
<u>Preserve Crownline</u>

"After about eight years of living in the Washington, DC area, I've had enough," Christopher mused. He had worked for Willard, Brendon, Miller, and Whitfield for almost five years and had received additional training. When he left the firm in October of 1995, he was working as a paralegal.

The senior partners of the firm were sad to see Christopher leave; he showed such promise. But Margaret wanted to see more of her son, and Christopher wanted to go back home. He figured, staying with his parents, it shouldn't take more than a month to find a job.

Christopher found work as a paralegal in Grand Rapids, about three hours from his parents' home, at the Law Offices of Sanders and Dempsey. He bought a small, one-bedroom condominium in the city near his place of employment. Using his time in the evenings wisely, he studied for his L.S.A.T., the entrance exam required to attend law school.

Two months after moving to Grand Rapids, Christopher received a letter from his mother. She informed him that

Crownline Glass was losing business and it seemed that the company was going to go bankrupt. "Your dad and I are trying to consider our options," she wrote, and she was hoping to see Christopher again soon.

The afternoon he received the letter, Christopher took off work early and headed over to his parents' home.

In their living room that evening, Christopher made a fire in the fireplace, and he and his mother talked over coffee and cake.

Margaret was happy to see Christopher. "Thanks come visit. Good see you," she signed hesitantly. She had lost some of her signing skills since Christopher hadn't been constantly nearby for years.

"Mom, I not come chitchat. I worry. You, Dad okay? Business, what happen?"

"Dad a lot stress, but we okay." Margaret explained that many customers had been leaving Crownline. It seemed there was another company that was underbidding them. Some customers had even canceled their contracts in order to work with this other company. The lost business had caused financial problems for Crownline. For the first time in 30 years, Crownline Glass was on the verge of closing its doors. It looked like they were going to have to declare bankruptcy.

Christopher was shocked. He couldn't believe what his mother was telling him.

After a few minutes, Christopher asked, "Where Dad?"

"He out town. He wrote you letter. He wanted me mail you, but I guess you read now." Margaret walked over to the kitchen table and picked up a large yellow envelope. Walking back into the living room, she handed it to Christopher.

"You know letter about?"

"Just read it."

Christopher opened the letter and read, "Dear Christopher, Your mother and I must get away for a while. We are going to New England to find peace. Enclosed are papers appointing you as Crownline's Vice President. You are now in control of Crownline Glass during my absence. Do what you want with the company. If you would rather be an attorney, then just file Chapter 11 and dissolve the business. Dad."

Christopher looked at his mom. "Dad wants leave because I deaf."

"Christopher, this nothing connect your deafness. We not leaving you. We love you."

Christopher thought maybe he was partially to blame for Crownline's problems. "Maybe I should try more work with Dad. He always want me partner him control company; instead I try my goals . . . ignore Dad's."

Margaret began crying. "Not your fault. Please blame yourself not." Running to her bedroom, she closed the door.

Christopher stood up, not knowing what to do. Should he stay in the living room or try to talk with his mom?

Sitting down in the chair near the fireplace, he reread his dad's letter. As he sat thinking about what his dad had said, he looked at the fire . . . the way the flames jumped up and down . . . how carefree they seemed to be . . . and he fell asleep.

The letter fell out of his hand and to the floor in front of the fireplace.

During the night, Margaret went into the kitchen to get a glass of water. Noticing Christopher asleep in the chair, she took the afghan off the couch and covered him with it.

The next morning, Christopher asked his mother to call his office to let them know he would not be in for the next two weeks because of a family emergency. He left early to visit Crownline Glass.

As Christopher entered Crownline's building, memories flashed back into his mind of when he was younger. There had always been many people busily moving around the office, but today there was only the receptionist. Walking past her, he went directly to his father's office.

Jack's office had been left untouched except for the pile of mail on his desk. Christopher began sorting through the mail. There were numerous bills from suppliers. Looking through his dad's desk and file cabinets, he tried to see if they would give him any clues as to what had gone wrong.

The receptionist came in a few times to see if there was anything Christopher needed. After a few hours, she came back to let him know that she was going to take her lunch break. He asked her if she could call the accountant after lunch and set up an appointment for them to go over the company's financial records. She said she would take care of it.

After the receptionist left, Christopher decided to go back to the factory. He wanted to see the level of production. Entering the factory, the grim reality of the loss of business hit him. The factory usually had over 100 employees working the equipment. Today there were only a dozen people.

The production manager, Frank, seeing Christopher, walked over to him. "It's not as you remembered, is it?"

Christopher shook his head.

Frank looked at Christopher, "It's not good."

Christopher stood silently looking around the factory and then he went back up to Jack's office.

Spending the entire weekend at Crownline, Christopher went through all of Crownline's files. He read through all the construction contracts that had been approved, rejected, and fulfilled. He examined payroll records and checked all the purchase orders for supplies. All of the factory's records were also reviewed. He was unable to find anything that gave any indication as to what had caused Crownline's downfall.

Monday, Christopher met with the accountant, who went over all the financial records with him. The accountant indicated that the production levels had steadily been decreasing since Frank took over as production manager last year.

Christopher was stumped since all the records he had examined over the weekend had indicated nothing out of the ordinary.

Thinking back on his childhood, Christopher remembered Frank working for his father. He knew Frank to be loyal to the company and to his father; however, the comment made by the accountant bothered him. He decided to meet with Frank that afternoon.

As usually happened when Christopher wanted to have a serious or technical discussion to learn something from those who didn't know sign language, he and Frank tediously wrote notes to each other for all but the simplest of communications. They discussed Frank's managerial qualifications and career goals.

Before he went home, exhausted by the day's long meetings, Christopher contacted a local interpreting agency to arrange for an interpreter to be at the office every day for the next two weeks to aid him in communicating with Frank and the other employees.

During the week that followed, Christopher and Frank reviewed all of the factory records together. As they went through the files, since Frank was very knowledgeable about everything that was manufactured by Crownline, he explained everything to Christopher. The more they talked, the more evident it became to Christopher that Frank was as dedicated to this company as Jack was.

Included in the factory records were glass designs, specifications, and formulas for special protective coatings for the glass. Some of the designs and techniques were patented. Other designs had patents pending. As Christopher and Frank went over the designs, Frank became concerned. He began frantically looking through file cabinets.

"What's wrong?"

Frank sat down and looked at Christopher. "There are some files missing. A few times, folders have been filed in the wrong cabinet, but I've looked through everything and can't find these."

"What kind of files?"

Frank explained, "As you know, our design team develops new glass designs and techniques for producing glass. Those designs and specifications are kept in these files. I just noticed that some of the designs that have been developed over the past few months are in the files, but the specifications for glass production are missing. I know the information has been put in the files, but now it's gone. We have not applied for a patent because we first wanted to see if we could readily get the supplies needed to produce this glass, and we wanted to calculate how cost-effective it would be to manufacture."

Frank and Christopher reviewed the remainder of the factory records, and then Christopher returned to what was now, at least temporarily, his office.

The next day when Christopher arrived at work, the receptionist told him that Frank wanted to see him in the factory office.

Frank apologized for not having all of the specifications available when he had met with Christopher the day before. "I looked through all the file cabinets again this morning and found the folders. They had been filed in the "Patented Design" file cabinet. I thought I checked that cabinet yesterday, but I must have missed it. I'm sorry." Frank proceeded to explain to Christopher the new techniques for producing glass and to show him the corresponding specifications.

Christopher seemed to have other things on his mind. While Frank was talking, Christopher had walked over to the office window and begun watching the employees. All of them were working at a steady pace; however, one man caught Christopher's attention. He was working much faster than the other employees.

"Excuse me Frank." Christopher and his interpreter went out into the factory to meet the young man who was keeping himself so busy. "Hello. What's your name?"

The employee looked nervous. "Oh, uh, my name is Jay Laredo." He turned around and went back to work.

Christopher was surprised at how reluctant to talk Jay was. He greeted a few of the other employees and then returned to Frank's office. "Frank, when you get a break, come to my office."

Fifteen minutes later, Frank came up to Christopher's office. Opening the door, he waved at him to get his attention.

Christopher stood up. "Please come in; sit down." Confidently, Christopher walked to the door, closed it, and then returned to his desk.

Frank sat quietly, waiting to hear what Christopher had to say.

Christopher was looking at a plant on his desk. He felt its leaves. "You know some plants, after time, can erode the strongest of crags. Look at ivy, for instance, it grows along a brick wall, and when it finds a weak spot, it breaks through. It continues to grow and push its way through until the brick splits apart. Frank, I think we have some ivy growing here at Crownline."

Frank looked at Christopher. "You mean someone has infiltrated our plant and is stealing our designs?"

"Exactly."

Christopher and Frank made arrangements to meet again in the evening, after the employees had all gone home.

After work, when the receptionist, factory workers, and the interpreter had left, Frank and Christopher got together. They reviewed the records of each of the twelve employees working in the factory, as well as the receptionist's records.

There was nothing unusual about any of the employees' records. All of the employees were productive workers, most of whom had been with the company for more than six years. There were two employees who had worked for the company for a much shorter time: one for two years, and the other for 18 months.

Discussing the fact that Frank and Jack were the only ones with keys to the factory office, the two men concluded that no one else should have been able to access the information therein. Christopher and Frank decided to set a trap to see if they could catch anyone going into the factory's file room.

The timing couldn't have been better to catch a thief, since Crownline's scientist and designer had just finished prints that afternoon for a new thermal-insulating window, which would save consumers thousands of dollars on their heating costs.

Before Christopher went to the expense of renting a surveillance camera, he and Frank wanted to try a simple homemade trap. They had found an old incomplete design on the computer, which they printed up and labeled as prints for the thermal-insulating window. They strung a piece of thread, dipped in mechanic's oil, loosely across the doorway to the file room, about three inches above the floor. They then locked the office door and went their separate ways.

The next morning, Christopher went to work at seven. Checking the trap, he could see that no one had tampered with it. He went to his office and began working on a plan to stimulate new business.

At about eight thirty, Frank came into Christopher's office and closed the door behind him. "We got him."

"What?"

Frank explained that when he got to work at eight, the string was gone and so were the fake prints.

Christopher was both excited and nervous at the prospect of finding the culprit. He instructed Frank to go back to work and act normal.

Christopher went down to the factory. Walking around with his interpreter, he greeted each employee. To those he didn't recognize, he introduced himself. Thanking each one for his continued support of Crownline, Christopher encouraged them to remain loyal to the company.

As Christopher met the employees, he looked for anyone with a horizontal grease mark on his pant leg. What he found was even better.

Christopher had met eight of the employees. When he approached the ninth, he noticed a greasy piece of string stuck to his pant leg. "Good morning Jay. How are you?"

Jay seemed nervous again this morning. "I'm great. How about you?"

"I feel great too!" Christopher stood watching Jay work for a few minutes.

Jay turned and looked at Christopher. "Is there anything I can do for you, sir?"

Christopher smiled. "No. I'm just checking up on my employees. Hey Jay, do you enjoy working here at Crownline?"

"Huh, oh, yes sir."

"That's good. We'll talk more later." Christopher stepped back and slowly turned around.

Jay seemed relieved as he went back to work.

Christopher then stopped, looked at Jay's pant leg, and said, "You've got a string stuck to your pant leg."

Jay looked at his pants, pulled the string off, and threw it on the floor.

"All right, you got it." Christopher turned and walked away.

Jay quickly returned to work.

All of a sudden, Christopher returned, picked up the thread, and examined it. He looked Jay directly in the eyes. "Have you been in the factory's file room today?"

Jay looked away, "Uh, no sir."

"No? I had a greasy string just like this one strung across the doorway of the file room . . . hmmm, but it wasn't you." Christopher walked away. He greeted the three remaining employees and gave them positive encouragement to continue working with Crownline.

After meeting all of the employees, Christopher went into Frank's office.

Frank, who had been watching Christopher as he met the employees asked, "Is Jay the thief?"

Christopher smirked. "He had the string stuck to his leg."

The two men kept watching Jay as he worked.

Jay had seen Christopher go up to the office, and he knew Frank was there. Aware that he was being watched, he periodically glanced toward the office. Each time, they were still watching him. He felt like a bird in a cage—trapped. Unable to stand it any longer, he just had to confess.

Jay reached a point where he could stop working. Looking up at Christopher and Frank, he motioned that he was coming upstairs. He walked up the stairs to the landing just outside of Frank's office. "We need to talk."

The three men, along with the interpreter, sat down in Frank's office. Christopher again asked Jay, "Did you go into the file room today?"

Jay put his head down and mumbled something.

Christopher looked at the interpreter, who had been unable to understand what Jay had mumbled, and then he looked at Frank. "What did he say?"

Frank's eyes had opened wide. "He said, 'Yes'!"

Christopher walked over to Jay and looked him in the eye. "You were stealing Crownline's designs and specifications for whom?"

Jay looked very scared, but he answered, "Rod."

"Rod who?"

"Rod Tyler."

Frank responded, "That makes perfect sense. Rod had been the production manager here for almost 20 years. Last year, your father caught Rod sending an application for a patent under another company's name. The other company was owned by Rod. Your father quickly fired him and promoted me to production manager."

Christopher looked at Jay, "What does Rod do with the files you give him?"

"Really, sir, I don't know. I only give him the prints or specifications, he copies them, and then I return them to the file office. I don't know what he does with the information."

"How much does Rod pay you?"

"Well, our agreement wasn't for money, per se. He had promised me that once I got him five sets of designs, then I would be made the general manager of his company with a $50,000 per year salary."

Frank interrupted. "How did you get into the file room?"

"Rod gave me the key." Jay apologized for the problems he had caused, handed over the key, and said that he would gather his belongings.

Christopher walked over to the door and held it open for Jay. "Get back to work."

Jay sheepishly walked past Christopher. "Thank you."

Christopher returned to his office. He couldn't believe, after all the years that Rod had worked for Crownline, that he would turn against the hand that had fed him.

Frank told all the factory workers and Christopher told the receptionist that, when they arrived at work the next morning, they should punch in and then go straight to the conference room for a company breakfast.

Having waited for the other workers to leave the locker room, Jay was emptying all of his belongings out of the locker as Christopher and his interpreter strode in.

Christopher asked, "Are you leaving us?"

Jay looked a little surprised that Christopher would even ask such a question, but he responded, "Yes."

"I am not a wolf in sheep's clothing. In all sincerity, I am saying this. You can leave, or you can stay with the company. It's your decision." With that, Christopher left the locker room and returned to his office.

Crownline's employees were quite pleased when they arrived at work the following morning. A long table had been set up in the conference room, and it was piled with Danish, donuts, bagels, croissants, and fruit, and there were three different kinds of juices and coffee.

Christopher looked around the room. It felt good to see all the employees eating and enjoying themselves.

Jay came into the conference room and walked up to Christopher, "I'm sorry I let you down, sir. It won't happen again."

Christopher could see that he was genuinely remorseful. Looking at Jay, he smiled and replied, "I'm happy you're becoming a team player. Help yourself to some breakfast."

Closing the conference-room door, Christopher asked everyone to take a seat. Through his interpreter he said, "I want to thank you all for your continued support of Crownline Glass. I know it hasn't been easy this past year, with declining production and profits, but I'm hoping to turn that around. If we all work together, I believe we can make this company bigger and stronger than it was before. Our design team has come up with a new thermal-insulating window, which will save consumers thousands of dollars. I believe the technology we are using to design this window will give us an edge over our competitors. I am also in the process of restructuring this corporation. After numerous discussions with the accountant, I have decided to make each of you a shareholder in Crownline Glass. The number of shares that will be given to you will be based on how many years you have worked here. I feel that this will give each of you the incentive to make Crownline Glass the leader in the industry. I want to thank you again for your support. Keep up the good work!"

All of the employees stood up and clapped. They were thrilled at the prospect of a bigger and better Crownline.

After speaking with a few of the employees, Christopher approached Jay. "I would like to see you in my office."

"Yes, sir." Jay followed Christopher and his interpreter back to his office.

"Please have a seat. I've decided that I will not take punitive action against you if you would be willing to cooperate with me on three matters. First, I want you to continue working at Crownline. I've seen how quickly and efficiently you work, and I can always use employees like that. Second, I will need you to testify in court against Rod Tyler. Third, I want you to set up a meeting with Rod. What do you say?"

"Yes; I will do whatever you ask."

"Great! I want you to call Rod right now and set up a meeting for this afternoon to give him the prints that you took."

Jay picked up the phone and called Rod. They made arrangements to meet for coffee at four o'clock at a little coffeehouse downtown.

When Jay entered the coffee shop, Rod was already waiting for him. "What do you have for me?"

Jay pulled the prints out of a cylinder. "I've got prints for a new thermal-insulating window. It's supposed to revolutionize the industry." He handed the prints to Rod, who briefly looked at them and then put them back in their cylinder. "I've kept my end of the bargain. That is the fifth set of prints I've delivered to you. When can I start managing?"

"Well . . . your providing new designs has helped Tyler Glass to increase business. I've been thinking that if we could get a few more window designs, we could become the leader in the glass manufacturing industry. I would be willing to make you vice-president of the company with all its perks. What do you think?"

"Wow, that's quite an offer."

Rod stood up. "Why don't you sleep on it. In the morning when you come to pick up these prints, let me know what you've decided."

As Rod left, Jay thought, "He's the wolf."

Shortly after his meeting with Jay, Rod went back to his office. Walking into the lobby, he greeted the receptionist.

A neatly dressed man wearing an Italian-made coat was walking down the hall to the lobby. As the man neared the lobby, Rod looked up at him and said, "Have a good afternoon."

The gentleman nodded his head and smiled as he walked past Rod toward the exit.

Rod thought the man looked vaguely familiar, but he didn't know where he had seen him. After watching the gentleman as he walked out to the parking lot, Rod walked past the receptionist and remarked, "Nice threads."

Rod went into his office, hung up his coat, and sat down at his desk. He opened the cylinder that Jay had given him and laid the prints on his desk. As he was looking over them, he noticed an envelope leaning up against his desk lamp. The envelope had Rod's name handwritten on the front. Opening the envelope, he removed a Polaroid picture of the meeting he'd just had with Jay at the coffee shop. On the bottom of the Polaroid, underneath the picture was written, "Nice company. Christopher Cline."

Rod was shocked to find out that Christopher was aware of his meeting with Jay and that the young buck had the audacity to come into his office and leave proof of it. He then realized that the nicely dressed businessman he had just met in the lobby must have been Christopher. He ran back to the lobby to see if Christopher was still outside, but he was long gone. Rod stood there staring out the window.

Within a week, Christopher had hired an attorney to represent Crownline in a case against Tyler Glass.

Writing to his father in Vermont, Christopher informed him how Rod had been stealing Crownline's designs and then was having them patented under his company's name. He also explained how he had caught Rod and his plans to sue him for damages incurred.

Jack never responded to the letter so Christopher was quite surprised to see him, eleven months later, in court on the day of the hearing.

Crownline's attorneys presented their argument that Tyler Glass, owned by Rod Tyler, had used Jay Laredo to steal designs and have them patented under the Tyler Glass name. The attorneys also argued that Rod Tyler was using his knowledge of Crownline's customer database in order to underbid Crownline and lure their customers away.

Tyler's attorney then argued that the evidence was circumstantial and that there was no hard proof linking stolen designs to Tyler Glass, because Tyler's designs couldn't have been patented if they were identical to Crownline's.

After a day of arguments and counter arguments, the judge ruled that the pictures did not reveal what, if anything had passed between Tyler and Jay, and therefore the evidence regarding stolen designs was Crownline's word against Tyler's and was thus inconclusive. Regarding Tyler underbidding Crownline and taking their customers, the judge felt that, though it was an unethical business practice, it was not illegal; therefore, he could not rule on that matter. Court was then adjourned.

Rod left the courtroom gloating that he had been vindicated in this wrongful lawsuit.

Crownline's attorneys immediately began discussing an appeal. Christopher thanked his attorneys for their help, but he decided that he wasn't going to waste company time or money working on an appeal.

Sitting quietly in the courtroom until it emptied, Christopher decided to head back to the office to finish up some paperwork.

As Christopher left the courtroom and walked down the hall, he saw his father sitting on a bench.

Jack stood up and walked over to Christopher. He looked exasperated with him. "My son, you are a loser. I deserve better than what you've given me." Jack turned and walked away.

His father's words cut him to the heart! Christopher had put his life, his career, and his goals on hold to rebuild Crownline for this man, yet it was not enough. It seemed that whatever he tried to do, it was never enough.

Chapter 36
<u>Increasing Demand</u>

Christopher had quit his job at Sanders and Dempsey immediately after his initial two-week absence. His number one priority now was to get Crownline back on its feet. He and his accountant completed the restructuring of the corporation, and all of the shareholders were giving Crownline 100 percent of their support.

As they began production of their thermal-insulating window glass, Crownline was contracted to provide new windows for a system of hospitals being built in Minnesota. The demand for Crownline's glass products was slowly increasing, but it still wasn't enough to save the company from bankruptcy. Something more was needed.

Christopher met with Frank and his design team, which consisted of one scientist and one designer. Since they had all been working in close proximity for the past year, Frank had become adept at signing and the other two men had learned enough sign language to communicate effectively with Christopher.

The four men were trying to come up with a new window design and were continually discussing possible new technologies that could be used on the glass. Unable to come up with any new ideas, it seemed that they had hit a brick wall.

As they were brainstorming, the receptionist entered the conference room. Because, as usual, she was carrying something that restricted her already limited ability to sign, Frank interpreted as she spoke. "Mr. Cline, someone is here to apply for a job."

"Have him fill out an application, and Frank will call him back in a day or so to set up an interview."

She handed Christopher a folder. "Sir, here are his application and his resume . . . I think you may want to meet with him now."

Christopher took the folder and began reviewing its contents. "He graduated Harvard with an architectural degree, and he minored in math and chemistry. Maybe we should invite him in. Thank you. Good thinking!"

The receptionist left the room and returned in a few minutes with a neatly dressed, clean-shaven young man in his mid 20's.

Frank continued to interpret for Christopher. "Please be seated."

The young man sat down confidently. He did not seem at all intimidated by the four gentlemen at the table.

Christopher reached out to shake the young man's hand. "Hello. I am Christopher Cline. What is your name?"

"My name's David Dietrich. It's a pleasure to meet you sir."

"Thank you. I looked over your application and resume. You seem to have the academic knowledge that would be useful on our design team. I am wondering, why you chose to apply for a job here at Crownline?"

"Well sir, I know Crownline's reputation. It has been an industry leader for over 30 years. I'm also aware that during the past two years there has been a decline in your production. I believe I have some ideas that can turn that around and put you back on top."

"Do you have any work experience in this field? You didn't list anything on your resume."

David's confidence waned slightly. "Truthfully sir, that is my biggest problem. I do not yet have experience in this field, so no one will grant me an interview or even look at my designs."

"Do you have a portfolio?"

"Yes, right here." David opened up his briefcase and pulled out three folders containing computer-generated schematics, scientific formulas, and specifications for three different window designs.

Christopher glanced through the papers and then passed them on to his designer and scientist. "What do you think?"

The scientist smiled. "Yes, yes. It's very impressive."

The designer studied the information. "He's got some very innovative ideas."

Frank signed to Christopher, "I think we need him."

Christopher looked at David. "You've got yourself a job. How soon can you start?"

"I can start right now."

"I would like to introduce you to our production manager, Frank Russo. This is Jake Smith, our scientist. And this is Matthew Bruebager, our designer. You will be working closely with these three men."

David shook their hands. "Nice to meet you."

"I will have Frank set up a work station for you. My receptionist, Becky, will bring you some papers to fill out, and she will explain our company policies and benefits. I believe you will be happy working with the Crownline team. Welcome Aboard."

"Thank you sir."

During David's first week of work, Jake and Matthew carefully reviewed his designs. Although a few minor adjustments had to be made in order to make them more cost-effective, copies of the reworked designs and specifications could be sent to the patent office for approval within just a couple of weeks. Only two months later, production on the new window designs had begun.

One day Christopher was walking by the design office when a crumbled piece of paper rolled into the hallway. Picking it up, he walked into the office and threw the paper into a burgeoning trashcan. Looking around David's workstation, he could see schematics hanging on the wall, calculations written in a notebook, and dozens of papers strewn over the desk.

David looked up and saw Christopher, "Excuse my messiness. I have so many ideas, I'm trying to get them all on paper so I don't forget them. I have a few new ideas I want to discuss with Jake and Matthew for windows with UV protection."

"Really?" Christopher positioned himself near David and saw that the apparent clutter did indeed contain several partial designs and lots of notes.

Pointing to different papers as he talked, David replied, "Yes. You know how some furnishings fade if exposed to regular sunlight? Our windows would guard against that. Another idea I had is for a light-diffusing window. Sometimes the sunlight will shine so brightly through the window, you might as well be standing outside. The light will be diffused as it passes through our windows. I also have a few ideas for actual window shapes and patterns."

Remembering how quickly the young man's language had changed from "your" to "our", Christopher gave him a thumbs-up and thanked him for joining Crownline.

"No; thank you, sir, for giving me a chance to prove myself."

Christopher patted David on the back. Smiling, he went back to his own office to find more ways to increase business.

Over the next year and a half, Frank met with some of the local retailers and contractors to show them Crownline's new line of windows. He was able to pique their interest and bring in a limited amount of business.

Crownline was finally expanding instead of contracting and had successfully staved off bankruptcy, but it still wasn't making its mark on the industry. Crownline needed to expand nationwide. Christopher felt that the only way they could reach retailers, building planners, and contractors nationwide was to invite them to an open house as had been his father's habit years ago.

Christopher met with all the company personnel, explained the former tradition of having an open house, and asked for suggestions on how to make it a success. A weekend in October was chosen, which gave them two months to prepare. It was decided that formal invitations would be ordered and a caterer would be hired to provide drinks and hors d'oeuvres. The designers would create window and glass displays. All of the factory workers would be trained in salesmanship and would give tours of the factory, which would include some technical information regarding the products Crownline manufactures and a little of Crownline's history.

Christopher went through all of the business files to get names of former clients. He also checked the Internet to get names of retailers and government contractors. Inviting half to attend on Friday and the other half on Saturday, a total of 1000 invitations were sent to businesses around the country.

Finally, the time came for the open house. Everyone was trained and everything was in place. The doors opened at 10 a.m. each day.

The turnout was incredible! Over 700 people attended on Friday, representing 416 businesses, and Saturday another 520 people attended, representing 362 businesses. Everyone was asked to sign the guest book, next to which was a slotted container for the business card of anyone who wanted more information.

In two days Crownline had received requests from over 750 businesses from across the country that wanted more technical information, pricing information, or bids for specific work.

Christopher and Frank got busy hiring more personnel. They hired over 100 new factory workers, 10 chemical workers, four designers, and one more scientist to meet consumer demands. Within a six-month time period, Crownline was on its way to being the number one glass manufacturer in the country.

Chapter 37
<u>Promote Respect</u>

For the first few months after Crownline's open house, Christopher had been working additional hours in the evenings and on the weekends, trying to keep up with Crownline's increasing demands. The hectic schedule had begun to take a toll on him.

Christopher needed time to pursue his own activities. Once again he started meeting with the Deaf club on the weekends. Nick was no longer the president of the club since he had married and moved to Ohio, but he and his wife would visit from time to time.

The new president of the Deaf club, Tommy Jackson, was very active when it came to Deaf rights or activities for the Deaf. He worked with a Deaf advocacy group and a local movie theater to set up open-captioned movies once a month.

Christopher enjoyed being able to see movies with captioning at the theaters rather than having to wait three or more months for the movie to come out on videotape.

The coming Saturday a new action adventure movie would be shown with open captioning. Christopher, purchasing his ticket early, went to a restaurant just off of the mall's food court to grab a bite to eat before the movie. He asked to sit near the window that looked into the mall, since he enjoyed watching people.

As Christopher watched the people passing by, he saw an older couple who obviously came to the mall for exercise rather than for shopping. They were wearing sweats, headbands, and gym shoes. Walking around the mall at a steady pace, they must have passed by him nearly five times while he ate his sandwich and salad. He saw groups of teenagers that seemed more interested in drinking pop and laughing with their friends than shopping. Next he noticed the mothers who were attempting to shop, all the while trying to keep their young children content. And then he saw the true shoppers, the ones for whom the phrase "shop 'til you drop" was coined. Mostly women who would scurry from store to store, they would find the best prices for the latest fashions, gadgets, or housewares. They could be identified by the numerous bags, from different stores, that were draped from their arms or the rented strollers that contained bags instead of children. He always found the variety of people at the mall amusing.

On this particular day, one man especially caught Christopher's attention. He would stop people as they walked by and would show them a small card. Some people would pull out a dollar and give it to the man in exchange for the card. Others would give him a dirty look, wave their hands, and walk away.

Soon a security guard approached the man and said something. He motioned toward his ears and shrugged his shoulders. The security guard pointed at his cards and shook his head. He gave the security guard a thumbs-up, put the cards in his pocket, and walked away.

It seemed that the man was deaf, but Christopher wondered what the cards were that he was selling. He would have to find out another time, since the movie would be starting in 20 minutes and he wanted to get some popcorn to munch on during the show.

While Christopher waited in line for popcorn, he noticed some Deaf moviegoers beginning to congregate nearby. He watched their animated conversation about the movie they were waiting to see.

Having paid for his popcorn, Christopher started walking toward the Deaf group when someone tapped him on the arm. It was the man with the cards. He showed Christopher one of the cards. It had the alphabet in sign language on one side and the sign for "I love you" on the reverse. In the corner of the card it had the price of one dollar. Pulling a dollar out of his pocket, Christopher bought one of the cards. As soon as Christopher paid him, the man approached a lady standing nearby and tried to sell another card, quickly moving through the crowd.

Christopher put his sign language alphabet card in his shirt pocket. As he walked over to the group of Deaf, he noticed they were all watching him. Smiling, he signed, "Hello!"

Most of the Deaf just looked at him. Finally, one of the deaf men asked him, "You deaf?"

"Yes. My name Christopher. Your name what?"

"My name Adam."

Christopher shook his hand. "Nice meet you."

Adam went back to watching the conversation of four or five of the Deaf. They were complaining about Keith, the man selling the alphabet cards. They said he was a bum that was just begging people for money.

One of the deaf women said Keith was like a little monkey wearing a toy hat and holding a tin cup for all the passersby to pity. All of the Deaf began laughing.

Christopher, not feeling comfortable in the company of those individuals, went into the auditorium where the open-captioned movie was to be shown and found a seat in the middle of the theater, toward the front. He pulled the alphabet card out of his pocket and was looking at it when a middle-aged woman sat down near him.

"You buy that?"

"Yes. Something wrong?"

"You deaf, right?"

"Yes."

"I surprised you willing buy card support Keith."

Christopher didn't understand why buying a card was so startling to everyone. "I never saw deaf person selling alphabet card. Other Deaf complaining. I not understand. I don't mind buy card."

"Other Deaf think Keith, he bum. I know Keith many years, not his fault."

"You mean what?"

"Keith's parents, they hearing. They learn sign language, communicate Keith, never. They spoil him. They give give money, food, clothes. He life easy until 18 years old, then they throw him out. He skill none, experience work nothing. He stuck sell cards, live shelter many years."

"How old Keith?"

"He 29."

Christopher was stunned. In spite of his experience with Donny, he still couldn't believe that anyone would treat his or her own child in such an unkind manner. He talked with the woman for a few more minutes, until the movie began.

When the lights came on after the movie, Christopher recognized a number of people from the Deaf club. Walking over to them, he began chatting.

The Deaf all decided to go to a small coffee shop in the mall, where they could relax and talk. Talking until the coffee shop closed, they moved into the mall and talked some more, until the security guard asked them to leave. The whole group then moved outside and continued talking, but the cold temperatures put an end to their conversation rather quickly.

As Christopher walked through the parking lot, he saw the same deaf man who had been trying to sell alphabet cards inside the mall, now trying to sell the cards to people as they walked to their cars. Approaching him, he introduced himself. "Hi. My name Christopher Cline. Your name what?"

"My name Keith Smith."

Christopher told Keith that he was acting president of a company that manufactures glass. He asked him if he would be interested in a job.

Keith looked at Christopher in disbelief, but said that he would like to work.

Christopher gave Keith a business card and wrote down directions to his office. He told Keith to come to Crownline for an interview Monday morning at nine. Shaking Keith's hand, he signed, "Nice meet you. See you Monday."

Keith stood there for a few minutes and then walked down the street smiling.

Monday morning, Keith arrived at the Crownline office a little before nine. He approached the receptionist and showed her Christopher's business card.

She signed, "I will inform Christopher you here."

Keith watched the receptionist in amazement as she put the phone receiver on what looked to be a small typewriter with a digital display—he recognized it to be a text telephone (TTY)—which she used to call Christopher in his office. After she typed something, she hung up the phone and then handed Keith a clipboard with a job application attached to it. "Please sit; fill out application."

Keith sat in the lobby and read over the application. He wrote his name and his birth date. He wrote 'Michigan' under state. Looking through the remainder of the application, he didn't know what to write. He didn't know the address of the shelter. Many of the words he didn't understand, such as occupation, salary, experience, and references. After staring at the application for a few minutes, he began wondering what he was doing there. He was considering leaving, when he saw Christopher come into the lobby.

Christopher approached Keith and shook his hand. "Good morning. I happy see you. How you?"

"Me nervous."

"Why nervous?"

"Me not know if get job."

Christopher noticed Keith glance down at the clipboard he was holding. He smiled. "Come my office. I help you fill out application, then you meet new boss."

Keith followed Christopher to his office.

After helping Keith fill out his application and the necessary employee documents, Christopher made a phone call using his TTY. "Come on. I show you office, factory."

As the men walked through the building, Christopher explained Crownline's history, what they manufacture, and the corporation's aim for the new millennium. After showing Keith some of the windows that were being produced, he led Keith upstairs to the factory office.

There were already two men in the office when Christopher and Keith entered. "I want you meet Frank Russo. He manager factory." Turning toward the other man, he continued, "His assistant, he Pat Harrington."

Frank immediately reached over to shake Keith's hand. "Hello. Nice meet you. Your name what?"

Keith was surprised that Frank could sign. "My name Keith Smith."

Pat likewise reached out to shake Keith's hand. "Sorry. Your name, I miss. I learning sign. Don't mind, again spell slowly."

Keith again spelled his name, much slower, for Pat.

"Nice meet you."

After a few moments of getting acquainted, the four men sat down to discuss a job for Keith. Christopher took the lead in the discussion. "Keith, you want work assembly line build windows?"

"I want, but I no skill. Many company don't want hire me because I deaf. I never learn."

Christopher understood the frustration and discouragement that Keith must have experienced. "Today, you new job. Frank, Pat will show you factory, find right job match you. They teach you, help you learn skill."

Christopher asked Frank to call the personnel department so that Keith could be added to the payroll and his benefits could be put into effect immediately.

While Frank was interpreting between the personnel department and Christopher, Pat began questioning Keith. "You drive?"

"Never."

"How you come work?"

"I walk."

When Christopher had finished making arrangements for Keith's benefits, he shook his hand. "Welcome. I happy you join Crownline. Why not we walk, more look factory? We show you different assembly lines."

As they walked through the factory, Christopher noticed that Pat and Frank were walking a few paces behind him and Keith. Pat seemed bothered by something and was discussing it with Frank.

At the first assembly line, Christopher asked Pat and one of the assembly line workers to explain in sign language to Keith what they were doing. Pat reluctantly did so.

Meanwhile, Frank began telling Christopher what Pat had been saying. "Pat thinks you hire Keith look like big joke. He thinks Keith bum live street. He said, 'Christopher serious? Keith, he bum, car none. Imagine! He 29 years old, can't drive! Many companies won't give him job—I understand. He deaf dumb. Dumb not mean can't talk. He completely ignorant!'"

After Keith got to see how the assembly lines ran, Christopher asked Frank and Pat to join him as he walked Keith back to the main office building. He again shook Keith's hand. "See you tomorrow morning, time eight o'clock."

"Thank you give me job." Keith walked out with a big smile on his face and a lot more confidence in his step than when he had arrived a few hours before.

After Keith left, Christopher turned to Pat. "Mock deaf man or talk against deaf man—DON'T! Many hearing people no job, can't drive. You mock him look like you mock me too!"

Pat was taken back by Christopher's rage. "I sorry. I not against you."

Christopher sent Pat home. He had it noted in Pat's employee records that he had been harassing a deaf employee and was suspended from work for a week without pay. Afterwards, Christopher went to his office to review the month's production reports.

Pat turned to Frank, "I didn't mean to hurt Christopher."

As the two men walked past the receptionist, Becky responded, "Keith isn't the only one who can't drive."

Frank turned to Becky, "What do you mean?"

"Christopher doesn't drive."

"Really?"

Pat asked, "How does Christopher get to work everyday?"

"He rides the bus or takes a taxi."

Near the end of the day, Frank went up to Christopher's office. Opening the door, he waved to get Christopher's attention.

"Hey, what's up?"

"I bring coffee." Frank handed Christopher a cup and sat down across from him.

"Pat want me inform you, he really sorry he mock Keith. He say won't happen again."

"I hope not."

They sat quietly for a moment and then Frank waved to Christopher. "Don't mind I ask you something personal?"

"Sure. What you want know?"

"Recently I found out you not yet drive. Why?"

"Well, who control my life?"

"Jack?"

Christopher raised his eyebrows and shook his head affirmatively.

"Why he not let you drive?"

"I deaf. He think if I drive, I will accident or dead. He let high school teach me drive, but he not let me street drive."

"You want learn drive?"

"How? I no car."

"Come on. You coat on. We go parking lot. You practice, drive my car."

For the next two weeks, Frank took Christopher out to practice driving.

Christopher also got his learner's permit and took a driving refresher course that lasted two days.

When Christopher completed his course, he borrowed Frank's car and took his driver's test. He was offered a videotape test that contained all the questions on the test interpreted into sign language. Frank had explained the reasoning behind the laws to him as he read the manual, so he didn't have any problem with the questions. Though his hearing could have impacted the driving part of the test, Christopher remained alert to his surroundings as he maneuvered around the city. He passed the written part of the test with a score of 100 percent and the driving part of the test with a score of 95 percent.

Christopher really enjoyed driving. At first he used the company car to drive back and forth to work, but soon he wanted to drive farther. The more he drove, the less restricted he felt. He soon found himself purchasing his own car. The freedom it afforded him was like nothing he had ever experienced.

Chapter 38
<u>Crownline Complex</u>

The spring following the open house was a busy time. Christopher had just signed 23 new contracts to provide windows for new constructions throughout the country, and he had purchased three large pieces of equipment to keep production in step with the increasing demand.

One day while Christopher and Frank were discussing Crownline's growth, the receptionist came into Christopher's office. "There's a gentleman in the lobby who's here to apply for a job. I think you might be interested in talking to him."

Frank stood up. "I'll take care of this."

Fifteen minutes later, Frank returned. "I hired new equipment repairman."

"Great! He interesting same Becky suggested?"

"Yes! You won't believe. He said he working Tyler Glass for two years. Last week he arrived work. Building locked. On door paper say bank take over property. He tried call office, but phone disconnected. He called bank, try find what happen. Bank told him Tyler Glass bankrupt. They no more business!"

213

"Good. Hmmm . . . Good!" Christopher, who had been standing by the window, returned to his desk.

Frank sat down across the desk from Christopher thrilled that this particular competitor was no longer in business, but wondering what had happened. "Maybe Rod not business-minded, not know how control money."

"No, that not problem."

"What you mean?"

"Last year, we determined Rod stole our customers; I take back. All contractors, retailers left us, I contact them. I discussed Crownline's reputation, our restructuring, our new products, our pricing. I build confidence, pull business back us. Only two companies not back. They small businesses, both owners retired."

Frank started laughing. "You destroyed Tyler Glass!"

Christopher smiled. "Okay, now we focus Crownline's growth."

Frank responded, "I think company too big, not fit this building. We already hired over 100 factory workers. We purchased three new machines. Now customer demand increasing, I need hire at least 50 factory workers. Factory not enough space for work smooth. Also warehouse full for while. Extra supplies, windows all around factory's perimeter."

"I agree. Same happen office. Two or three chemical workers, designers must share office. Look like we two choice. We can buy property new build, or we can buy new warehouse, office building. Why not you meet realtor, check if any buildings or property sale. I go bank see how much money we can borrow. We information can explain board members."

After a week of researching Crownline's options, Christopher and Frank presented their suggestions to the board. It was decided that Crownline would buy property and build a large multimillion-dollar complex consisting of a four-story office building, a two-story factory, and a large, 32,000 square-foot, warehouse.

By mid-November, construction was completed. All equipment, files, and personnel had been moved to the new complex. The old factory portion of the building was converted to a parking garage and service station for the Crownline trucks. The old offices were used for storage of office supplies and old files.

After the first day of production in the new Crownline complex, Christopher reflected on all the changes he had effected since becoming vice president four years earlier. Considering that Jack had not been back to Michigan since the court case against Tyler Glass, he wondered how his father would react to the company's growth and if his success would meet with his father's approval. He had tried to tell his father what he was doing at different times, but they still had a hard time communicating, and Jack never seemed to be interested; Christopher was sure Jack didn't have a clue what was going on.

Chapter 39
<u>Communication Vital</u>

It had been almost four years since Jack and Margaret had moved to Vermont.

Christopher would call his mother monthly, but that was always frustrating and time consuming. He would use his TTY to call the relay service. They would then call his mother. The relay service would tell her what he was typing on his TTY and then they would type to him what she was saying. Oftentimes there were misunderstandings.

Christopher preferred communicating directly with his mother, rather than through a third party. He hadn't seen his father since Crownline lost the lawsuit against Rod Tyler, and he hadn't seen his mother for an even longer time. He decided to pay them a visit. He made all the arrangements to spend two weeks in Vermont.

The plane departed from Metro Airport half an hour late, due to inclement weather, which caused him to miss his connecting flight in Cleveland.

When Christopher finally arrived at the Burlington airport in Vermont, Margaret was at the gate, eagerly awaiting his arrival. She looked very happy.

Christopher approached her and gave her a hug and a kiss. "Hi Mom."

"Oh, dear Christopher, it is so good to see you!" Since there had been no one that Margaret could sign to on a regular basis for almost ten years, she spoke slowly and tried to enunciate her words as she attempted to sign. It was clearly a struggle for her to remember the correct signs. "I am sorry. I not sign good any more."

Christopher appreciated her effort. "It okay. Hey, Dad where?"

"He wait home for you."

Christopher picked up his luggage at the baggage claim area, and they headed out to his mother's car. Since he didn't want to interfere with her driving, they rode home in silence.

When Margaret and Christopher arrived at the house, Jack was sitting in the living room reading his newspaper. Christopher walked over to his dad and gave him a firm handshake. He tried to vocalize the best he could, since his dad didn't know any sign language. "Hi Dad. It good see you."

Jack didn't even get up from his chair. "Welcome home son."

Christopher sat on the couch near his dad. "How everything here?"

"Everything's fine."

"You know Crownline recently contract provide windows for schools near here."

"Good for you." Jack then picked up his newspaper and continued reading right where he had left off.

Christopher was disappointed that his dad hadn't asked him anything about his life or the business. He wanted to tell his dad about Crownline's expansion and the new complex, but it was obvious that this was not the time.

Jack had invited his fishing buddy and his wife to come join them for dinner that evening. Christopher tried to be pleasant, but inside he felt like he didn't belong. His mother kept forgetting to interpret for him, and when she did, she couldn't remember many of the signs. His father kept busy entertaining his company.

After dinner, Christopher went out on the porch. Since his parents lived in a small town, the night sky was not lit up by streetlights, but by the celestial bodies. He was standing looking up at the stars, when he felt someone put an arm around his waist. It was his mother. She held him close to her side.

When Christopher looked at his mother, her face was as he remembered—full of love, tenderness, and compassion.

She signed "I miss you much."

"I love you too." Christopher looked back up at the stars.

After a few minutes, he looked toward the house. He could see his dad through the window, talking and laughing with his friend. "You know I push aside my career. I work hard build Crownline for Dad, but he never appreciate my effort."

Margaret kissed Christopher on the cheek. "That is your father's decision. You must get on with your own life and do whatever you need to do to be happy."

The next day, Christopher overslept. When he woke up, he found homemade cinnamon rolls on the counter with keys and a note.

"My dearest Christopher, the nursing home needed assistance today. I had to go help out. Dad went fishing with his friend. The car is out back if you need it. I'll see you later. Love, Mom."

Christopher wasn't in the mood to stay home alone. He took a drive to a neighboring town an hour away, where they had a small mall.

Before Christopher left Michigan, he had bought his father a Rolex watch and had even had an inscription put on the back. It read "Crownline 35 years 1964-1999". He wanted to have it gift-wrapped for his father.

While Christopher wandered around the mall, he noticed a young girl with Downs Syndrome with her father. She looked to be about nine years old.

As the girl and her father were passing the pet store, she turned around, ran over to a bench, and sat down. She patted the bench and said, "Dad sit." As she spoke, Christopher noticed she signed sit.

The girl's father looked confused. "Why?"

"I watch cat." As she spoke to her father, she signed, "Look."

Holding out his hand, the father said, "Come on." He pointed to the pet store. They stood up and walked into the pet store.

Christopher wondered if she was deaf. He followed them into the pet store. "Excuse me, your daughter deaf?"

The girl's father looked surprised, "No."

As her father answered, the girl also said "No," but as she did, she also signed, "No."

"I sorry. I deaf and I notice your daughter sign language."

"Really?" Her father looked at her, "You know sign language?"

"Little."

Christopher asked the young girl where she had learned to sign.

She said and signed, "School."

Her father was shocked. He had no idea the school was teaching her sign language.

"My name Christopher Cline. I live Michigan; visit here."

"It's nice to meet you. My name is James Hill."

The two gentlemen shook hands.

"This is my daughter, Julie."

"Hi, Julie. You like animals?"

She signed, "Yes."

They were standing near the puppies. Christopher pointed to a puppy that was barking. He signed dog and then used his hands to imitate the dog's mouth barking while he said "Woof, woof."

Julie started laughing, and then she tried to imitate Christopher.

Christopher next pointed to the kittens. He signed cat. Using his hand to imitate a cat's small mouth, he said "Me-youuu, Me-youuu."

Julie again copied Christopher, which made her laugh even harder than before.

James watched in amazement. He couldn't remember ever seeing Julie laugh like that.

Christopher and Julie looked at a few more animals and then James asked Christopher if he would like to join them for ice cream.

"Sure."

Walking with them into the food court, Christopher sat with James and Julie after they bought their ice cream.

James wondered how Christopher could communicate with Julie so well.

He told James that he remembered that in school they would use sign language with some of the kids with Downs Syndrome. The visual connection helped them to better understand, and it gave them a way to respond when they didn't know the words to express themselves.

James said he felt he was missing something because he couldn't communicate well with his daughter. Christopher suggested he learn sign language. He could get a sign language book, take an adult education course, or visit a Deaf club.

"I think I will look into that." James turned to Julie, "You want Daddy to learn to talk with his hands?" As he said that he wiggled his fingers.

A big smile came across Julie's face, as she said and signed "Yes!"

James thanked Christopher for joining them, and then he and his daughter left, hand in hand.

Christopher sat at the table alone for a while, thinking about James and Julie. It must have been hard for James, having a daughter with Downs Syndrome, but he seemed up to the challenge. He was even willing to go the extra mile for her so that they could better communicate.

How Christopher wished his father would reach out to him! He was saddened that he had made special arrangements to visit his parents, and they had just left him to fend for himself rather than take the time to be with him. What disappointed him even more was that he had put his life, his career, and his goals on hold to take care of his father's business, yet his father didn't seem to appreciate or care about the sacrifices he had made.

As Christopher was leaving the mall, a homeless person was sitting outside asking for money. He gave him the watch he had bought for his father and then walked to the car.

Chapter 40
Pursuing Companionship

During the next few days, Christopher struggled to communicate with his parents. Though he made every effort to speak with his father, Jack seemed to keep himself busy around the house. Margaret tried to relax and spend time with Christopher, but still of the mindset that each meal had to be home-cooked, much of her time was spent in the kitchen. Every afternoon Christopher would help his mom in the kitchen, and then while the food was baking, they would catch up on each others' lives.

Margaret asked Christopher if he had a girlfriend.

"I always busy working. No time for girlfriend."

Margaret got up to check the bread in the oven.

"Mom, you remember long ago, neighbor girl name Nicole?"

"Yes. I remember; why you ask me?"

"I often thinking her. Sometimes I wonder, 'Where she now?'"

"She's teacher for the deaf at a school in Maryland."

"Really! Why you never told me?"

"I didn't know you interested. Her mother, Susan, and I have kept in touch with each other."

Christopher's countenance completely changed. "You have her address?"

"I can get it from her mother."

"I can't believe! We best friends long ago! You get address now?"

"Just relax . . . Relax . . . I'll call Susan." Margaret spoke on the phone for a few minutes. She wrote something down and then hung up. "Susan said Nicole would love to hear from you." Margaret handed him a piece of paper with Nicole's TTY phone number and her address.

"Thanks, Mom."

"Christopher, don't get too excited. Susan also said Nicole recently engaged."

"Okay. Thanks, Mom." Christopher ran to his room and returned a few minutes later with his duffel bag. He grabbed the car keys and gave Margaret a kiss. As he was leaving, he bumped into Jack in the hallway. "Oops, sorry. You good day, Dad." He got in the car and left.

Jack walked into the kitchen where Margaret was still sitting at the table. "What's his rush?"

"A woman."

"Really?" Jack sat across from Margaret.

Both Margaret and Jack sat pondering Christopher's new interest.

Christopher drove the hour and a half to the airport, where he had seen a TTY. By the time he arrived at the airport, it was nearly five o'clock. He tried calling Nicole, but he got her answering machine. He left a message. "This your best friend. See you soon. Christopher."

Christopher hung up the phone and ran over to the nearest airline. He wrote a note asking if they had any flights to Baltimore, Maryland. Relieved that they had a few seats available on their six o'clock flight, he bought himself a ticket.

On the way to the gate, Christopher saw another TTY. He called his mom through the relay service. "Mom, I hope you not need car few days. I going Maryland. I back few days."

"No, I don't need my car. You be careful, Christopher. I love you."

"I love you, Mom." Christopher hung up the phone and ran to the gate just as they began boarding the plane.

During the flight, Christopher couldn't stop thinking about Nicole. He wondered what her life had been like, if she was happy, and how she would feel about seeing him after all these years.

When Christopher arrived in Baltimore, he rented a car. After asking for directions to Nicole's home, he drove to her apartment and rang the bell. There was no answer. He decided to stay at a hotel nearby, and then he would come back to Nicole's tomorrow.

The next day was Thursday. Christopher drove by Nicole's apartment early in the morning, but then he realized she would already be at work if she were a teacher.

Stopping at a coffee shop to look at a phone book, Christopher found the address of Nicole's parents' home. After purchasing a map, he was able to locate their house. It was much larger than the house they used to live in when they had lived next door to the Clines. The neighborhood was very ritzy.

As he rang the bell, Christopher questioned his reason for seeking out Nicole. He was ready to turn around and walk away, when the door opened. A woman dressed in a blue pantsuit stood there. "May I help you?"

As clearly as he could he said, "I deaf. Nicole here?"

The woman smiled. "Nicole doesn't live here. This is her parents' home."

Christopher showed the woman Nicole's address. "She not home." He shrugged his shoulders.

"No, she's working now." The woman took the paper and wrote, "Wilson Junior High School."

Christopher smiled, "Thank you." Turning, he walked back to his car.

The woman tried to get Christopher's attention to ask him his name, but he didn't notice. Getting in his car, he drove off.

On the way to the school, Christopher stopped at a florist. He wanted to get some long-stem red roses for Nicole. Walking up to the counter, he motioned toward his ears. "I'm deaf."

The woman behind the counter told him to wait a minute.

Another woman approached Christopher. She signed, "Hello, I Kim. I help you what?"

Christopher was surprised. "You deaf?"

"Yes."

"Nice meet you. I Christopher. I want box 12 roses, red, long-stem."

"Okay." Kim went behind the counter and got a long white box. Carefully placing white tissue paper in the box, she neatly laid 12 fragrant red roses interspersed with baby's breath on top of the tissue paper. "You want write note?"

"Yes, please."

Kim handed Christopher a note card and a red pen.

Christopher wrote, "Nicole, We will always best friends. Love, Christopher." He put the card in the envelope, and Kim placed it in the box.

As Kim put the lid on the box and tied a shiny red satin ribbon around it, she asked, "Nicole your girlfriend?"

"We grow up together. We best friends."

"Nicole, last name what?"

"Coleman."

Kim got excited. "She interpreter, teach deaf right?"

"You know her?"

"Yes. We went university together. Now we best friends."

"I can't believe!"

Christopher and Kim chatted for a few more minutes. She then gave him directions to Wilson Junior High School, and he left.

Christopher had no trouble finding the school. When he arrived, he went straight to the main office. Trying to use his voice, he signed and said, "Excuse me. Where Nicole Coleman?"

"Nicole is teaching a class right now."

"I old friend. I want give flowers then I go."

"All right, that should be fine. She's upstairs in room 202."

As Christopher went upstairs to find Nicole's classroom, he began to experience a nervous sensation. He wondered if she would recognize him and how she would feel to see him again.

The classroom door was closed. There was a small window in the door through which he could peek inside the classroom. He saw about 15 students but no teacher. As he was looking around the classroom to locate Nicole, he felt someone tap him on the shoulder. Turning around, he saw her standing in front of him. She was more beautiful than he had remembered— her brilliant blue eyes, long flowing brown hair, shapely figure, soft skin, and kindly expression—she was simply radiant!

Christopher was so flustered at seeing Nicole so unexpectedly that he dropped the box of roses. As he bent down, she too bent down. Picking up the box, she handed it back to him.

"Thank you." He said with his voice, but no signs.

Nicole recognized that Christopher was deaf, but she didn't realize with whom she was speaking, though he did seem familiar to her. She signed and asked him if he wanted her to give the box to someone in the class.

Not knowing what to say, since the flowers were supposed to be for her, Christopher nodded his head and handed her the box of flowers.

"Me give who?"

Christopher couldn't do it; he couldn't get up the nerve to tell Nicole that the flowers were for her. He looked back in the classroom and saw a shy-looking girl in the last row. Pointing to the girl, he signed "Girl, short hair brown, shirt blue."

Nicole smiled. "Me give," she did a name sign with the letter K by her mouth.

Christopher nodded his head.

"What your name?" At that moment the light began flashing in the classroom and students streamed out into the hallway. "I must back teach class. I will give," she again signed a K by her mouth.

Nicole went into the classroom and gave the flowers to the girl Christopher had described. The girl was surprised to get a box of roses. Opening the card, she read it. She then waved to her teacher. "Flowers mine not. It yours."

Nicole walked to the back of the classroom. The girl handed her the card. She read it and looked up at the door. Running to the door, she opened it and looked up and down the hallway. He was gone—Christopher was gone. She hadn't expected him so soon after his message, so she had ignored the feeling that the young man seemed familiar. She just figured she had seen him at one of the parties she'd been attending lately to celebrate her engagement. Now she couldn't believe her stupidity!

Christopher returned to the hotel. He knew Nicole hadn't recognized him, but he was still anxious to see her again. Borrowing the hotel's TTY, he called the school and left a message with the secretary to give to Nicole. "Please tell Nicole I will meet her in office at noon, then we go lunch."

"Ok SK" and then the secretary hung up without asking who was calling.

Christopher thought that was strange, but he didn't concern himself with it. He glanced at himself in the mirror and then got back in his car and once again headed toward the school.

Christopher got to the school a few minutes before noon. Standing in the hallway, he waited to see if Nicole would respond to his message. He was thrilled when he saw her coming down the stairs. Standing back so as not to be seen right away, he watched her as she walked into the office.

Christopher's heart was beating rapidly. He was excited to get this chance to once again be with Nicole.

As Christopher walked down the hallway toward the office, he could see her through the window. She was hugging another man. He stopped dead in his tracks. Standing off to the side, he watched her.

She signed to the man she was with, "I happy you want out lunch. I need break."

The man signed back to her, "School Secretary called, said found message 'Brian meet Nicole here lunch.' She wanted be sure I got message. I thought you bring lunch." He shrugged his shoulders, and both of them started laughing. "Come on. We out eat." He grabbed her hand, and they started walking toward the hallway.

Christopher stepped into a nearby classroom so Nicole wouldn't see him. How he wished he was the one walking hand-in-hand with her!

After Nicole and the other man had left the building, Christopher went into the office. He wanted to find out who the man was that had left with her.

Approaching the secretary, Christopher told her that he was deaf and he was supposed to meet Nicole for lunch.

Looking confused, she told him that Nicole had just left with Brian.

Christopher asked, "Who Brian?"

The secretary wrote on a piece of paper, "Brian Finch, her fiancée."

"Okay. I will contact Nicole later. Thank you." Christopher gave the paper to the secretary and walked out of the office.

As Christopher walked through the empty hallway, he kept thinking how it could have been he hugging and holding hands with Nicole. If only he had known she was in Maryland sooner. He thought of all those wasted years he lived and worked in the DC area, not knowing that she was so near to him.

Christopher decided to return to the hotel until school let out, and then he would try again to catch up with Nicole.

After lunch, Nicole stopped by the office to copy some worksheets for her class.

The secretary mentioned that the man who had come earlier in the day had returned to have lunch with her.

"Really? You mean the same man that brought me the roses this morning?"

"Yes, that's the one."

Thanking the secretary for the information, Nicole returned to her classroom. She sat down at her desk. Surprised that Christopher had come back to the school to see her, she began thinking about their good times when they were younger and wondered what his life had been like. She wondered if he knew that she was engaged. Thinking about how different her life would have been if her family had not moved to Maryland, she started to wonder if she would have ended up with Christopher . . . then the bell rang, and her students began entering the classroom.

Christopher drove over to Nicole's apartment at four o'clock, hoping to catch her as she arrived home from school. As he pulled up in front of the building, he noticed Brian getting out of his car.

Brian, walking over to the apartment, rang the bell. A minute later, Nicole came down in a red dress with a flowing skirt.

To Christopher, Nicole looked like royalty.

Brian gave Nicole a kiss on the cheek, and then they got in his car and left.

Christopher couldn't help himself. He had to see Nicole again, so he followed them to an expensive-looking restaurant overlooking the Chesapeake Bay.

Brian and Nicole went into the restaurant and were seated near the window. The atmosphere was romantic, and they seemed to be completely wrapped up in each other.

As they waited for their dinner, the waiter approached them with two glasses of champagne. Handing Nicole a note, he said, "This is from the gentleman over there. Oh, he's gone . . ."

Nicole opened the paper and read, "Enjoy your evening. Christopher." Her eyes opened wide. Shocked that Christopher was there, she began looking around the restaurant.

Brian asked what the note had said.

"Enjoy your evening."

"Note from who?"

"I not sure." Nicole sat in her seat anxiously looking around. She was so excited, she began to tremble.

Excusing herself, Nicole went to the restroom, all the while searching for Christopher. She wasn't able to find him. Was he still in the restaurant watching her, or had he left? She didn't know what to do. She tried to calm herself, and then she returned to the table.

"You okay?"

"Yes, I'm fine."

Nicole and Brian sat quietly eating their dinner. Afterwards he dropped her off at home.

Nicole kept hoping to see Christopher. As she drove to school the next morning, she watched for him. Throughout the school day, she would look outside or down the hallway to see if he was there. She checked with the office a few times during the day to see if she had any messages from him. Since all she could think about was Christopher, she had a difficult time teaching, but he never came to the school or called.

School finally let out. Nicole gathered her personal belongings and left the classroom. Wanting to see if she had any messages, she checked with the secretary one last time before going home, but there was still nothing. She walked down the long corridor to an adjoining hallway that would take her to the parking lot. Since the students always left school quickly on Fridays, the halls were now empty except for a few teachers.

As Nicole neared the door, she noticed a man standing against the wall looking down at a brochure. He was a nicely dressed, professional-looking man. She was about ten feet away from him when he looked up at her.

Nicole stopped dead in her tracks. It was Christopher. He looked her directly in the eyes, and suddenly she felt self-conscious. Looking down at the ground, she pushed her hair behind her ear, and then she looked back at him.

Smiling, Christopher signed, "Happy see you."

Nicole couldn't hold her excitement in any longer. She ran up to Christopher and threw her arms around his neck. They stood there holding each other, hoping that this moment would never end.

Chapter 41
<u>Affections Emerge</u>

After the emotional reunion at the school, Christopher asked Nicole if she would like to go out for coffee.

"Yes, I like catch-up talk."

Dropping her car off at her apartment, Nicole climbed into Christopher's car and directed him to a little coffee shop just outside of Baltimore.

Christopher and Nicole sat and talked about all that had happened since they had last seen each other, almost fourteen years earlier.

Thinking back to when Nicole's family had moved, Christopher asked, "I wonder . . . your family move DC area why?"

"My dad works under government. His job transfer."

"You not tell me family move. Why?"

"My parents last-minute inform me. I wanted see you, but . . ." Nicole shrugged.

"I went your house looking you."

"I know. Mom told me. I with Dad go DC."

"You not good-bye me why?"

"I want, but parents thought better I go. Not matter . . . happen long ago."

"I understand . . . because I deaf."

"My parents worry I too much associate Deaf. They want me more friends hearing, but I never give up signing. I always look friend deaf. Anyway, that finished. How your mom, dad?"

"They fine; live Vermont."

"How you, dad communication?"

"We fine."

"You honest tell me . . . your dad learn sign?"

"No. He same same. He wants me read lips. I must follow his way. Seem he satisfy my effort—never."

Christopher and Nicole talked about school and how they had both attended the same university but at different times. She couldn't believe he had lived in the DC area for almost 10 years, and they had never run into each other.

"Now you come DC why?"

"You."

Nicole blushed, "You thinking me why?"

"My whole life, I stop thinking you—never. You, me best friends. That worth remembering. Recently, I found you live Maryland. Everything drop, come see you."

"Nice you thinking me, but you know that I engaged. Sorry."

"I understand. I want you happy, your life satisfied."

Nicole smiled.

Sitting quietly for a few uncomfortable minutes, Christopher and Nicole wouldn't look at each other, but instead looked around the coffee shop.

Glancing down at his watch, Christopher realized that he and Nicole had been talking into the evening. He suggested that they go grab a bite to eat. She found a phone and ordered a pizza, which they picked up and took to a nearby park on the Chesapeake Bay.

After eating, the two friends talked more about their experiences and goals until the early morning hours.

Christopher, dropping Nicole off at home shortly after

two, informed her, "Monday I back my parent's home. I hope we can together again."

"Yes, I like. You wake, call me TTY."

Walking Nicole to her apartment, Christopher said, "Good night."

"Thanks searching for me. I really enjoy." With that, Nicole turned around and went into her apartment.

Later that morning, Christopher again picked up Nicole. Since it was Saturday, they could spend it sightseeing in Baltimore. They visited the aquarium and the science center, and then they took a boat ride on the bay. The sky had been clear all day, the sun would soon be setting, and the air was crisp. It was a perfect evening for a boat ride.

Christopher and Nicole talked about the good times of their younger years and how they had been best friends.

Christopher told Nicole how, becoming lonely when she had moved, he had found life difficult without his best friend. Gazing into her eyes, he then reached out and took her hand. "I happy we together again."

Nicole could sense how alone Christopher had felt.

The two of them sat in silence the remainder of the boat ride, hand-in-hand.

Though the sun sets every evening, that particular sunset seemed amazingly beautiful—the way the sky was illuminated in shades ranging from bright golden yellow to deep orange.

The boat docked, and knowing the evening would soon be over, Christopher looked into Nicole's eyes and then at their hands. He appreciated the ease of being with her, and he didn't want to do anything that would jeopardize their friendship. "Thank you. Today wonderful." Leaning toward her, he kissed her on the cheek. "Come on, I take you home."

Nicole had invited Christopher over to her place for dinner on Sunday. All day Christopher could think of nothing else. He couldn't get Nicole out of his mind. After fourteen years of no contact, he was amazed that they could pick up right where they had left off and feel even more comfortable with each other than they had before.

Nicole had always made Christopher feel confident. She had accepted him for who he was and was supportive of his choices and goals. Christopher felt that he could trust Nicole with his deepest feelings, knowing that she wouldn't reject him, and she felt likewise. There was no one else with whom Christopher would rather be.

He realized that he was so in love with Nicole that he couldn't bear the thought of losing her again. Wanting to let her know how he felt before he left for his parent's home the next morning, he decided to open his heart and bare his soul.

Christopher arrived at Nicole's just before five. He rang the bell and a minute later she came down the stairs. She was wearing a royal blue dress that made her eyes sparkle.

"You beautiful!" Handing her a long white box with a red ribbon around it, Christopher said, "For you."

As Nicole took the box, the fragrance from the roses filled the air. "Thank you."

Christopher and Nicole went upstairs to her apartment. As she put the roses into a vase, he looked around.

Nicole's apartment was small, but she kept it neat. In the dining area the table was set for two, lit only by candles. The living room had a couch, a chair, and two end tables. There were no knick-knacks, but there were candles burning on the tables and two pictures on display. One picture was of Nicole and her parents. The other was a picture of her and Christopher when they were children.

A few weeks before Nicole's family moved to DC, she had gotten her first camera as a gift from her parents. Bringing it up to the tree house, she had shown it to Christopher. They'd had fun taking pictures of each other. Wanting a picture together, she had put her face next to his, held the camera out at arm's length, and snapped a picture.

Christopher couldn't believe Nicole still had that picture. He wondered if she always displayed it, or if she had just put it out while he was there. There were no pictures of Nicole and Brian. Was that done for Christopher's sake, or did she not have any of the two of them?

Nicole and Christopher enjoyed dinner together. The food was delicious, but the company was what made the meal so pleasurable.

During dinner, the two talked about their dreams for the future. Nicole spoke of how she wanted to marry. If she married a hearing man, he would have to have the same love of sign language and make himself a part of the Deaf community as she had. If she married a deaf man, it would have to be one who didn't use his deafness as an excuse for laziness but was a success despite being deaf. She wanted to be with someone who could love her for who she is and who would let her love him unconditionally.

Christopher found it interesting that Nicole never mentioned Brian as being in her future.

After Christopher and Nicole cleared the table and washed the dishes, they went into the living room and sat on the couch. Her beauty dazzled him.

Feeling a little uneasy, Nicole stood up and grabbed the picture of Christopher and her off the table. "You see?" Handing the picture to him, she sat down in the chair.

"Yes, we lot fun together." Christopher, returning the picture to its place on the table, kneeled down in front of Nicole. "I missed you so much."

"I missed you. Long ago we young, I happy we met."

"Before, I lost you. I feel I can't bear lose you again." Christopher then held Nicole's hand and kissed it tenderly. "I love you much. You give me chance show my feelings?"

Looking down, Nicole pulled her hand back and signed, "I can't. I sorry."

"You love Brian?"

"We engaged."

"I know, but you love him?"

"I thought yes, but you show up. Now my life, my world upside down."

"You know me better than anyone. You know I deep care you. I willing do anything give you happiness."

"I know . . . I can't. Next year I, Brian will married."

"I understand. I want you best life. I hope you much happiness."

"Thank you."

"I should leave. Thank you, enjoyable evening. I never forget you."

As Christopher opened the door to leave, he turned around and handed Nicole a small white box with a red ribbon on it. Then he went down the stairs and left the apartment building.

Nicole watched Christopher as he drove away, and then she sat down on the couch his gift still in her hand. Removing the ribbon, she opened the box. There was a gift card and a jewelry box inside. The note on the card read, "To Nicole—my first and only love. Christopher." Opening the jewelry box, she saw a beautiful gold pendant in the shape of two intersecting hearts with a solitaire diamond where the hearts joined together. Knowing Christopher held a special place in her heart, she could no longer hold back her emotions; she gave way to tears.

Chapter 42
<u>Love Realized</u>

Nicole called in sick on Monday, since she had hardly slept the night before. She had choices to make. Her heart told her she was in love with Christopher, but she was already engaged to Brian. She realized now that she had always subconsciously sought out people like Christopher, and she had probably accepted Brian's proposal because of his similarities with Christopher. It shocked her to discover that her heart had always been Christopher's. She knew what had to be done, but how could she do it?

Shortly after nine, Nicole's doorbell rang. Thinking it might be Christopher on his way to the airport, she ran downstairs. It was Brian. He looked upset and began signing emphatically, "Weekend, where you? We plan go Deaf club party Saturday. You remember?"

"I sorry. I forget."

"Saturday I try contact you, but not home. I left TTY message. I call relay service left voice message. I wait wait, you never call me. Today I went school; they say you sick. I see . . . you look fine. What's up?"

"I sorry. I a lot busy."

"No. You not sorry. You with other man!"

"How you know?"

"You think me deaf-dumb?" He knocked on his head, "Hello, hello . . . Kim told me old friend visit, buy box roses . . . Twice!"

"We best friends since young. Recent he found I here. Fourteen years he never contact me. I thought he not care me, but really he not know I here. We talk talk, my heart grow love him." Nicole removed the engagement ring from her finger, handed it to Brian, and said, "I sorry, sorry!" Turning around, she ran up to her apartment crying.

Brian stood at the door in shock. He knew Nicole never made important decisions rashly, and she must have been thinking about her situation all night. Realizing it was over between them, he spun about and walked to his car. He passed a trash can at the curb, dropped the ring in, got in his car, and drove away, knowing that he would never see Nicole again.

Nicole had made her choice. Christopher's plane was due to take off at ten. If she hurried, she might be able to catch him before he left. Fortunately it was the end of rush hour, so she made good time getting to the airport.

Knowing which airline he was flying out on, Nicole asked an attendant the number of the gate from which his plane would be leaving. It was in a concourse on the other side of the airport, and they were presently boarding the plane. She ran through the airport only to be slowed down at the security checkpoint: she set off the metal detector as she walked through it. She had forgotten to remove her keys from her pocket. Taking them out, she went through the metal detector again. This time there was no alarm. Walking quickly past security, she heard someone call, "Miss, Miss. You forget your keys." Nicole ran back. "Thank you," she gasped.

It was 9:59 am. Running as fast as she could to the gate, she approached the attendant. She could see a plane pulling away

238

from the building. Pointing to the plane, she asked, "What flight is that?"

"That is flight 159 to Burlington, Vermont."

"Oh, I missed him!"

"Can I help you ma'am?"

"No, thank you." Nicole sadly walked over to the window to watch the plane leave.

As she watched the plane, Nicole became vaguely aware of someone running up to the counter. She could hear the attendant say, "Yes, that's your plane. You missed it. Don't worry; I will get you on the next flight."

Feeling sorrier for the poor passenger who had missed the flight than for herself, Nicole glanced at the attendant behind the counter and then at the man standing with his back to her. Christopher! It was Christopher standing there. Relieved, she walked over to him, where he could see her.

Not expecting Nicole to be at the airport, Christopher was taken off guard. He immediately tried to explain himself. "I missed plane. Seem breakfast finished, I fall asleep . . . uhhh . . . Last night I difficult sleep . . . My plane left." As Christopher's head cleared, he looked at Nicole, "You here why?"

Nicole smiled. "I, Brian broke up. I decide I want best friend. I love you." Putting her arms around Christopher's neck, she leaned forward and kissed him.

After holding each other for a few minutes, Christopher asked Nicole to sit down. He started rummaging through his duffel bag. He put something in his pocket, zipped up his bag, and knelt down in front of Nicole. Holding her hand and kissing it tenderly, as he had done the night before, he said, "My whole heart loves you. I feel without you my life worthless. Will you marry me?"

With tears in her eyes, Nicole signed, "Yes. My heart belong you."

Christopher pulled a ring box out of his pocket. Taking a one-carat diamond ring out of the box, he slipped it on Nicole's finger. The joy of knowing that all of their dreams were about to come true was almost more than they could bear!

Chapter 43
<u>Wedding Blues</u>

The next few months flew by rather quickly as Christopher and Nicole planned for their wedding and their future together. Nicole and her parents made preparations for the wedding to be held in their backyard when all the spring flowers would be in bloom. While Christopher made plans for the honeymoon, Nicole and Kim went shopping for dresses. The guest list and invitations, as with many weddings, would prove to be a challenge: they both wanted to invite everyone they knew, but the backyard would only hold so many people.

About two months before the wedding, Nicole and Christopher went to visit his parents' home in Vermont. At dinner, Nicole told Jack and Margaret about their wedding plans. As she spoke, Nicole interpreted everything that was being said, including Jack's conversation with her.

"Why are you signing everything that you and I are discussing?" Jack wanted to know.

"I want Christopher to be involved in our conversation."

"We didn't invite you to dinner to work. Enjoy your dinner. Christopher did fine growing up. He learned to be patient and accept the fact that his deafness would limit his involvement in conversations."

Nicole, becoming irritated with Jack's apathy toward Christopher's situation, responded, "So . . . Christopher missed half of his life."

Sensing Nicole's irritation, Jack straightforwardly replied, "There were no interpreters to walk Christopher through the real world. He had only a few friends and his mother who could sign, but he managed. I insisted that he learn how to read lips so he could communicate, and he did. Rather than miss out on life, I think he was in a better position to live life to the full."

Nicole knew the truth of the matter was different from Jack's opinion, but she did not pursue the subject any further.

After dinner, Nicole helped Margaret clear the table and clean up the kitchen.

By way of thanking her, Margaret told Nicole how special Christopher was and how pleased she was that he had found such a wonderful, caring woman. "It's not going to be easy being married to a deaf person. Are you sure you're up to the task?"

Nicole spoke very positively about her relationship with Christopher. "Christopher's being deaf or hearing doesn't matter to me. I see the effort he's put forth in caring for himself, his family, and the business. He has learned the skills needed in order to care for life's responsibilities. We have similar goals, and we love each other. What more do I need?"

Margaret appreciated Nicole's honesty. "I know you and Christopher will find much joy in married life."

"Yes, I know; we look forward to spending our lives together."

"I just wish Jack could share in Christopher's joy."

After the kitchen was clean, Nicole went into the living room. Jack and Christopher were having a heated discussion, but they stopped when she entered the room.

Jack told Christopher to think about what he had said, and then he went to the kitchen to see if dessert was ready.

Christopher didn't look happy.

"What wrong?"

"We wedding signing."

"What you mean?"

"You know my dad feelings, sign language. He not want interpreting—nothing." Nicole couldn't believe Jack's demands.

Jack didn't want any interpreting done during the ceremony, but Nicole's grandparents were to be at the wedding. Since they were deaf, a debate ensued. After much discussion between the two families, Jack had to concede that Nicole's grandparents and the other Deaf persons in attendance could be seated in the front on the far right. During the ceremony, one of Nicole's friends would be seated facing the Deaf, interpreting.

At the wedding, both Christopher's and Nicole's grandparents were there, along with a few other relatives. There were some friends of their parents in attendance along with a number of Crownline employees and some of the teachers from Nicole's, now former, school. The few deaf friends that Jack would permit them to invite were also in attendance.

Christopher and his best man, former high school buddy Mike, stood under a floral arch waiting for his bride.

Nicole walked down a stone pathway with her father. She looked like a goddess to Christopher. She was dazzling!

Though the surroundings were beautiful and everyone was smiling, Christopher felt as if they were attending a funeral rather than such a happy occasion. He was thrilled to be marrying Nicole, but Jack's attitude toward their deaf friends and his restrictions on interpreting at the wedding had dampened Christopher's joy.

During the ceremony, Christopher couldn't understand what the Justice of the Peace was saying, since the interpreter was seated behind him and off to the side. He just kept staring at Nicole thinking how fortunate he was to be loved by such a wonderful woman.

After a few minutes, Nicole squeezed Christopher's hand and said, "I do."

Christopher looked at the Justice of the Peace. When the Justice stopped speaking, Nicole administered the prearranged signal to Christopher's hand again. Gazing deeply into Nicole's eyes he said, "I do."

The Justice closed his book and Nicole squeezed Christopher's hand yet again. Christopher lifted her veil and kissed her.

"I would like to introduce to you Mr. and Mrs. Christopher Cline."

The hearing in attendance clapped, while the Deaf and those who worked with Christopher applauded by waving their hands in the air.

As Christopher and Nicole walked down the stone pathway, Christopher looked at his father.

Jack looked happy.

Christopher couldn't help but wonder if Jack was happy for him or happy to be relieved of his supposed responsibility for him. He hoped that Jack was satisfied with the way Christopher's life had turned out, because he was tired of trying to please his father. From now on, he was going to concern himself with pleasing his wife.

To that end, Christopher took Nicole on a two-week European honeymoon and then back to their newly built home in Michigan to begin their life together.

Chapter 44
<u>Unexpected Return</u>

During the next year and a half, Christopher and Nicole had made several trips to Vermont to visit Jack and Margaret. Each time they visited, Christopher tried to explain to his dad about the corporation changes, technological improvements, and building expansion of Crownline Glass, but Jack never seemed interested. It was as if he thought Christopher was exaggerating to try to impress him, until one day he received a note from Christopher with a corporate check for $250,000. Jack's curiosity was finally aroused.

Jack and Margaret decided to take a trip to Michigan. While Margaret checked on Christopher and Nicole, Jack wanted to check on the business.

Jack and Margaret's trip was unannounced, so there was no one to greet them when they arrived at Metro Airport. They had rented a car and drove to a restaurant they used to frequent before they had moved east.

After an enjoyable lunch, Margaret suggested that they stop by the office and surprise Christopher.

Jack thought that was a terrific idea, since he hadn't seen the Crownline office for nearly five years. The last time he had been in Michigan was when Crownline was on the verge of bankruptcy and had lost in court to Tyler Glass.

Taking the scenic route to the office, Jack and Margaret shared a lot of memories of the "good old days". They reminisced about the way life used to be and how much the neighborhood had changed.

As Jack turned the corner onto Fifth Avenue, he and Margaret were shocked to see the Crownline building. The parking lot was empty, except for a few cars. The factory windows had all been painted black. Through the lobby windows, they could see boxes stacked along the wall.

Margaret remembered how she had come every spring and planted annuals along the front of the building. Now there were only patches of wildflowers. The seeds must have been dropped in the fields of grass by birds as they tried to decide which they needed more—food for their hatchlings or grass for their nests.

Jack stopped his car on the side of the road. He stared in utter disbelief at the company that he had worked so hard to build up, for almost three decades, now lying in relative shambles. How he wished he had paid more attention to what Christopher had tried to tell him about the business! Resting his elbows on the steering wheel, he hung his head.

As Jack was feeling sorry for himself, thinking about all those wasted years, Margaret tapped him on the shoulder. "Jack look!" One of the garage doors on the side of the building had opened, and a brand new truck had pulled out. "Look at that truck!"

Jack followed Margaret's eyes. As the truck left the parking lot, he could see it had the Crownline logo on the back and sides. Amazed, he commented, "We never had a truck like that . . . It's brand new!"

Both Jack and Margaret began to get excited.

"Jack, follow that truck. Let's see where it's going."

Turning the car around, Jack followed the truck about eight miles to the other side of town. The truck turned onto Meadow Hill Road.

There was no way Jack and Margaret could have prepared themselves for what they saw next.

Down the road, on the right, was a large, white, three-building complex, neatly landscaped, with a parking lot full of cars. Along the side of the second building was a fleet of about 30 trucks, half of which were semis. As they pulled into the main parking lot, they passed between two beautiful stone walls bearing Crownline's name and company logo.

Jack couldn't believe what he was seeing. Assuming that there was no way Christopher could have brought the company from bankruptcy to what he saw standing before him, he decided that Christopher must have sold the business, and the check that he had received was proceeds from the sale.

Jack and Margaret got out of the car and approached the office building; they were impressed with the architectural design of the lobby's atrium. Entering the lobby, Jack stared up at the window glass.

Margaret looked around the lobby and then commented, "What an impressive way for a glass manufacturer to display its product."

Jack nodded his head in agreement.

Walking over to the receptionist's desk, they were greeted with a smile.

"Welcome to Crownline Glass." Then, recognizing them, the receptionist continued, "Mr. Cline. Mrs. Cline. Hello. It's so nice to see you."

"Becky, is that you?" Becky and Margaret hugged each other.

"Is Christopher here?" Jack interrupted.

"Yes. He is meeting with the board members. Would you like me to let him know you're here?"

"No, I'll find him."

As Jack headed into the interior, Becky and Margaret began catching up on what had been happening in their lives.

Jack walked down the hall mumbling, "Board members?" Seeing many people scurrying about the office reminded him of a time when Crownline was one of the leading glass manufacturers in the Midwest, except now he didn't know any of these individuals. He finally asked someone for directions to the conference room where the board members were meeting.

As Jack approached the conference room, through the window he could see a large table with nine people sitting around it. There were sets of schematics on the table at each place. The end seat was empty. Frank was the only person Jack recognized.

Opening the door, Jack saw Christopher standing near a window display. He was writing some figures on a dry-erase board.

Christopher turned around to go back to his seat and saw Jack standing in the doorway. "Hi. Uhhh . . . you want join us?"

Jack looked around the room and then left without saying a word.

Christopher asked Frank to continue with the agenda and fill him in later about what transpired.

Catching up with his dad, Christopher showed Jack around the office, the warehouse, and the factory. Except for the few times when he gave a brief description of the area or the equipment, he and his dad walked silently around the entire complex.

Jack was astonished as he saw the size of the plant, the rate of production, and the additional personnel.

After the grand tour, the two men headed back to the main office building. Jack gazed at Christopher. Before he could say anything, Christopher smiled nervously and said "Surprise!"

"Congratulations, but why didn't you discuss these changes with me?"

Just then, on his way back to the factory, Frank met up with Jack and Christopher. "Jack, it's good to see you." He shook hands with Jack and then turned to Christopher and signed, "Board accept new window design."

Christopher nodded in acknowledgment.

"Excuse me, I must get back to work. It was good to see you again Jack." Frank turned to walk away.

"Frank, where did you learn sign language?"

"Christopher. He's a good teacher."

Jack rolled his eyes, "Oh, that's great!"

Christopher tried to be positive. "Dad, let me show you to your office."

As they walked into the lobby of the office building, Christopher saw his mother.

Happy to see her son, Margaret asked, "Is okay we hug at your work?"

"Of course." Christopher gave his mom a big hug and a kiss on the cheek.

Clumsily, Margaret signed, "Christopher, everything here . . . wow, it's amazing! How you do this?"

"I work hard make business grow for both you."

"Oh Christopher, you did great job!"

Jack interrupted, "Where did you get the money to do all this?"

"I restructured the corporation."

"Why didn't you discuss any of these changes with me?"

Christopher was becoming aggravated at his father's harping about his lack of communication regarding business matters, especially since he had on numerous occasions tried to speak with his father about everything he had planned and done.

Margaret could feel the tension mounting. "It doesn't need to be discussed right now. This is not the time or the place."

Heatedly, Jack replied in a rather loud voice, "I thought it would be nice for father and son to work together."

"Dear, let's discuss it later, okay? I'm sure Christopher can explain everything."

Turning to Christopher, Jack said, "So where's my office?"

Christopher showed his parents to Jack's office and then, after offering the hospitality of his home to his parents during their visit, he retreated to his own office. While he was regrouping, Frank came in.

"You coping okay?"

"Long ago I should business sell you . . ." Standing up, Christopher put his coat on, and went home.

Jack and Margaret stayed with Christopher and Nicole for almost two weeks before they headed home.

While Nicole was at work, Margaret would keep herself busy by visiting her old friends until midafternoon and then she would hurry home to prepare dinner for everyone. She made the most elaborate meals—it looked like a banquet every night of the week.

Jack went to work every day, usually arriving earlier than Christopher and staying later. By the end of his stay, Jack had made it known to all that he was no longer a visitor to Crownline, but the returned president of the corporation.

A month later, Jack returned to Michigan to look for a house. By mid-March, he and Margaret were once again permanent residents of Michigan.

Chapter 45
<u>Hope Realized</u>

The weather was becoming warmer, and the scent of lilacs filled the air. It had been a month and a half since Christopher and Nicole's Caribbean cruise. What a relaxing way that had been to celebrate their second wedding anniversary.

Nicole had not been feeling well for the past few days, but she wasn't concerned. She and Christopher had been trying to conceive a child. The pregnancy test she had taken in the morning had turned out positive.

Knowing she wouldn't be able to wait until Christopher came home from work to tell him the good news, she decided to call him at work on the TTY.

"Hi Sweetie. What's up?"

"I want out lunch together same dating. You want?"

"Sure. Work slow. I bored. You want me pick you up?"

"Yes. See soon. Sksk" Nicole hung up the phone.

After Nicole packed a picnic lunch, Christopher picked her up and took her to a nearby park. As they ate, they reminisced about how they had finally gotten together after years of having no contact.

Nicole couldn't help but smile with an expression that Christopher immediately recognized. It was the kind of expression she had whenever she wanted to surprise him and she wasn't going to be able to contain herself for much longer. She looked like she was going to explode from the excitement.

"You big smile, why?"

"You love me?"

Christopher looked at Nicole. "You know I cherish you. Come on tell me, what's up?"

Looking down at her stomach and then at Christopher, Nicole smiled. "I pregnant."

Christopher looked at Nicole with that same dumbfounded look he had given her years before when she had taken him to her tree house and first signed her name to him. After about 15 seconds, which seemed like 15 minutes to her, he responded, "We will baby." Smiling, he leaned forward, kissed her tenderly, and signed, "I love you."

Christopher and Nicole sat holding each other. It was the moment they had been dreaming of since their marriage. They would have a child of their own. It would be a child they would love unconditionally, and one to whom Christopher would teach his language and culture.

After lunch and the news that he would be a father, Christopher decided to take the rest of the day off of work.

Christopher and Nicole discussed how they would go about telling their parents the news. She wanted to do something special. He agreed that such a special occasion required a very special announcement. They found a specialty store that would embroider designs onto shirts. The tee shirt for Nicole's mother was to have baby booties and the words 'I'm an expectant grandma!' embroidered on the front. They chose to have embroidered on the tee shirt for her father a teddy bear and the words 'Grandpa-to-be'. After placing their order, they headed home to make their plans for the upcoming weekend.

Contacting the airline, Nicole made arrangements for Christopher and her to fly to Washington, DC on the weekend to see her parents. They planned on taking her parents out for dinner and then surprising them with their gifts and the good news. Within a matter of hours, Nicole had everything set to inform her parents about her pregnancy.

The parents-to-be were bursting with excitement. They wanted to share their good news with someone. Feeling that they were too excited and could not possibly keep their news a secret until the weekend, Nicole and Christopher decided to tell Jack and Margaret that evening.

Christopher wasn't sure how his father would react to their news—especially since there was a possibility that their child could be born deaf. Nicole's grandparents on her father's side were deaf, and his great grandparents and great uncle on his mother's side had been deaf. If they both carried the recessive gene for deafness . . .

The fact that their child could be born deaf did not bother Christopher or Nicole, but Christopher, in particular, wondered how his father would react. Would Jack be able to accept his grandchild with all the love that a grandfather is supposed to show, or would he treat his grandchild the same way he had treated his son? These were troubling thoughts for Christopher.

Nicole wanted to get a gift for Jack and Margaret, but Christopher felt that their news would be exciting enough for his parents. After some persuasion, Nicole convinced Christopher to shop for a gift for his parents. They bought two bibs—one stated 'I love my grandpa!' and the other, 'I love my grandma!' Having the bibs boxed and gift-wrapped, they headed over to Jack and Margaret's home.

When Christopher and Nicole arrived at Jack and Margaret's, they went in through the side door. Nicole called, "Hello!"

The aroma of freshly baked cookies permeated the house. It was obvious that Margaret was in the kitchen doing what she enjoyed most—baking. "I'm in the kitchen, dear."

Nicole grabbed hold of Christopher's hand and excitedly led him into the kitchen where Margaret was wiping off the countertop. She looked like such a perfect homemaker, with her apron around her waist, freshly baked cookies on the table, and clean dishes in the strainer.

Nicole approached Margaret and gave her a hug. "Hi, Mom."

"What timing!" Margaret looked at Christopher, "I made cookies—your favorite. Can you stay?"

"Yes."

Before Christopher could say anything else, Margaret had put some cookies on a plate and filled four glasses with lemonade, calling, "Jack! The kids are here." Looking toward Christopher and Nicole, she invited, "Come on in the living room."

The three of them went to the living room; Christopher and Nicole sat on the couch while Margaret sat in a chair across from them. Jack was in his favorite chair, reading the newspaper.

"We got a little something for you." Nicole handed the gift to Margaret. She had that same excited look on her face that had been there when she had told Christopher he was going to be a father. She looked like she was ready to burst.

Looking at Nicole, Christopher grinned.

"That is so sweet!" Margaret said as she carefully removed the wrapping paper from the box.

Nicole sat on the edge of her seat, smiling from ear to ear.

Margaret opened the box and looked at the gift. She stared at it and then suddenly jumped out of her seat. "Jack! Jack! They're going to have a baby! Look! Look!" She showed him the bibs. "Oh, this is wonderful news!" Margaret ran over and gave Nicole a big hug.

Jack looked at Christopher. "Congratulations." Getting up out of his chair, he also gave Nicole a hug. "I'm very happy for you."

"Thanks, Jack."

Margaret, who had sat down next to Nicole, began asking when she was due and what names she and Christopher had picked out.

Nicole laughed. "We haven't had a chance to discuss it. We just found out today."

Margaret began reminiscing about how excited she had been when she found out that she was pregnant with Christopher and the preparations she had made for his arrival.

"At least with the advancements in medical technology, you won't have to deal with the problems that come with having a disabled child," piped in Jack.

Christopher asked, "What you mean?"

"Well, it wasn't easy for us. You know, your being deaf and all."

"Jack! That's enough!" Margaret was a little irritated by his negative comment.

"Margaret, you have to admit it was difficult for both of us."

Margaret conceded. "We just didn't know what to do."

Nicole knew Jack's comment was upsetting to Christopher because it also upset her. She responded, "That's where we have the advantage. We understand the needs a deaf child would have, especially the need to be able to communicate in sign language."

"Well, you don't need to worry. I'm sure your baby will be fine," replied Jack.

Christopher couldn't hold back any longer. Having Nicole voice for him, he questioned his dad, "What if our baby is deaf? How will you feel?"

Jack smiled, "I will love your baby even if it's deaf, but I don't think that's going to happen. Your deafness wasn't inherited. It was from your mother being exposed to rubella."

Christopher and Nicole looked at each other and then he continued, "It's true that my deafness may not have been inherited, but no one can be sure and deafness does run in both of our families. There is a strong possibility that our child could be born deaf . . . then what will you do?"

Jack sat back in his chair. "Well . . . let's just wait and see what happens."

Everyone sat silently for a moment. Christopher, standing up, said, "We should be leaving. We are going to DC this weekend, and we need to make our preparations."

Nicole and Margaret followed Christopher to the door.

Jack remained in his seat, wondering why Christopher had put a damper on such a happy occasion.

Chapter 46
Smart Dog

Since Jack had come back to work six months earlier, Christopher found himself coming home in the evenings feeling tense. Working at Crownline was no longer enjoyable. He wanted to go back to studying law, but he had put so much time and effort into establishing Crownline as the leading manufacturer of glass in North America that he found it hard to just walk away.

This day in particular, Christopher decided to relax by sitting on the porch swing, waiting for the sun to set. Yearning to feel accepted by his father, he thought about their relationship. He and his father had so much in common, they could share so much if only Jack would put forth as much effort to communicate with him as he had put forth to communicate with his father. Crownline employees who worked with Christopher only a couple of hours a day had put forth more effort to communicate in sign with him than his own father had during his entire lifetime.

Christopher could not comprehend how his father, who claimed to love him, could not give such a small part of himself to his son. He sat, reflecting on his relationship with his father.

After a few minutes, Nicole brought him a glass of wine, hoping that it would ease his pain. Sitting down with him on the swing, she put her arm around him, and they sat quietly relaxing.

Nicole had to go back into the house to check on dinner. That's when Christopher's cocker spaniel, Joey, who had been lying at his master's feet, decided it was time he got some attention. The dog walked over to Christopher, who scratched his chin and behind his big floppy ears and then gave him a pat on the side. Then, leaning back in the swing, he closed his eyes.

Joey started pawing Christopher's leg, but Christopher had other things on his mind. His thoughts had reverted to his dad and how they could improve their relationship.

After Joey had pawed Christopher's leg persistently, Christopher could no longer ignore him. Looking at Joey, he signed, "Wrong what?"

Joey jumped onto all fours. He became so excited that it wasn't just his tail wagging from side to side, but the whole rear end of his body.

Christopher signed to Joey, "out out."

Joey ran off the porch and onto the grass. He began running around the yard with his nose to the ground. A minute later, he returned with a stick in his mouth.

Christopher really wasn't in the mood to play with the dog, but he gave in because Joey seemed so happy to be with him. Walking over to the kitchen window where Nicole was inside cutting vegetables, he tapped on the window and signed, "Joey want out. We back soon."

Nicole nodded her head and smiled.

Christopher and Joey walked to the back of their property, which was alongside a park; there they played fetch. Afterwards they walked around the city block to get back home. Christopher hadn't really stopped thinking about his communication problems with his father. Playing with the dog had underscored how he had taught his dog to understand and respond to sign—yet his father, who is far more intelligent than Joey, could not sign. Joey had been able to learn signed commands for a treat, but how much more valuable it would have been for Jack to learn sign so that father and son could really share what was in their hearts. What a sad situation! Why did it have to be this way?

As they arrived home, Christopher ran in the house shouting, "Nicole! Nicole!"

Nicole, running out of the kitchen thinking that there had been some kind of accident, signed, "What wrong?"

"Nothing. We home. You, me talk."

"Good, dinner ready."

Sitting down to eat, Christopher explained to Nicole his feelings about his father—especially since Jack had never put forth any effort to learn sign language. He told her that he wanted to show his dad how Joey responds to sign to exemplify how Jack could just as easily, with practice, learn to communicate with Christopher.

Nicole thought it was worth a try. She called Jack and Margaret to see if Jack was home.

Margaret told Nicole that Jack had called earlier to let her know he would be staying at the office for a few extra hours so that he could finish up some paperwork.

Christopher put Joey in the car and headed over to Crownline. When he pulled into the parking lot, he could see Jack's car parked in the same reserved parking spot it had been in since the morning. He opened the lobby door and he and Joey walked in. They went upstairs to Jack's office, but it was empty. Shutting the hallway lights off, he secured the building and then they headed over to the factory.

The factory was dimly lit, since only the night security lights were on, but the main office on the second floor overlooking the factory was lighted. Christopher turned on a few of the factory lights nearest the office. Then he and Joey walked toward the stairs.

Jack had heard the door close and noticed the extra lights. Walking over to the window, he saw Christopher and Joey coming toward the office. He waved to Christopher to come on upstairs.

Christopher waved back.

At the bottom of the stairs, Christopher bent down and placed something on the ground.

Jack opened the door and then returned to the desk where he had been studying specifications for a new window design.

Joey darted in and ran straight over to Jack, who responded by rubbing his back. Christopher entered the room a few seconds later.

"Hello. What are you doing here so late? Is there a problem?"

Christopher smiled, "No, just visiting. You work hard—huh?"

Jack nodded his head. "Yep. I always work hard to support my family."

Christopher sat down across from his father.

Jack continued petting Joey.

"I taught Joey new tricks."

"Really? Show me."

Christopher clapped his hands. Joey ran over and sat in front of him. He signed "close door." Immediately Joey ran over to the office door, put his front paws on the door, pushed it until it slammed shut, and then ran back over to Christopher and sat down. Christopher gave him a dog biscuit.

"Wow! That was great! That hand movement you did meant close the door?"

"Yep. You want see more?"

"Sure."

Christopher looked at Joey and signed, "shake hands him," as he pointed to Jack. Jumping on the chair in front of Jack's desk and then onto the desk itself, Joey sat in front of Jack and held out his paw.

"He wants to shake." Jack began laughing as he shook Joey's paw.

Barking, Joey then jumped off the desk and sat in front of Christopher waiting for his treat and the next command.

After giving Joey a biscuit, Christopher opened the office door and signed "pop, go."

Joey immediately ran down the stairs.

Standing up, Jack looked out of the window to see where Joey was going. He saw the dog grab something at the bottom of the stairs and carry it back toward the office. As Joey neared the office door, Jack could see that he was carrying a plastic bag.

Joey, carrying the bag in his mouth, approached Christopher.

Looking at Jack, Christopher signed, "pop". He then took the bag from Joey opened it up, and removed two cans of pop. He handed a can to his father.

"Thanks."

"Pop not enough!" Christopher looked at Joey and signed, "bowl".

Joey excitedly ran downstairs.

Jack again watched Joey through the window. Grabbing a bowl at the bottom of the stairs, the dog carried it upstairs and dropped it in front of Christopher.

Joey wagged his tail as he awaited his treat, but instead of a treat, Christopher signed, "No. Bowl go table." Joey picked up the bowl, jumped on a chair, and then onto the desk. He placed the bowl in front of where Jack had been sitting and then jumped down and sat in front of Christopher. After eating his treats, Joey waited patiently for Christopher's next signs.

Jack couldn't believe it. He sat back at his desk, "That's incredible!"

Christopher pulled a bag of peanuts out of his pocket and poured them into the bowl. Looking at his dad, he signed "nuts" and then pointed at the bowl.

"That's great how you taught Joey to follow your hand movements!"

"Those not hand movements! Joey know sign language."

"Really?" Jack started laughing. "How does he sign back to you with his little paws?" He made two fists, clapped them together and then circled his fists around each other as if they were paws signing.

Christopher was angered by his father's thoughtless joke. "I sign Joey, he understands—that more than you know! You never learn sign language for precious son; why?"

"I never had a chance to learn, and now I'm too old. I always worked hard to build up this company so that I could support our family. I love you and your mother, and I've always worked hard to give you the best. This company will take care of you and your family long after I'm gone."

Christopher was clearly unhappy since Jack had missed the point. He didn't know what else he could say, so he sat quietly watching his father.

Jack continued, "We never needed sign language. You did well reading my lips. Maybe when I retire, I'll be able to learn a little sign language."

Christopher thought that by the time Jack made an effort to learn sign language it could be too late.

Jack put his paperwork aside. "Let's grab some ice cream before we head home."

Christopher and Joey started down the stairs while Jack locked the office door. He wasn't comfortable with Jack's willful ignorance of his need to communicate with his father.

While Christopher and Jack walked toward the exit, Joey excitedly ran circles around them and then ran ahead of them. He turned back to wait for Jack and Christopher to catch up with him.

Jack tapped Christopher's arm. "Okay, teach me a sign that I can show Joey."

Christopher showed Jack a sign.

Jack imitated Christopher's hand movement. "What's that mean?"

"Go ahead. Show Joey. You see . . ."

Jack called Joey, who immediately ran to him, and then he made the sign. Joey squatted where he was and pooped on the floor. "Joey! What—"

Christopher started laughing.

Jack wasn't sure why Christopher thought Joey's mess on the floor was so funny. "Why are you laughing? Did I tell Joey to do that—huh?"

Christopher smiled mischievously.

Jack started laughing. He thought it was cool that Joey could poop on command. "Just leave it. We'll let someone else take care of it."

Chapter 47
Appreciation Lacking

During Jack's absence, and even since his return, Christopher had cared for Crownline's finances. For almost seven years he had worked closely with Crownline's accountant and attorneys to restructure the corporation, build up company stock, and reinvest monies to the benefit of the corporation.

Jack had questioned Christopher at different times about the corporation's finances—especially regarding the initial investment used to restructure Crownline. Worrying that there were outstanding loans that were suddenly going to become due and fearing that Crownline would be set back severely if large sums of money had to be repaid, he decided to meet with the accountant.

Knowing Christopher would be hurt even further by his father's worries, Margaret urged that he get Christopher out of the office so that he could freely review Crownline's finances without Christopher feeling Jack's mistrust. Jack didn't see what the problem was. He didn't mistrust Christopher; he just worried that his son might have gotten in over his head. To keep his wife happy, he gave Christopher a week off and plane tickets to Washington, DC so that he and Nicole could visit her parents.

While Christopher was gone, Jack reviewed the corporation's financial records for the past seven years. He was sure he would be hit with a number of unpaid loans. To his surprise, he found that Christopher's idea to give each of the employees stock in the company had been a real incentive to work harder and had helped to increase Crownline's assets. Still, he wondered how a corporation on the verge of bankruptcy had been able to give stock to its employees.

After almost a week of reviewing finances, it seemed to Jack that the accountant was hiding something. Whenever he would ask about a few large deposits made to the corporation bank account, the accountant would direct his attention to some other financial document.

By the end of the week, every last penny had been accounted for with the exception of three large deposits made in the first two years after Christopher took over Crownline. Jack confronted the accountant and told him that he needed to know who had provided these funds.

"They were gifts to the corporation."

"From who?"

"The benefactor wanted to remain anonymous."

"Who would give over a quarter of a million dollars to a company on the verge of bankruptcy?"

After much coercion, the accountant finally admitted, "It was Christopher."

"Christopher . . . but how?"

"Shortly after taking over the corporation, Christopher sold his condominium and moved into an efficiency apartment. He took the money from the sale of his condo and what was in his savings account, and he invested it in Crownline stock—which was the $100,000 deposit. The following year, he took out a personal loan for $125,000 and gave it to the corporation. The $75,000 deposit was saved from his earnings the next year and reinvested in the company."

When Christopher arrived home from an enjoyable week visiting his in-laws, his former employer, and some of Nicole's friends, he was disturbed to receive a message from the corporation's accountant. He found out that Jack had met with the accountant to review all of the corporation's financial records including Christopher's investment in the company. Why couldn't Jack trust him?

The next morning Christopher, furious, went to the office to talk to his father. The receptionist informed him that Jack was over at the factory, meeting with Frank. Going straight to the factory office, he approached the two men and signed to Frank, "Excuse me. Jack and I need talk. Don't mind, you interpret for me?"

Frank looked at Jack, "Christopher would like to talk with you, but he would like me to stay to interpret."

Jack nodded. "What's on your mind son?"

"Why did you meet with the accountant?"

"I just wanted to make sure our books were in order."

"Reviewing the records for the past year or two would've been sufficient to see that our books are in order. Why did you feel the need to review the company's records for the past seven years?"

"Because you never explained to me how Crownline went from bankruptcy to where it is now. Why didn't you confer with me before you poured your hard earned money into the corporation?"

"Confer with you? You left town and dumped a bankrupt company into my lap. I gave up my goals, my dreams, and my career . . . I gave up my life! I worked hard and gave everything to make Crownline successful—for YOU! Why can't you appreciate what I've done for you? Why can't you be proud of the success I've given you? Why can't you just say 'thank you'?" With that, Christopher turned around and left.

Jack sat back in his chair and thought about how he had worked relentlessly to support his family. How dare Christopher accuse him of being unappreciative! He thought about

Christopher's deafness and how he could not be held accountable for his son's inability to hear what he had said over the years.

As Jack was deliberating, he heard a horn honk, tires screech, and glass shatter. Jumping up, he looked out of the office window. He could see that a forklift had stopped suddenly and dropped its half-ton load of glass. Someone had been injured and the employees were screaming for someone to call 9-1-1.

Frank, who had left the office just before the commotion began, yelled, "Jack! Get down here!"

Jack ran down the stairs and over to where the forklift was stopped.

One of the men who had been working on the assembly line near the accident yelled, "Help me get the glass off him!"

The others quickly swarmed around and removed the large sections of glass that had fallen off the forklift.

As Jack looked on the ground, there was Christopher underneath fragments of broken glass; he wasn't moving. Blood was streaming onto the floor. The smaller pieces of glass around Christopher's body were swept away.

Jack could see Christopher was in a lot of pain.

Christopher's eyes were open and focused on his father, but he wasn't able to move his limbs because they were so badly cut. He was also having difficulty breathing.

Removing his coat, Jack covered Christopher to keep him warm.

There was a large gash on Christopher's shoulder.

After removing a piece of glass from his son's shoulder, Jack applied direct pressure to stop the bleeding. Leaning over Christopher, he very slowly said, "You . . . will . . . be . . . okay . . . just . . . hang . . . on . . ."

Dazed, Christopher just stared at Jack not knowing what he was saying or what was happening around him, but his father's was a familiar face—the only one that could bring him any kind of comfort.

When the ambulance arrived, the paramedics took over. They bandaged the wound on Christopher's shoulder and his left leg, but they seemed more concerned about his going into shock and pulmonary arrest. Putting him on a gurney, they wheeled him out of the factory, lifted him into the ambulance, and left for St. John's Hospital.

Jack stood there looking at the blood on his hands—some his own, but most Christopher's. For the first time in his life, he became scared that he might lose his son.

Chapter 48
Heart Opens

At the hospital, Nicole, Jack, and Margaret sat in the surgical waiting area. Nicole sat on a couch wringing her hands, while Jack and Margaret sat nearby whispering to each other.

Jack admitted to Margaret, "Maybe I didn't always do things right by Christopher. I just wanted him to be prepared to face the hearing world. I've been sitting here thinking about how the accident happened . . . Christopher rushing, not able to hear even that piercing, nerve-shattering horn of the forklift, the load shifting as the driver slammed on his brakes . . . I've been watching the people here in the hospital talking and all the activity, trying to read their lips . . . I can see, now, Christopher has been very patient with me."

Margaret tried to speak reassuringly, "When Christopher gets better, he can teach you sign language, and then you and he will be able to converse and build your relationship. You will be able to tell him how much you love him."

"You're right! That's what I'm going to do when Christopher gets home."

Christopher was in surgery for nearly four hours. The doctors worked hard to keep him alive.

After another two grueling hours, the chief surgeon came out to the waiting area. "Well, he's alive, but the next 24 hours are going to be crucial." Looking at Nicole, the doctor continued, "Your husband suffered internal injuries from the weight of the glass that fell on top of him. His ribs were broken and one of them punctured his lung. His spleen ruptured. Along with that, he lost a lot of blood from the lacerations to his shoulder, arms, and especially his thigh. We've done all that we can. I honestly don't know if he'll be able to pull through this. If he survives the next 24 hours, there's a 75 percent chance he'll fully recover."

The reality of the doctor's words, that her Christopher may not be with her much longer, was difficult for Nicole to face. She started crying.

"Christopher's awake if you would like to see him." The doctor led Nicole to the surgical ICU.

After an hour, the doctor walked back to the nurse's station. Jack and Margaret, seeing him, approached. "How is Christopher?"

"He's not responding as well as we had hoped. Why don't you go see him."

Margaret began crying. Jack put his arm around her, and they walked down the hall to Christopher's room.

Through the door, what they saw was almost more than they could handle. Christopher had an oxygen mask covering his mouth and nose, numerous fluids being pumped into his bloodstream through an IV, electrodes stuck to his chest to monitor his heart, and bandages on his head, shoulder, midsection, and leg. Pale and hardly moving, he looked as though he were already drained of life. Nicole was at his side, holding his hand.

When Jack and Margaret entered the room, Nicole told Christopher his parents were there.

Jack stood by the foot of the bed.

Margaret approached Christopher. Trying to be brave for her son, she leaned forward and kissed his cheek; she looked him in the eyes and signed, "Christopher, I love you so much."

She held his hand until she could no longer hold back her emotions. With tears streaming down her face, Margaret looked at Nicole and sobbed, "I'm sorry," as she turned and left the room.

Nicole, never having left Christopher's bedside, looked into his eyes. Without speaking, they knew how much they loved each other, but she didn't want to leave it at that. She wanted him to see how she felt. "You, me best friends long time. I much happy you chase, catch me. Recent two and half years we married—that best years my life. My heart belongs you. I love you."

It took a lot out of Christopher, but he managed to smile at Nicole.

Margaret, having composed herself, came back into the room and stood near Nicole, holding her hand.

Christopher looked at his father and motioned for him to come closer.

On the opposite side of the bed from Nicole and Margaret, Jack held Christopher's hand.

Christopher's breaths became shallower. It was obvious he wasn't going to be with them much longer.

Jack looked into Christopher's eyes and said, "I'm sorry."

With obvious difficulty, Christopher raised his left hand and made a sign with his thumb, index finger, and pinky finger sticking up; the two middle fingers remained bent down. Then he lowered his hand, still in that shape, back to the blanket.

Jack had seen Christopher make that sign before, but he had never understood what it meant. He looked up at Nicole, "What does three fingers mean?"

Before Nicole could respond, Christopher's hand that had so tightly held Jack's hand now relaxed. His breaths became still shallower, and his heartbeat had become faint enough to set off the monitor.

"What does three fingers mean?"

Through her tears, Nicole said, "It means I love you. Christopher loved you very much."

The nurse came into the room and turned the heart monitor off. She said, "The last thing to go is the hearing, so keep talking to him."

It was too late. Jack wanted to tell Christopher how much he loved him, but his son couldn't hear him. Making the sign for "I love you", he moved his hand up to where his son might be able to see it. As he did, Christopher gasped for air, exhaled, and was gone.

Jack stood there in shock.

Margaret and Nicole held each other and cried.

~ ~ ~ ~ ~ ~ ~ ~ ~ ~ ~ ~ ~ ~ ~ ~ ~ ~ ~ ~

Some weeks after the funeral, Jack visited the cemetery. He had ordered a special gravestone in the shape of the "I love you" hand sign to be put on Christopher's grave, and it had finally arrived. Approaching the gravesite, he stood silently, wondering why he hadn't seen it before now. He leaned forward and touched the stone. It was a cold, hard testimony to the fact that Christopher's silent ears had caused Jack to silence his heart. What a missed opportunity! If only they could have a second chance . . . but there would be no second chances. Christopher was gone. There was no going back. The life he had worked so hard to achieve was truly a waste without his beloved son.

Jack fell to his knees and sobbed.

Epilogue

After the funeral, Nicole's parents tried to convince her to go back to Maryland with them; however, she didn't feel ready to give up the life that she and Christopher had built together. Staying in their house with their dog, she continued making preparations for the baby's arrival.

It was on a frigid morning in February that Nicole gave birth to a 6-lb. 10-oz. baby boy whom she named Jonathan Christopher. It was the name that she and Christopher had chosen for a boy. It was Jonathan's privilege to bring a measure of happiness back to a sad family.

Jonathan was a beautiful boy, who in many ways resembled his father. He had his father's hair, his eyes, his smile . . . and his deafness.

Though Jonathan was a constant reminder of the son he had lost, Jack resolved not to allow deafness to interfere with his communicating with his beloved grandson; on the contrary, he worked hard to learn sign language so that he could share his heart with his grandson in a way that he had never done before with anyone.

~ ~

Now, as Jack stood silently in the cemetery, remembering his son, he felt the young man at his side tap his arm. He looked down at young Jonathan.

"Papa, you okay?" the young boy signed.

Jack smiled and nodded his head. Bending down, he hugged his grandson and then looking directly into his eyes, he signed, "I love you."